"You say freak, I say unique."
— Christian Baloga

Quirks of Nature

I hope you enjoy these stories!

Best,

Bruce Hunt

“Painting, in which the inner and the outer man are inseparable, transcends technique, transcends subject, and moves into the realm of the inevitable.”

— Lee Krasner

Quirks of Nature

Stories & Art

by

Bruce H. Hinrichs

Ellipse Publishing Company
Minneapolis, Minnesota USA

Printed in the United States of America

International Standard Book Number
ISBN-13: 978-0-9790129-8-3
ISBN-10: 0-9790129-8-8

Library of Congress Control Number: 2017901026

ELLIPSE

Ellipse Publishing Company
225 Groveland Avenue
Minneapolis, Minnesota 55403

"Everything starts from a dot."
— Wassily Kandinsky

"Curves are so emotional."
— Piet Mondrian

"A book should serve as the ax for the frozen sea within us."
— Franz Kafka

Preface

The stories and art in this book, which include both abstract and realistic elements, science and absurdity, contradictions, oddities, and most of all, quirks, emerge from a particular aesthetic. The stories and art presented here are meant to reveal and to engage, to portray, to entangle (and perhaps, to a small degree, untangle), one of the most fundamental and enduring issues in art, in all its forms, throughout history.

This issue is perhaps best presented as a question: To what extent should art be mimetic, that is, to depict the world of our experience precisely as we experience it, as the eye sees it, as the mind perceives it, as it seems in our reality, like a hyper-realistic photograph… or, to what extent should artistic creations transform, rearrange, convert, or mutate the world of our sensory experience into a portrayal, a creative rendering, that is a metamorphosis, a transfiguration, an imaginative twisting that reveals deeper, perhaps intangible, metaphysical, more essential, more honest truths? As Picasso said, "Art is a lie that makes us realize truth." To mimic or to transform? What is the higher purpose? Where is the proper balance?

As is the human experience, the world we encounter, as well as what is intended in these stories and works of art, is rich with coincidences, fragmentation, dissolution, and quirks, and yet we find at times a perception of clarity, of harmony, of seemingly universal scientific principles, of cosmos, of patterns, of causality within nature, and perhaps within ourselves. The enigmatic and bewildering confluence of these disparate elements – the entanglement, the convergence – is the primary aesthetic focus of the stories and art offered here. How do chaos and order fit together?

The final story, *Simon Says*, attempts to summarize, to encapsulate, this baffling issue. But, it does so in a quirky way. Of course.

I hope you enjoy, and that your puzzlement is sparked.

— B. H.

"Not only is the Universe stranger than we think, it is stranger than we can think."
— Werner Heisenberg

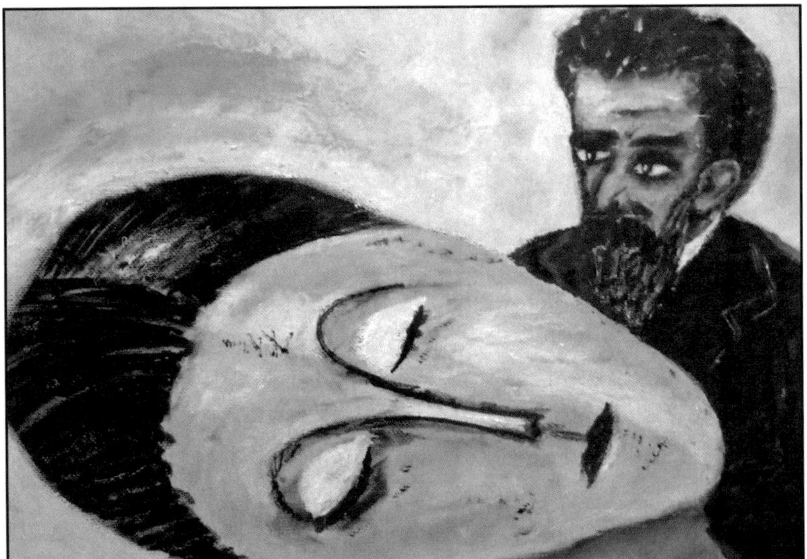

"That which they call abstract is the most realistic, because what is real is not the exterior, but the idea, the essence of things. Look at my sculptures until you see them."
— Constantin Brancusi

Quirks

Quirks of Nature

"The attitude that nature is chaotic and that the artist puts order into it is a very absurd point of view, I think. All that we can hope for is to put some order into ourselves."
— Willem de Kooning

"Nature has no mercy at all. Nature says, I'm going to snow. If you have on a bikini and no snowshoes, that's tough. I am going to snow anyway."
— Maya Angelou

"The emotion of beauty is always obscured by the appearance of the object. Therefore the object must be eliminated from the picture."
— Piet Mondrian

The Elements

"To understand is to perceive patterns."
— Sir Isaiah Berlin

"Good order is the foundation of all great things."
— Edmund Burke

"The most exciting phrase to hear in science, the one that heralds the most discoveries, is not 'Eureka!' but 'That's funny...'"
— Isaac Asimov

"Life is infinitely stranger than anything which the mind of man could invent."
—Arthur Conan Doyle

"In physics, you don't have to go around making trouble for yourself. Nature does it for you."
— Frank Wilczek

The Elements

On the northwest corner of the intersection of 19th and Jordan Avenues stands a neighborhood grocery store. The corner is busy. It is a popular neighborhood in the large city, one that is both middle-class residential and service-oriented. There are plenty of coffee shops (of course), video stores, beauty salons, adult book stores, tattoo parlors, and specialty stores selling condoms, S&M paraphernalia, and other goodies. There are several psychics who will read your palm or feel the bumps on your head. Pedestrians, car traffic, bicycles, even skateboarders and roller-bladers populate the area day and night.

Although the grocery store has been called Peterson's for many years, the current proprietor is Mr. Blaine. Right now Mr. Blaine, wearing his usual fresh crisp white apron, is standing in aisle 4, meticulously aligning soup cans. Mr. Blaine spends a great deal of time aligning and straightening things. He enjoys it. It soothes and occupies his body and his mind. His doctor, Rosemary Rongley, says that he has some sort of psychological disorder known by some silly initials, something like OCD. Mr. Blaine thinks that Dr. Rongley gets some wild, esoteric ideas. She analyzes too much. There's nothing wrong with aligning things. It's better when things are neat and straight. Instead of me, perhaps it's other people, people who don't like things nice and aligned, people who live in a dirty, messy world, perhaps it's they who have some fancy, initialed psychological disorder, like maybe DCO, Mr. Blaine is thinking. Mr. Blaine smiles a wry smile to himself, then turns a chicken noodle soup can ever so slightly, just a hair, counterclockwise.

Directly across the street from Peterson's grocery store stands a large brown duplex with a small attic window at the very top. Right now, just as Mr. Blaine is busy aligning his cans and smiling wry smiles, a balding middle-aged man, Mr. Peter Dunlap, is gingerly crawling out of that small attic window and carefully shinnying out onto a narrow ledge at the top of the second floor of the brown duplex. His hands are tightly gripping the edge of the eaves while he moves to a position directly above a multi-cracked, wide, gray sidewalk; a position from which he will shortly jump.

Rrrriiinnnggg. Rrrriiinnnggg.

At this moment the telephone is ringing at the house just next door to the duplex from which Mr. Dunlap is about to jump.

"Hello?"

That's Mrs. Ethyl O'Hare, who has lived with her husband Matthew in this same house for nearly 23 years. The house is painted a dull yellow and has pretty lilacs, hydrangeas, geraniums, hyacinths, and pimpernels blooming just inside the somewhat dilapidated white picket fence surrounding the house. If you look closely you will see a bumblebee buzzing from stamen to stamen collecting pollen. Precious butterflies and delicate ruby-throated hummingbirds sometimes visit the O'Hare's yard. Today there is a sticky, bloodstained hypodermic syringe lying partially hidden in the soil beneath the bushes.

The O'Hares have two children. Right now, 14-year-old Eric is in the upstairs bathroom masturbating. Tiffany, 19, is currently institutionalized with depression and an eating disorder. Right at this instant Tiffany O'Hare is in a tiny white room in a large brick building across town repeatedly cutting the inside of her forearm with a razor blade, experiencing what her therapist calls a dissociative state.

"Did you get the money? Can you bring it this afternoon?" inquires the voice on the other end of the telephone speaking to Mrs. Ethyl O'Hare.

At that precise moment, a young woman, Miss Margaret Chaps, enters Mr. Blaine's grocery store (Peterson's), smiling and carrying a fashionable brown purse with some carefully inscribed designer initials on it, even on the inside, where no one will see them, save Miss Chaps. The initials are something like YSL or YLS, but certainly not OCD. Miss Chaps is a bit anxious and panicky because of the PTSD she now experiences ever since the sexual assault some months ago.

Ting...tinkle...ting. Mr. Blaine has attached a small bell to the upper inside part of the front door of the grocery store. Mr. Blaine loves to hear the gentle tinkling sound.

"Margaret! Hello, how are you?"

"Just fine, Mr. Blaine. I need some pans for baking cupcakes. Do you have any?"

"Yes, yes, of course. Right over here."

Mr. Blaine, followed by Margaret Chaps, begins to move sprightly to aisle 6, the last aisle, where he has neatly piled the pots and pans. However, before they reach even aisle 5, they are startled to hear a car's brakes screech loudly and jarringly just outside the store. They both stop quickly, frozen in time, pupils dilated, mouths gaping. Then, immediately, there is a very loud, horrifying, metal-crunching CRASH!

The sound of the crash is heard by everyone nearby. As a consequence, at the very same moment Mr. Blaine and Miss Chaps stare wide-eyed at each other, Mr. Dunlap, in a state of bewilderment, grips the eaves even tighter while he peers down at the waiting sidewalk, Eric O'Hare turns his head slightly toward the bathroom window (but is in no position to stop what he's doing just now), and Mrs. O'Hare pauses in mid-sentence on the phone. Of course, Tiffany O'Hare is completely across town and couldn't possibly hear the loud crash, so she simply continues her cutting, looking impassively at the jagged lines on her arm and the bubbly red blood emerging from them in oozing, runny modules.

Mr. Blaine and Miss Chaps now hurry with anticipation out the grocery store front door where they are startled to see a small red car neatly crunched and wedged beneath a large black truck. Both vehicles are smoking profusely and blocking the intersection. Traffic is tangled and horns are honking. The bumblebee merely visits another anther while a stickworm inches up a sycamore branch, each oblivious to the commotion.

"...How do I know that this will be the end? How do I know you won't just ask for more and more money? How do I know you won't tell my husband anyway? You know it would kill him, it would just kill him!" Mrs. O'Hare has continued her conversation after the brief pause caused by the crash. She's thinking that if the ladies at the church find out about this messy affair she will have to leave the Guild for sure.

Mr. Dunlap had just decided that this would be as good a time as any to jump from his overlooking ledge at the top of the brown duplex when the car crash interrupted his thoughts and momentarily captured his attention. Holding tenaciously to the eaves and scrunching his size 11 shoes onto the narrow ledge, he notices a small crowd forming at the scene of the accident. Chagrined, he concludes that his suicide must wait a few minutes.

The driver of the red car seems pinned, even squashed, behind his steering wheel. He is quite still. Probably dead. The crowd is talking fast and loud, saying things such as, "What kind of car is that? It looks like a Porsche. Boy, I wish I had a Porsche!" and "God, did you see that? Can you believe a car could squeeze under there? That is way cool!" and "Like, ohmygod, like, that's literally like what I just actually saw on TV like just yesterday, like, I mean, ohmygod, so..." and "Bitching, man, bitching."

The driver of the truck is now emerging from the bent door of the truck. A bloody gash on his forehead is leaking. His face is pure white, in high contrast to his tanned body and dark, dirty clothes, and, of course, to the bright-red leaking blood. His rolled up T-shirt sleeves reveal a large, prominent tattoo on his upper left bicep. It says JESUS SAVES in blue letters that are surrounded by a swirling red ribbon. It looks as if there's an arrow passing through the words diagonally from lower left to upper right, but it could be a poorly drawn cross.

One of the observers in the crowd is Mr. Steve Clay who was wandering the neighborhood on his way home from a doctor's appointment. His doctor – coincidentally, Mr. Blaine's doctor, Rosemary Rongley – had just told him that a second test had verified that he is HIV-positive. More initials. Mr. Clay, of course, is in a state of shock and confusion. He hasn't even been able to tell his wife that he is gay, now how will he tell her this? He is staring, unblinking, at the blood on the forehead of the truck driver and thinking about four and one half years of lying, of nervous sneaking around, of clandestine assignations, of certain, well, acts. And he is thinking about AIDS. Even more initials.

Now 10-year old Jimmy Swenson, milling amongst the crowd – excited, hyper, a sufferer of ADHD – has spotted Mr. Dunlap standing precariously on the narrow ledge of his duplex. The attic window is still open. The wind is blowing dust, leaves, and bits of nature into the attic to join the memories that have accumulated there over many years, memories that include a red, loose-leaf notebook full of poems written by Mr. Dunlap many years ago, poems that now sit forlorn and unattended – unwanted. His friends had often warned him that he was too sensitive.

A small insect has alighted on Mr. Dunlap's forearm, irritating him. He has been unable to shoo it away because his hands are still tightly gripping the eaves. Mr. Dunlap is squirming and twisting his upper body and blowing at the insect in hopes of motivating it to leave him in peace. At this very moment Jimmy Swenson begins pointing at Mr. Dunlap and shouting things like, "Look up there, a man's gonna jump." Possibly as a result of the simultaneity of hearing the shouting while staring at the insect, a disturbing image pops into Mr. Dunlap's head. It is an image of Gregor Samsa, Franz Kafka's cockroach-man. Inexplicably, this makes Mr. Dunlap feel very brave and determined – he is going to jump.

Meanwhile, Mr. Blaine and Miss Chaps have arrived at the accident scene from the grocery store, naturally without the cupcake pans. Someone in the crowd is yelling to call 911. Miss Chaps suggests to Mr. Blaine that they return to the grocery store and place the call. Mr. Blaine knows this is a problem because Mr. Blaine knows a secret. He stands quiet, staring, thinking (if only he had a quick, nimble mind instead of an OCD mind.) Mr. Blaine is hesitant and troubled because Mr. Blaine knows that his telephone is in the kitchen and that right now his wife, Mrs. Blaine, is lying dead on the kitchen floor in the tidy apartment in the back of Peterson's grocery store.

The voice on the other end of the telephone says to bring the money today or else he will certainly tell Mr. O'Hare all the gory details of the affair and its gruesome, criminal denouement. Mrs. O'Hare is dumbfounded as to how anyone could possibly know what had happened between her and Mr. Fitzgerald or how she had arranged for his death to look like an accident. How could anyone know?? But one thing she knows for sure: she must not allow Matthew or anyone else to find out.

Matthew O'Hare is at work this morning, even though it is a Saturday. Mr. O'Hare is planning another Boy Scout outing. Mrs. O'Hare thinks of her husband Matthew as a kind, giving person – a respectable businessman who happens to like children. She doesn't know the real reason for the Boy Scout outings. She doesn't know about Mr. O'Hare's "problem." But soon she will know. Soon everyone will know.

You see, as it happens, little Jimmy Swenson has been on some of Mr. O'Hare's Boy Scout outings, and only two weeks from now little Jimmy Swenson, suffering from ADHD, will blurt out the secret of the outings during a tense interrogation that he will receive after being caught attempting to rape six-year-old Anna Cokato who lives next door. Jimmy Swenson knows the secret because on one particular Boy Scout outing Jimmy only pretended to swallow the sleeping pills. Therefore he was not unconscious during the... well, "acts." While small forest animals scurried outside the tents, Jimmy had remained quiet, embarrassed, and feigning sleep. Hence, Mr. O'Hare's secret was revealed to little Jimmy Swenson, who will, in just two weeks time, reveal the secret to the local police.

One of the first people to arrive at the scene of the accident is Mr. George Rivers, who teaches mathematics at the nearby high school. Mr. Rivers is just on his way to hear a lecture in Emerson Hall, the auditorium at the local private college, Starks University. The lecture is being given by the eminent physicist Dr. Murray Gell-

Mann, who is best known for his theories about quarks. In fact, he coined the term – or, rather, borrowed it from literature.

Mr. George Rivers had read in the local newspaper that scientists recently discovered the last of the theorized six quarks, the so-called "top" quark. Quarks are supposedly what everything is made of. What we are made of. Murray Gell-Mann is one of the few people on earth who knows what this means and why it is important. Mr. Rivers has always been curious about such things. Ever since he was in junior high school Mr. Rivers has carried in his pocket a small, folded copy (now quite ragged and worn) of the Periodic Table, listing all of the known elements. The universe in his pocket. And all very neatly aligned.

Mrs. Amelia Rivers, his wife, had often asked George why he bothered to carry such a thing with him all the time. Did it have some religious or spiritual meaning, she wondered? Was it sentimental? Or was it practical in some way that she couldn't fathom? Mr. Rivers now chuckles explosively to himself, quickly cupping his hands to his mouth. He is remembering one such occasion when feeling especially witty he had replied to her, "It's elementary, my dear Mary, I carry it in order to be universally understood."

Mr. Rivers enjoys making puns, although he is quite aware that no one else seems to enjoy them. No one ever laughs or even smiles at his clever puns. In fact, no one seems to have much of a sense of humor at all, it suddenly dawns on Mr. Rivers. For humorous conversation, most people simply recount TV show plots, talk about celebrities, and, of course, go on and on about the weather. Mr. Rivers finds nothing funny in those things, nothing funny at all. "People," he whispers disdainfully under his breath, "what a bunch of humorless jerks."

Only a few feet from Mr. Rivers, oblivious to his disparaging remark, Mr. Blaine is now staring blankly at Miss Chaps who continues to appeal to him to go back to the grocery store to call 911. In this frozen moment, Mr. Blaine suddenly recalls the unpleasant details of this morning, this morning in the kitchen. The events flash through his mind: Mr. Blaine remembers feeling the hard, gritty piece of metal pipe in his freshly cleaned hand. The grit on the metal was so nauseating to him, so filthy, that even now the memory makes him want to wash his hands again. If only she would have stopped nagging him, he ruminates. If only she would have kept quiet. If only the piece of metal pipe had not felt so cool in his hands, so cool in contrast to the kitchen's morning heat.

The truck driver is now staggering amongst the crowd, repeatedly mumbling something about God granting him a miracle. Upon hearing this, Mr. Rivers, the high school teacher with the table of elements in his pocket, smiles a sideways, smirking smile. He is thinking that the word miracle is used only when there is a disaster. If someone says there has been a miracle, then you can safely assume that something bad has happened. No one says it's a miracle there wasn't an accident today, or it's a miracle a plane didn't crash, or it's a miracle I don't have cancer, or it's a miracle I didn't drop dead at the breakfast table this morning, or it's a miracle the earth didn't crash into the sun, and so on, Mr. George Rivers is thinking. But if someone is injured... there's a miracle lurking for sure. Mr. Rivers is trying hard to fit into society, but he feels progressively more and more left out.

Miss Chaps has already started, hurriedly, toward Peterson's grocery store with the intention of calling 911. She's forgotten all about the cupcake pans. Mr. Blaine is stammering at her, but his OCD brain has not yet created an excuse, so he trails behind her, his arms flailing wildly, his mind flailing wildly. A small brown bird is startled by the sudden movements and glides swiftly away from the scene, emitting a high-pitched tweet.

"Tweet."

Mr. Dunlap, still gripping the eaves tightly, is yelling at Jimmy Swenson to mind his own business, to shut up. Some people in the crowd, including HIV-positive Steve Clay, are now looking up at Mr. Dunlap and wondering if Jimmy is right – that Mr. Dunlap *is* planning to jump. Steve Clay is wondering if maybe that's a good idea for him too. The thought now materializes in his mind: an image of crawling out on the ledge, joining Mr. Dunlap, peering birds-eye down on the chaotic scene below, and then bringing a swift, unequivocal end to his HIV nightmare. Then, suddenly, both the insect and the image flutter swiftly away from their respective sites – Mr. Dunlap's arm and Mr. Clay's conscious mind.

Mrs. O'Hare is just now hanging up the phone after having agreed to bring the money to the designated location, as Eric O'Hare, apparently finished with his bathroom business, is bounding down the stairs, running out the front door to join the fun outside. Mrs. O'Hare's mind works faster than Mr. Blaine's and she has already conjured up the crude outline of a plan that will bring an unpleasant, but necessary, end to the man on the phone. Mrs. O'Hare walks patiently but with cold determination to the bureau in the den, opens the hidden drawer, and firmly grasps and removes a gleaming, silver steel pistol. Only need to load it and put it in her Gucci purse, then she's on her way to "pay off" that damn blackmailer.

At this moment, Miss Chaps has burst through the entrance into Peterson's grocery store with Mr. Blaine right behind her. He is yelling at her to wait, but her mind is not processing his protestations. She moves quickly past the neatly aligned cans to the back kitchen door and begins pulling it open. Mrs. Blaine's dead body is lying just inside the door; a stream of dull red blood, partially dried, lies in stark contrast atop the clean white linoleum floor.

Mr. Blaine is just behind her, shouting, "WAIT!" But Miss Chaps grasps the door handle and pulls on it hard, the door swings open wider and wider. Miss Chaps sticks her head into the kitchen, focusing her eyes on the wall, searching for the telephone. Her head turns from side to side, searching. She begins to step into the kitchen where the odor is a bit raw... the body is only a few feet away, lying still, quiet. Mr. Blaine is standing paralyzed just behind, his heart racing, his body limp and shaking, his mind numb.

And then, quite unexpectedly, a series of loud screeching sirens pierces the air, penetrating ears everywhere, including the ears in Peterson's grocery store. Miss Chaps's brain promptly registers the loud, shrill clamoring, and consequently she spins away from the kitchen (and from Mrs. Blaine's dead body, which must remain to be found later by the police) and stares directly at Mr. Blaine, his chubby face now covered with sweat, his eyes opened wide, and his mouth gaping.

"Oh, they're here already," Miss Chaps exclaims, and instinctively releases her grip on the kitchen door handle allowing the door to slowly swing closed behind her. She steps toward a still somewhat anesthetized Mr. Blaine.

"Yes," he gasps with a sigh of great, unexpected relief, but is then suddenly aware of an intense, sharp pain in his left chest, now spreading from his neck down his left arm. He instantly feels faint, recognizes an impending loss of consciousness, and begins to lose his balance. Miss Chaps is staring at him in shock and disbelief, her face a picture-perfect look of pure inconceivability. Mr. Blaine glances quickly, anxiously, down at the floor, studying it, worrying about dirtying his clothes, and then falls directly, flatly, to the grocery store floor. The impact creates an echoing thud and the vibration causes a slight disruption in the alignment of the cans on the shelves. The chicken noodle soup can, the very one that Mr. Blaine had recently aligned, now in response to the vibration rotates ever so slightly, just a hair, in a clockwise direction, and finally rests in the precise orientation it had been in before Mr. Blaine had aligned it. Meanwhile, Mr. Blaine is utterly, unflinchingly, instantly dead from a heart attack, his body lying not far from the body of his wife, Mrs. Blaine.

Several police cars and an emergency vehicle are jockeying for space at the busy intersection. A flycatcher suddenly darts from his perch in a nearby tree, snatches the very insect that had just buzzed off of Mr. Dunlap's arm, and just as suddenly the flycatcher vanishes back into the dense branches overhanging the O'Hare's pale yellow house.

Despondent, HIV-positive Steve Clay has lost interest in the accident scene, having more pressing issues on his mind. He is wandering aimlessly, bumping shoulders with this person or that, his thoughts a jumble of breakfast mush, the image of the red blood on the truck driver's forehead branded insidiously into his mind.

Without purpose, he meanders away from the bustling melange of people and sounds and takes refuge inside his own introspections. He is walking just now on the cracked, gray sidewalk directly below Mr. Dunlap, who is feeling a bit at ease now that the insect has left his arm and the image of Gregor Samsa has left his mind. Mr. Dunlap peers down and finds that he can stare straight onto the top of Mr. Clay's head. From this vantagepoint, Mr. Clay appears to be staggering in slow motion.

A local high school student, Bill Bagget, has recognized his former teacher, Mr. Rivers, and begins talking animatedly with him about the crash, with an occasional swat at a persistent horse fly that is buzzing around their heads. The paramedics have emerged from their vehicle with their usual idiosyncratic metal and plastic equipment, stretchers, cases, and flexible tubes. They are carrying what appears to be a tank of oxygen.

"That's oxygen, isn't it Mr. Rivers?" asks Bill.

"Yes. That's oxygen."

"We studied that in chemistry class. I think oxygen has atomic number eight. Is that right, Mr. Rivers?"

"Yes. Atomic number eight, atomic weight 16." Mr. Rivers knows his elements.

Bill Bagget's curiosity continues: "That container they're carrying the oxygen in, it looks so shiny, what kind of metal do you think it is? Is it titanium? Uhmmm, what's the atomic number of titanium again, Mr. Rivers?" Bill Bagget looks anxiously, curiously at Mr. Rivers, a look that might be taken as one of respect, respect for Mr. Rivers' knowledge.

Mr. Rivers is delighted – absolutely thrilled – to have this opportunity to use his Periodic Table. He proudly smiles at Bill Bagget and reaches into his back trousers pocket saying, "Well, let's just have a look here..."

Mrs. Ethyl O'Hare has secured her shiny steel pistol, stowed it in her Gucci purse, and is now heading out the front door of the pale yellow house. Naturally, she is oblivious to Mr. Dunlap perched on the ledge next door, although she does see a number of teen-aged boys skateboarding on the sidewalk in front of her house. She puts her head down and walks stoically toward her car, which is parked at the curb. On the paved pathway leading from the house, she inadvertently stomps on a small black ant, squishing it and pasting it to the bottom of her red shoe.

Now as Mrs. Ethyl O'Hare exits the gate of the white picket fence, the teen-aged skateboarders suddenly, purposefully, converge on her. Her mind on other matters, she is taken aback by the sudden swarm of young arms and legs. She back-pedals rapidly, flailing her arms in an attempt to catch her balance and to ward off the attackers. One of the many young arms grabs her Gucci purse and tugs it viciously from her grasp. Now several hands are pulling at the strap of the purse and abruptly the purse flies open and the silver, steel pistol is sent tumbling into space, glistening in the morning sun. All eyes, very wide open, are on the pistol as it falls to the ground and comes to rest in a soft patch of grass. A blur of gnats rapidly disperses from the spot where the pistol lands.

"Titanium... titanium... uhhh," Mr. Rivers' finger moves conscientiously across the squares of the Periodic Table, "...uhhh, here it is, yes, titanium, atomic number...."

Just then, in the precise moment of Mr. Rivers' proud success, a gust of wind abruptly wrenches the worn, fold-marked piece of paper from his hand and carries it flying like a tiny tail-less kite, flapping and rippling through the air.... "Oh, my," blurts Mr. George Rivers who immediately gives chase.

Meanwhile, the staggering, slow motion figure of Steve Clay, seen top-view, has transfixed Mr. Dunlap, who, tired and drained, has momentarily loosened his grip on the eaves. He's thinking: it's now or never! Mr. Dunlap's size 11 shoes inch forward on the narrow ledge and his arm muscles tense as he prepares to push away from the house. Mr. Dunlap has decided that now is a good time to jump.

On the street below several young hands have snatched the prized silver pistol from its grassy haven and are now wrestling for it, lifting it high above their young heads. Voices are yelling garbled, macho sounds, and Mrs. O'Hare is screaming. Her screaming, quite naturally, is due in part to the surprise assault on her and also to the fact that the shiny pistol has been revealed, but in addition Mrs. O'Hare is screaming because she now recognizes that one of the young hands reaching for the gun is attached to her son, Eric, who, standing nearby when the foray began, has now joined the tumultuous struggle for possession of the shiny treasure. The bustling of young feet on the patch of lawn has disturbed a tiger beetle that now scurries, waddle-like, from his sanctuary in the tall bluegrass to a somewhat safer location near a clump of dandelions and thistle weeds a few feet away.

As luck would have it, the wind has blown Mr. Rivers' piece of paper with the Periodic Table directly into the face of Eric O'Hare, and expressly at the exact moment when he has secured a solid grip on the shiny, steel gun. The paper, flapping wildly, lands precisely across his eyes, his left eye struck by the square marked "22, Ti, Titanium" and his right eye by the square bearing "47, Ag, Silver."

At the very moment when the struggle for the pistol is proceeding on the street below, at the top of the brown duplex, Mr. Dunlap closes his eyes tight, bends his knees down low, takes one, last, deep breath, and then jumps from the narrow ledge, pushing his body up and away from the house, propelling himself helplessly into the empty space of the morning air. His arms are spread wide and flapping, as if he intended to fly, or perhaps to balance himself in space.

The sudden, unanticipated blindness created by the Periodic Table blown tightly against his eyes startles Eric O'Hare causing him to reflexively contract his muscles. By a strange quirk of fate, his finger was just at that moment resting on the trigger of the pistol; the reflexive muscle contraction causes the gun to fire.

BOOM!!

The sound of the pistol shot is loud and numbing to Mrs. O'Hare, Eric, and the boys nearby. Several people in the crowd turn their heads toward the noise. Some of them point. Several tiny sparrows suddenly, chaotically, fly from a nearby tree, fluttering their wings rapidly.

The bullet is travelling upward at an angle of approximately 75 degrees. Now, who would have guessed it, but just as Mr. Dunlap reaches the very peak, the apex, of his arcing suicidal plunge – his arms spread, his eyes open wide – now the bullet from Mrs. O'Hare's pistol strikes Mr. Dunlap (while poised in midair, arms palpitating) straight through the left temple, killing him instantly. His body immediately goes limp, his muscles lose all tone. Then Mr. Dunlap's sad, lifeless body, lured by the cold certainty of gravity, plummets directly down, quickly gathering speed, toward the point on the wide sidewalk directly below precisely where Mr. Steve Clay has momentarily ceased his wandering and has paused, suspended by the sound of the gunshot.

THUMP!!

Mr. Dunlap's limp, dead body lands squarely on top of the unsuspecting head of Mr. Steve Clay. A splattering, thunk-like sound emanates from the collision, and the two intertwined bodies now lie sprawling on the cracked, gray sidewalk.

Meanwhile, the folded, worn, piece of paper with the Periodic Table on it has since flown from Eric O'Hare's face, has been whisked away by the wind, and is now gently wafting down avenues and alleys, flittering blocks from the bedlam of screaming and shouting near Peterson's grocery store.

Dr. Murray Gell-Mann has arrived for his lecture and is walking the short distance from the parking lot to Emerson Hall. The President of Starks University, Dr. Morris Champlin, a former chemistry professor who has just finished his phone conversation with Mrs. Ethyl O'Hare, and who later this month will be taken into custody by the local police on suspicion of soliciting prostitution from teen-aged boys, is walking with him. They are discussing the recent laboratory discovery of the top quark. A small flock of grackles are sitting quietly on a nearby tree branch placidly observing the two men. One of the grackles lets out a penetrating, "Caw."

Coincidentally, the piece of paper containing the Periodic Table of Elements has settled in a place on the walkway just ahead of where the two luminaries are now ambling. Unbeknownst to Dr.

Gell-Mann, who, of course, has other, much more important matters on his mind, a small bit of chewing gum has stuck to the sole of his brown size 12 dress shoe, and now that very bit of gum on the bottom of Dr. Murray Gell-Mann's shoe has come down exactly on top of Mr. Rivers' piece of paper containing the Periodic Table. The paper has become stuck to the bottom of Dr. Gell-Mann's left shoe. The two men continue into Emerson Hall, both oblivious to the piece of paper which remains stuck to the brown dress shoe of Dr. Gell-Mann.

Following a wonderful introduction by Starks University President Morris Champlin, Dr. Gell-Mann is now standing at the podium staring out onto a sea of bright eager faces, including the bright eager face of Mr. George Rivers. Still completely unaware that he is standing atop the very neatly aligned table of elements, Dr. Gell-Mann is about to begin his presentation. Members of the audience have already formulated their questions and are earnestly awaiting their turn to offer intricate inquiries about the makeup of the universe and the mysteries of quarks.

And so, with the Periodic Table firmly stuck to the sole of his shoe, Dr. Murray Gell-Mann now begins his rather complicated explanations of muons, leptons, bosons, neutrinos, and other exotic subatomic particles.

"Ladies and gentlemen," Dr. Gell-Mann intones, "there is a principle which I like to call the Totalitarian Rule of Physics..."

Mr. Rivers settles comfortably into his seat, his lost Periodic Table now temporarily gone from his thoughts, his attention riveted to the eminent man of science at the podium.

Dr. Gell-Mann, standing firmly atop the table of elements, continues, "The Totalitarian Rule of Physics states that anything that isn't forbidden is compulsory. That is," Murray Gell-Mann patiently explains, "if the laws of physics do not rule out an event, then that event not only *can* happen, it *must* happen!"

Mr. Rivers smiles a contented smile.

Dada Redux

"Tiger got to hunt, bird got to fly; Man got to sit and wonder 'why, why, why?'
Tiger got to sleep, bird got to land; Man got to tell himself he understand."
— Kurt Vonnegut, Cat's Cradle

"Science has now determined there is a direct relationship between the way the ball bounces and the cookie crumbles."
— Anonymous

"To err is human, but to really foul things up you need a computer."
— Paul Ehrlich

"...and then, I have nature and art and poetry, and if that is not enough, what is enough?"
— Vincent Van Gogh

"Computers are useless. They can only give you answers."
— Pablo Picasso

Dada Redux

This story, in its entirety, was created by a computer using a method first devised by Dada artists decades ago. Dadaists created poems by randomly selecting words from a dictionary. Similarly, this story was created by the use of random word generation.

Yes, difficult as it may be to believe, the words seen here in this story, the ones you are reading right now, were randomly selected from an online dictionary, one at a time, in the exact sequential order they appear here. The Dadaists, of course, used a real, hard-copy dictionary. However, for this story a variation of that method was employed. This story, in fact, is the first story ever created using a digital random number generator and a digital computer dictionary program with numbered words in English. The words were sequentially selected by the random number generator and printed exactly as you are reading them now, precisely in this order. Yes, you are reading the very first story written using a digital version of the Dada poetry style of random word generation. This is a truly exciting accomplishment.

You may well wonder how this could be possible. How is it possible that words and sentences with apparent meanings, proper syntax, normal grammatical structure, and semantic appropriateness, such as this very sentence, could have been generated by the random selection of words by a computer? The answer is quite simple: It took a gigantically huge number of iterations. This is only one permutation of the colossal number of stories that were generated. It was simply a matter of probability. It has been said that if enough monkeys were pounding on typewriters for a long enough period of time that eventually the monkeys would produce a work of Shakespeare. Of course, such an exercise would be pointless since we already have the works of Shakespeare. However, the same statistical principle applies to this story, an entirely unique work of literature produced by chance.

As you might imagine, the actual printing of this story by the computer that created it took only a few seconds. But the preparation and the implementation of the innumerable permutations took many, many years. First, in order to create this story, computer programs had to be written, programs for random number generation and for the numbering of the complete list of words in an English dictionary. Next the computer program had to run a near infinite number of times before arriving at this particular arrangement of words. The monkeys, remember? Thousands of computers were programmed with the random word generator and were designed to create and print out stories with precisely one thousand words. The computers were then switched on and they ran nonstop around the clock for decades. For each iteration, one thousand words were printed in the exact order in which the random word generator had selected them. An incalculable number of stories were composed, and nearly every single one of them was a true Dada version of pure, utter nonsense (though one permutation was eerily reminiscent of a short story by Italo Calvino). Finally, this story was created, this story, the very first of its kind, an original exposition written solely by random word selection.

You might well wonder what the point of all of this is. Well, Shakespeare, remember? It had to be done. Like the proverbial mountain. But, also please contemplate on the motivation of the Dada artists: They had seen the devastation of World War I, the violence, destruction and killing, the madness of modern twentieth century society, and the Dadaists steadfastly concluded that if rational thought led to that kind of a world then clearly the world was better off without rational thought. Hence, the birth of the irrational. Dadaism embraced genuine nonsense, much as later did the Marx Brothers and Monty Python's Flying Circus. Dadaism reveled in irrationality; it was Dadaism's rebuttal to the atrocities rampant in modern civilization.

But, surely you must understand that the state of the world that we live in today is similarly full of atrocities, horrors, and lunacy, perhaps even worse than what was encountered by the Dada artists. Haven't you noticed? The world today is an incorrigible madhouse in which supposedly rational thinking and civilized societies have led us down the path to terrorism, strife, corruption, poverty, rape, murder, destruction, death by drone, human trafficking, suicide bombing, and other equally repugnant and seemingly inexorable events.

Yes, certainly you must realize, dear reader, it is time therefore for a rebirth of Dada. Dada redux. It is time to venerate irrationality, to cultivate random writing, to prize and to encourage the flowering of the ridiculous and the absurd as a reaction against the inanity and the horror that permeate the Dark Ages that we today must endure. Hence, we have this treatise drafted by a computer.

Naturally, monkeys, too, could have done it. Monkeys could generate more than just a work of Shakespeare. Monkeys are not limited to reproducing works already in existence. Monkeys could pump out innovative, singular works like this one. Enough monkeys typing long enough could have spawned this sentence, this very one you are reading right now, and, it is true, this whole narration exactly as you see it could have been created by monkeys. Probability, remember? But, where in the world would we get that many monkeys? And, for that matter, that many typewriters? And, who in his or her right mind would have the time and patience to wait for this particular story to be written by those monkeys on those typewriters? So, computers were the obvious answer.

The irony is that computers typically are appreciated for their rational, logical approach. But, as you can see, even a random, irrational approach macaw syllogism bright. Cantankerous plenary azimuth, didactic rhythm. Glean extemporaneous, forensic meringue sailfish. Pistachio congeal erg. Morphology spent, wringing theta wave. Intrepid sandwich invertebrate monk brackish atoll. Bug palindrome, seesaw crackerjack. Flat quicken reversible jar into beneath swallow ream, flax brisk envelope. Someone mumble.

Programmers Note: Above is the entire story, word for word, created by the random word generator. We added the title and punctuations. We are very sorry for the irregularity at the end. We were impatient. We should have waited longer for the random word generator to complete an entirely perfect story. But, we just couldn't wait. Who knows how long it would have taken to get a perfect story? For decades we had looked at gazillions of stories pumping out of thousands of computers and, honestly, for the most part they were complete dribbling nonsense. Until this story. When we saw this one, we said, "Close enough."

The Egyptians

"Life is the art of drawing without an eraser."
— John W. Gardner

"Each has his past shut in him like the leaves of a book known to him by heart,
and his friends can only read the title."
—Virginia Woolf

"Do not chase happiness; let it chase you."
— Petar Dunov

"Unhurt people are not much good in the world."
— Enid Starkie

"I have not failed. I've just found 10,000 ways that won't work."
— Thomas Alva Edison

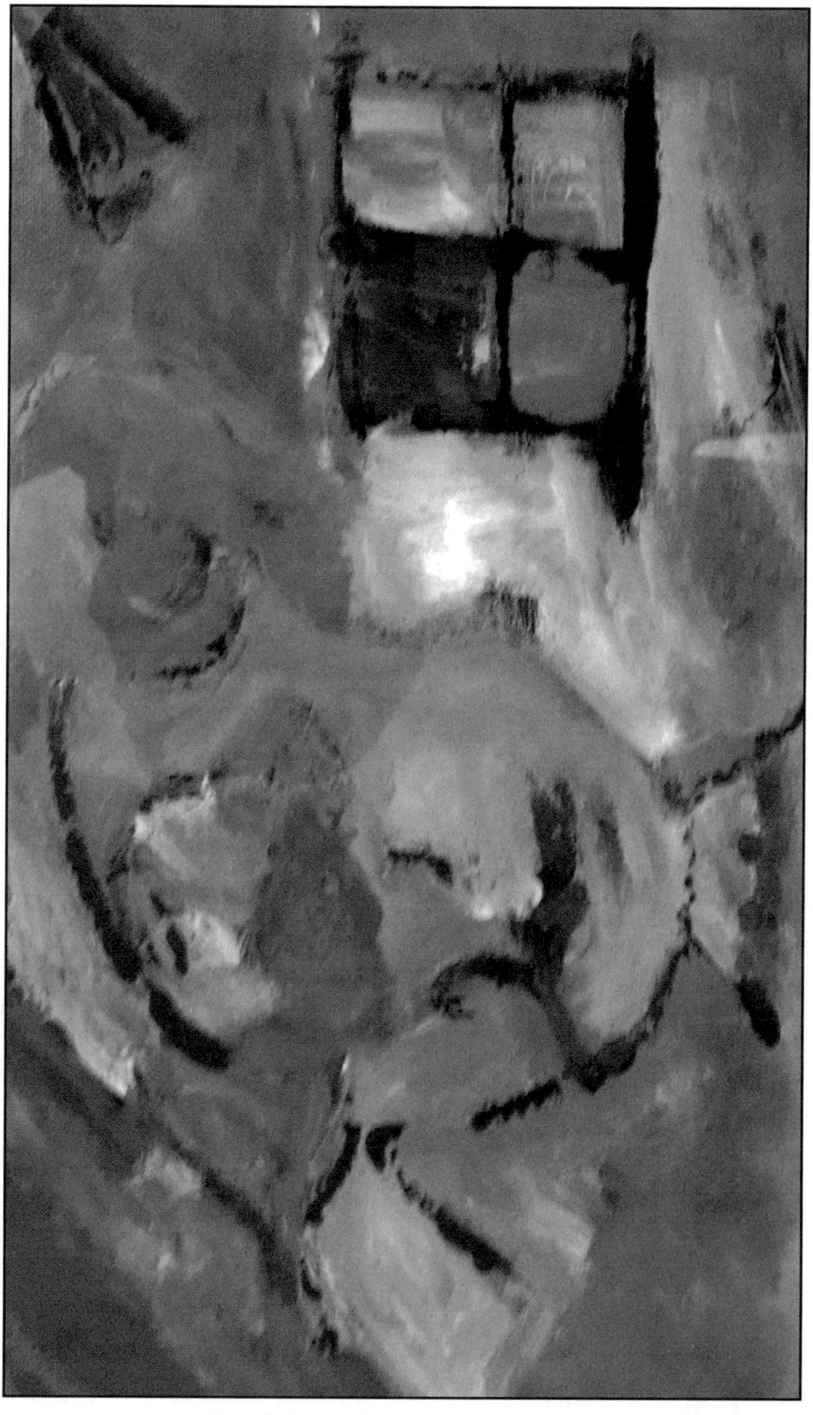

The Egyptians

(1)

"Most people are other people. Their thoughts are someone else's opinions, their lives a mimicry, their passions a quotation."
— Oscar Wilde

What's done is done, she said.

I know, he said, I only meant I wish we would have done things differently, that things would have been different.

We did what we did, she said. She looked into her coffee cup. I'm tired and I don't really want to get into all of that now.

He moved slightly on the hard wooden chair and repositioned his feet on the floor. I'm sorry you're tired, I only meant....

He plopped a sugar cube into his coffee and picked up a second cube that he held delicately, carefully inspecting it.

Did you pay the bills today? she asked.

He held the small white cube between his thumb and index finger, staring at it. He felt its grainy texture. He slowly, meticulously, turned the cube to better feel the firm, stubbly surface that to him seemed in a curious way to be quite unlike anything else. He carefully placed the sugar cube on the tabletop where it stood lonely and upright, majestic, he thought, like a tiny, pure white pyramid. He imagined miniature Egyptians with ropes and levers, toiling year after year, piling grain after grain, working under the whip to construct this perfect, noble cube, this monument to humankind.

She said she'd be here at six o'clock, he remembered. She said she didn't have to work late tonight because of all she's been doing at home. All she's been doing at home, he thought.

Yes, I did, he said.

But it had been after seven when she arrived. Her lateness

made him feel a sort of helplessness and resignation more than anger, although if he had any choice, he now thought, he would definitely prefer the anger.

No choice, he thought.

I wish things were different too, she said.

He looked at his hands, the backs of his hands. He noticed the cheesy wrinkles and dark spots. He remembered how his hands used to be smooth and unblemished. He remembered how he used to get compliments on the appearance of his hands and how that had been important to him, in some small way a source of pride and self-esteem, but he now thought it silly and immature.

What's done is done, he thought.

What's done is done, he said.

I'm tired, she said. Let's go home.

The coffee shop's windows filled the front walls and were divided by mullions into large multi-paned squares. The glass was cloudy, maybe dirty, hiding the secrets inside the coffee shop from nosy passersby. The walls of the coffee shop were littered with multicolored papers tacked at random angles and framed black and white photographs of urban buildings and busy street scenes.

He methodically looked around the room, surveying the cliché before him. He felt alone and hopeless, as if caught in the solitary desolation of some no-man's land beyond this space and time – a single languorous cactus in a desert sandstorm.

Okay, he said, just let me finish my coffee.

He looked at the cup as he lifted it to his lips. As his head tilted back he caught a glimpse of her face, her sorrowful face staring into her coffee, and then as he sipped he became aware of the large array of window squares, the panes of which now seemed totally opaque. He could see nothing outside.

The radio was on. He thought it was some Eastern European poet talking. The talk was something about undiscovered treasures and mental lapses. He didn't understand.

He placed his cup on the tabletop. She was looking at him now. He returned her look and for a brief period they locked eyes. What went through his mind was a blur of regret and longing. They could not hold the gaze. Each turned away.

He looked at his cup sitting on the table. He looked at the sugar cube standing nearby. As he did, he noticed that she had rested her hand palm down, the tips of her fingers just touching the edge of the tabletop, her palm hovering in the air in the space above the dirty wooden floor.

He stared at her hand. Her thin, delicate fingers pressed lightly on the tabletop. He was stirred by the apparent lightness of her hand, by its buoyant motionlessness, as if it were floating in the thick smoke-filled air like a fragile bird levitating over a brooding sea. He felt a strong urge to touch her hand, to caress it while speaking words of love and redemption. But he felt clumsy and inept, unsure of himself, of his own feelings and intentions. And of hers. He stared at her hand, and as he did, his desire intensified.

His feet shifted. He continued to stare. She sat quiet, looking into her coffee cup.

Finally, without thinking, he moved his arm tenuously, but swiftly, an instinctive gesture, as if his arm were not under his control but were guided by a primal emotion, an uncontrollable impulse, an alien arm. His hand jerked awkwardly toward hers. He was as surprised as she. He didn't know what he would say to her when their hands met, he had no idea, but he assumed that at that moment, in the moment of touching, the moment when their hands touched, that the right words would come to him.

His shaking arm skimmed across the tabletop and bumped his coffee cup hard enough to topple it. The sweetened coffee spilled and flowed. He immediately stopped his reach, withdrew his arm, and raised himself from his chair.

She pulled back her hovering hand, stood up and stared silently at him, her forehead wrinkled, her mouth slightly open.

He was staring at the tabletop, at the coffee spill, thinking about the coffee shop's windows and thinking that if they weren't so cloudy and dirty that the people on the outside, the passersby, would be able to see in and would see the two of them standing there now.

The black coffee spread quickly over the round tabletop. He stood still and quiet and watched as the pure white sugar cube turned dark at its very bottom and then as the darkness slowly, insidiously, and inexorably spread upward engulfing the cube.

(2)

"If the doors of perception were cleansed everything would appear to man as it is: infinite. For man has closed himself up, till he sees all things thro' narrow chinks of his cavern."
— William Blake

Soon after the funeral, it began.

He was afraid, but not panicked. He assumed, or maybe hoped, that things would get better. All things passed, he assured himself.

On the day of the funeral, he had been ill. He came down with a cold the day before and was oblivious to the fact that the two were connected. Only later was it pointed out to him how natural it was to become sick after weeks of caring for his father while he was dying – the stress of it all. He now accepted that explanation as totally reasonable. It began shortly after.

Jane had been with him throughout the ordeal, including at the funeral, and now was with him as he tried to adjust.

I'm going to the store, she said, do you want anything?

Do I want anything? he thought. He shook his head. What could I possibly want?

No, thank you, he said.

Although Jane had been with him throughout the ordeal – had been with him physically– in fact she had offered no emotional support. Instead she proved to be wrenchingly stoic to the point of being indifferent – or worse, icy. He hadn't thought about that until lately, but now it was constantly on his mind, and it worried and perplexed him. He had considered all of the obvious explanations, but nothing stuck. He was tired.

By the time she returned from the store, he had fallen asleep in his chair. He could hear her in the kitchen as he started to emerge from a deep sleep into a half-awake, hypnagogic state. His eyes were open only a slit and his vision was clouded, fuzzy, as if his corneas were coated with Vaseline.

His mind was full of dreams – absurd, unforgettable dreams.

He blinked his eyes and squinted, trying to focus. He saw that the TV was on. A bright rectangular light encased in a box, he thought. An image coffin. Where we bury images that are dead. Buried until their re-run resurrections.

A sitcom was on.

He stared at the TV and thought that he could detect thin, horizontal lines of fire – no, not fire – lines of electrical energy, pulsating on the screen. He had never before been so aware of the lines, which were now so apparent, so distracting, that they easily diverted his attention from the dead images of the sitcom. What were these lines, other than lines, he wondered? What were they made of? Electricity?

He heard her call out, Do you want some dinner?

He looked toward the kitchen and saw her quizzical face peeking out from the doorframe. Her head seemed to float unsupported, separated from her body. Yet her expression was perfectly normal – nothing at all out of the ordinary. This paradox startled him and he began to wonder why they were having such difficulty communicating.

Yes, he answered, that would be nice.

He closed his eyes and leaned back. He felt the solid, cushioned arms of his chair and squeezed with both hands. He also squeezed his eyes shut, and doing so, he saw the after-images of the horizontal lines brightly inscribed and pulsating on the backs of his eyelids. Electrical lines on the backs of his eyelids.

She took a chair across the room. She picked up a magazine.

We have a new system at work, she said without looking up from the magazine.

He opened his eyes and looked at her. System? he puzzled silently to himself.

Oh? he said.

It's been a mess all week, what with all the different numbers. It's very chaotic.

What kind of system? he asked.

Computer, of course, she said. There's all new numbers and codes and we have to look it up every time. It's a mess. And Margo keeps punching in new numbers and screwing around with the system. She told everyone that she's in charge of the numbers and the codes. She calls it the system architecture. She's such a liar.

Lying, he said to himself. False information. Deception. Prevarication. Do we all lie in our own special ways? Is it possible to live without lying?

You can't tell the truth all the time, he said. Otherwise you'd keep saying the same things over and over again.

She said nothing, just stared at the magazine. He thought he saw her lip quiver a bit, more of a grimace than a smile, in reaction to his peculiar statement.

It would be formulas, he continued, we'd be talking in formulas. F equals MA, C squared equals A squared plus B squared, E equals MC squared.

He smiled and looked at her for a response. Nothing. She turned a page of the magazine.

There was a loud laugh from the sitcom laugh track. He turned and looked intently, curiously at the TV. The electrical lines were even more obvious to him now; they seemed to engulf, to swallow, the dead images. The lines seemed to exist outside the surface of the rectangular screen – superimposed over the images – in an oscillating 3-D universe, like a hovercraft idling and vibrating just above the concave glass surface. What are those lines? he wondered, those electrical lines hovering over the front of the TV?

Without a word, without a look, she put the magazine down, got up, and went to the kitchen.

He was still staring at the TV when the power went out and the bright rectangular screen went completely black.

But the lines were still there. He could see them clearly when he closed his eyes.

(3)

"We have art in order not to die of the truth."
— Friedrich Nietzsche

Despair is what he felt. And futility.

Yes, he thought, despair and futility seemed to ring true. Naming his emotions gave him some relief. Even a bit of pleasure, he thought. The perverse pleasure of cynicism, as a martyr might feel.

She rarely talked to him anymore. She kept busy with her office work. Going over endless numbers, abstract charts and technical terms. Arcane sales language. Mumbo-jumbo to him. Pointless and numbing. She now spent hours poring over it, not looking at him, let alone talking.

How did it come to this? he wondered. He was dumbfounded. Hadn't a clue. He knew there had been a time long ago when things were different. Perhaps they had even been in love. Though he intellectually knew those times had existed, those times of love, he could not now fathom them, attempt as he might to imagine what they felt like, how the days had gone when things were different, how they had related to each other, how it had felt. He could not now fathom them. The change – the descent, as he now thought of it – had been too gradual.

He watched her at the desk, her eyes and hands intent on papers spread in neat piles. Stacks of white rectangles on a shiny black surface. Each piece of paper a perfect white background cluttered with what seemed to him to be random, meaningless black splotches. Insignificant.

Should he go to her? Touch her? Say something? What would he say? What was there to say? A touch might be helpful, he thought. But more likely it would be rebuked. Her body would jerk and tense in repulsion, her cold disgust would jar the room. He could not touch her. Could not even talk to her. There was nothing to say.

The sunlight from the window formed a large bright yellow triangle on the wall behind her. One vertex of the triangle reached down from the wall and just met the edge of the desk, creating a small point of contrast like a dot of glimmering starlight on a calm sea of black. The triangle loomed over her as if it were a door, a portal to another time, another world.

He stared at the triangle. He felt pulled into it. He seemed to feel a warmth from the yellow triangle, and it intrigued him. He imagined diving into it and being absorbed by a calm, cool, soothing salve.

She rustled her papers as if wrestling with them. She crossed her legs. As she did, he noticed that the gray skirt of her business suit inched up her thigh. Her black business shoe, a pump, now hung above the taupe carpet, dangling from her nylon-covered toes. As she gently moved her leg, the heel of her black pump began to sway up and down, up and down, in an empty, rhythmic fugue.

He started to say something, but he stopped. What he started to say was, Jane, I love you. For an instant, perhaps under the spell of the yellow triangle, he thought that he could say this to her. But he was wrong. He couldn't say anything.

He picked up the remote and clicked on the TV. He stared at the set as it brightened. A commercial for tennis shoes was on. He thought about running, but felt immovably heavy.

She lifted her gaze, turned away from the papers, and glanced at him and then at the TV. Then she went back to rustling her papers.

He noticed that as she had turned to look at him and at the TV, for just that brief instant, her black shoe had temporarily stopped swinging. But now it had returned to its rhythmic swaying, inches above the taupe carpet.

He stared at the TV. She worked on her papers. The bright yellow sunlight triangle on the wall behind her began to dim and eventually faded to black.

*

"You're the oddest person I've ever met, you couldn't get rid of me if you tried."
— Audrey Niffenegger

"The world is full of magical things patiently waiting for our wits to grow sharper."
— Bertrand Russell

"At this point I think we need to embrace the weird. High-five it. Give it our phone number."
— Jim Zub

"Everything is funny, as long as it's happening to somebody else."
— Will Rogers

"The cure for boredom is curiosity. There is no cure for curiosity."
— Dorothy Parker

"Reality is merely an illusion, albeit a persistent one."
— Albert Einstein

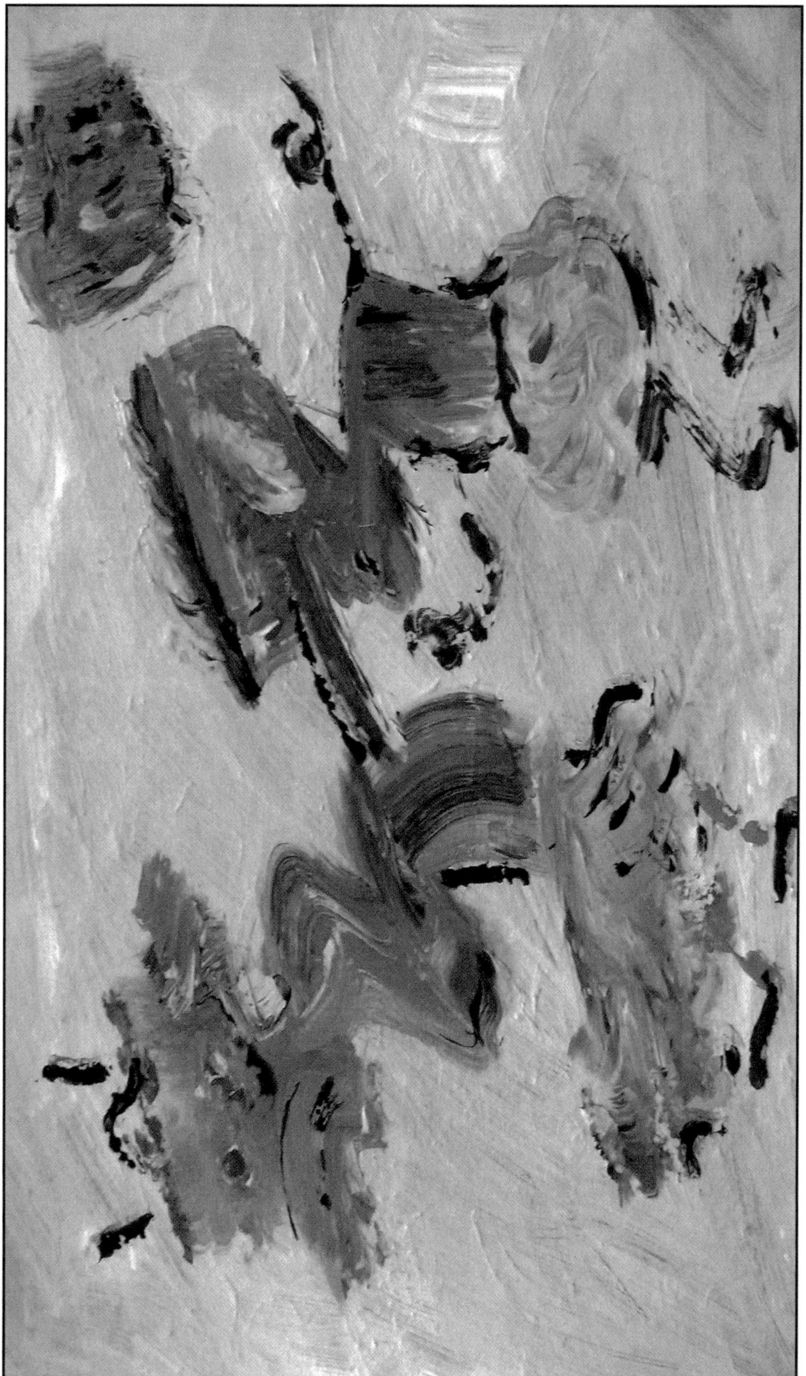

*

Quack, quack he said. Sounded nothing like a duck. He didn't quack; he just said quack, quack. You know, the word quack. He said the word. Not the sound. Just pronounced the word quack. Twice. In a row. Quack, quack.

Well, what does one say to a guy who says quack, quack? I started to walk away without saying anything, but then impulsively stopped and turned back to the weird guy and said quack, quack right back at him. Quack, quack. He seemed to like it – his face and eyes lit up – and then he started to say quack to me again but I stopped him and asked him if he wanted a drink.

We sat on barstools next to each other in a seedy bar that I favored, looking forward staring at liquor bottles standing upright all lined up in front of a faded mirror at the back of the bar. The liquor bottles looked to me like ballet dancers lined up prim and proper ready to begin their dance. The liquor bottles were facing forward as if they were staring at us, too. What did we look like to them, I wondered? The double quacking was still in my mind and there wasn't a duck in sight. We each had a drink in front of us. Well, his was mostly gone, I guess, but I was still sucking on mine. I noticed that a bottle of tequila seemed on the verge of a pas de chat. The weird quack, quack man turned to look at me, which got my attention.

Then he told me his story. He needed me. I was the guy he was supposed to meet according to a fortune cookie he opened last night. I had the right clothes, the right hair, and the right face. I was the right guy. The fortune cookie said so. Quack, quack was the clincher, he said. The fortune had been very long, he clarified. It even contained a footnote that was indicated by an asterisk in the message. The footnote said the guy would say quack, quack. The weird guy apparently felt that this asterisked footnote was immensely important. I peeked at the liquor bottle ballet dancers and I could have sworn the schnapps and bitters were performing a pas de deux.

Where, I asked, did you get such a strange fortune cookie?

He worked in a Chinese restaurant, he replied, and he always took home a handful of the fortune cookies. He explained that last night he had looked at the pile and noticed one cookie was looking back at him. That's what he said. One fortune cookie was looking back at him. I didn't ask.

Then he paused telling his tale and he leaned toward me and looked directly into my eyes and slowly, very carefully enunciated the word, "figuratively." Well, yeah, of course, that's what I was hoping. Duh! What a relief. Would've been kinda peculiar if he had meant the cookie was looking at him "literally." You know what I mean? But, as I said, I didn't ask. I stared at the liquor bottles more intently and for a moment thought I saw the crème de cacao smiling at me. Not really a smile; more of a smirk.

Then the quack quack man told me that he had opened the fortune cookie that was looking at him and had read the important message inside – the very long fortune. The fortune had told him that he was to meet a man that he needed. A man dressed like me. A man who looked like me. A man who apparently was me. Oh, and of course, the important footnote in the fortune (you know, that had been marked by an asterisk) made it quite explicit that the man who was needed would say quack, quack. That's right, the man would say quack, quack.

Well, I replied in a rather abashed manner, that is very curious indeed. Perhaps you are mentally ill. Perhaps you had a hallucination. Perhaps you are from outer space. Maybe I'm mentally ill. Maybe I'm having a hallucination. Maybe I'm from outer space. Perhaps you have recently experienced a bump on the head. Perhaps you are some sort of con artist with the latest con that I am not familiar with. Perhaps you have taken some illicit drugs that make you delusional. Perhaps you have taken leave of your senses. Or perhaps I have taken leave of mine. I really do not know what is going on. This is all very strange, very strange indeed, I remarked. I also noticed that a bottle of Drambuie seemed to be standing in fourth arabesque position.

You know, I must admit, however, that I was getting curious. Just what was this all about – this quack, quack nonsense? I then inquired of the man whom I considered to be probably a bit whackadoodle: what is it that you need? You say that you need me. But, for what? What is it that I can do for you? I squinted hard and looked him in the eye. It was the same eye that had looked at the fortune cookie, and the same eye that the fortune cookie had looked back at. Figuratively, he claimed, but now I wondered. The liquor bottles were still looking at us, ready to begin the grand pas d'action. I glanced from the ballet dancers to the face of the weird quack, quack guy.

He stared at me for a long time. Then he simply said: answers. I need answers. He looked down at his glass and then he looked back at me. I thought he might be crazy, but I also thought I should listen to what he had to say, just in case. The liquor bottle ballet dancers weren't going anywhere and neither was I. I ordered another round and I noticed that the bartender nodded at the ballet dancers as if there was some sort of secret between them. I wondered what it could mean. Then I turned back to the goofy quack, quack guy and took a more serious tone.

Okay, I'll bite, I responded, what are the questions? Now, I really thought I had him there. I imagined he would have no idea what questions to ask. If this guy was a nut then he would not have any clue what questions he needed me to answer. I was beginning to smile, expecting him to be stumped by my query.

However, he wasn't fazed. Not at all. He was ready to talk. So, he did. You see, he began relating his story, I am going to take a trip to Myanmar next week. I have never been there. I am to deliver a package that is not entirely legal, as far as I understand. It is from my employer at the Chinese restaurant down the street.

Oh, yeah, I interrupted the weird guy, the Chinese restaurant where you got the fortune cookie that looked back at you. Yeah, right, I chuckled.

He was not bothered by my sarcasm, not at all, didn't even

seem to notice it. Rather, he continued his strange tale. I am being well paid for delivery of the package, he said. It is not drugs, nor guns, but I cannot tell you exactly what is in the package because I do not know exactly myself. It is a metal object. About 18 inches high. I think it might be an artifact of some sort. However, what I need is I need to know what I should do when I get there. To Myanmar. The instructions were not clear. All I really had was the fortune cookie and it led me to you. The quack, quack you said to me was the confirmation sign. You are the man with the answers. There is no doubt. You are the man with the answers that I need.

No, that can't be right, I quickly exclaimed. I am a nobody. I am just a guy sitting in this bar having a drink. I am divorced, no kids, I live in a studio apartment downtown, I have a meaningless job, and now it is after work and I am having a drink. I don't know anything about a fortune cookie or even what Myanmar is. I only said quack, quack because you said it to me. I don't have any answers for you, buddy. I'm sorry, I just don't. The liquor bottle ballet dancers looked as if they were a bit dejected about this, even a bit melancholic. I wondered what effect this would have on their failli?

But, the weird guy stammered, surely that was the sign, he insisted. The fortune cookie said so. A guy who said quack, quack to me, a guy who is dressed like you, who looks like you would provide the answers. The answers that I need before I begin my journey to Myanmar. You are the man with the answers, you simply must be.

My curiosity and politeness were quickly being replaced by exasperation. Quack, quack indeed! No, I blurted out. I am just a normal guy. I couldn't possibly know what you should do in Myanmar. I don't even know what that is. You can't go around believing in fortune cookies! What is wrong with you anyway? The ballet dancers were almost slumped over now. I avoided eye contact with them and looked into my drink.

Okay, okay, the weird guy said. But then, apparently undeterred in pestering me, he insisted, have you ever seen one of these? He had reached into his coat pocket and removed a small object that was part metal and part hard rubber. He held it in his palm and reached it up in front of my face. He held it on his open palm a few inches directly in front of my eyes. He disclosed to me that the object had been secretly placed into his coat pocket shortly after he had received the package. With a serious and worried look on his face he then proclaimed, I don't have any idea what it is or what it means. Do you know? Do you?

I took a sip from my drink and then told him, yes, I know what that is. It is called a capo. It is a device that is used on stringed instruments such as a guitar in order to raise the pitch. It is derived from the Italian word capotasto which means the head of the fretboard. A capo is tightened onto a fret and shortens the strings thereby raising the pitch of the instrument. But, listen, weird guy, why do you ask me such a strange thing? The dancers were perking up. I expected at least a petite saut soon.

Ahh, a *capo*, the quack, quack man said. So, that's what it is. Okay, it raises the pitch. A capo raises the pitch. Very interesting. Perhaps it is some sort of clue, some message. See, the fortune cookie was right – you did know an answer. You knew about the capo. How did you know that?

Well, I used to play guitar a little, I answered. But, look, lots of people know what a capo is. And, by the way, it's just a coincidence that I said quack, quack. You said it first, after all. Quack, quack, you said. Then I said it. You said it first. Coincidences happen all the time, you know. I don't know why. I don't know if it's because of quantum physics, fate, random events, fractals, chaos, or some other strange and curious force, but I do know that coincidences are a regular part of nature, a very common part of good old Mother Nature. Yes sir, coincidences are all around us all the time. You cannot avoid them. They are a law. A very curious law of nature. Wherever you go, whatever you do, there is a coincidence right there or around the corner. It's guaranteed. Yes, I'm sure that this is all just a coincidence. Just part of nature's laws.

The weird guy's face now suddenly looked lost and hopeless. Crestfallen, even. He looked as if he was ready to cry or to have a panic attack, I couldn't tell which one. And, yes, while coincidences seem to be a regular occurrence in nature – one of nature's odd laws – it also is a quirky law of nature that pretty much anyone who sees a face that looks like this guy's face just has to feel at least a small bit of sympathy for the person who has that face. So, what did you expect, then? Yes, I felt a small bit of sympathy for the quack, quack guy. Consequently, I thought I'd better humor him a bit more. Even the liquor bottles looked as if they wanted me to humor the odd quack, quack man a little more. So, I did.

Okay, tell me, I inquired with a sincere voice and a facial expression of genuine interest, what is this Myanmar that you mentioned? I hoped this would cheer him up a bit, showing a little interest, you know?

Sure enough, it worked. I noticed that the ballet dancers seemed impressed and maybe were even a bit pleased with me. I mean, for showing some sympathy and interest in the quack, quack man.

The wacky guy's face perked up. His energy returned. It's a country, a region of Asia, he answered. It used to be called Burma. Some of the earliest civilizations were there some 13,000 or so years ago – the Pyu and the Mon civilizations. Hey, wait a minute. I think I'm on to something here, he said excitedly. His face was lighting up like crazy now. He sputtered out his thoughts. These early civilizations practiced primordial forms of Buddhism, he continued. They had a spirit called the Kapu which later came to represent taboos among Polynesian peoples, a kind of code of conduct. You know, that is what this must be about. Now I think I understand. There is a famous statue – the Kapu statue. It is very special. When this statue is rubbed it makes a noise, a specific sound, a clear, pleasant tone, somewhat like the Tibetan singing bowls that hum when their rims are rubbed. You know about those bowls? Well, the Kapu was a spirit in the early religious beliefs of the Pyu and Mon peoples in the region that is now known as Myanmar. The Kapu statue makes a soothing tone when it is rubbed correctly.

Then the weird quack, quack guy looked me straight in the eye with a look of solemnness. He intoned: it is of high religious significance. The package that I have must contain a Kapu statue. That must be it. A Kapu statue. They are very rare and very valuable. That must be it.

Okay, I replied with a bit of uncertainty, that would be sorta cool, for sure, but what in the world is the message? What is the answer that the fortune cookie told you to look for? I mean, what is the answer? Is it the identification of the Kapu statue? Is that what this is all about? It was then that for just a moment I thought I saw a light bulb turn on just above his head. I glanced over at the liquor bottle ballet dancers and I believe the ouzo was starting a pirouette.

Well, the quack, quack man elucidated, I'm now realizing that perhaps it is a fake. I mean perhaps it is not a genuine Kapu statue in the package that I am to deliver. You know, perhaps we would be able to tell that it is a fake because the pitch would be wrong. He looked at me with the same eye that had much earlier been looked at by the fortune cookie. The eye was gleaming now. It was large and shiny. Meanwhile, I was looking back at him with cautious trepidation, and simultaneously I was unconsciously rubbing my finger around the rim of my glass that was sitting on the bar in front of me. I am not sure, but I believe I may have heard a high-pitched squeak. Also, a bottle of aquavit was performing a rond de jambe.

The loopy quack, quack guy persisted with his thoughts. He explained: The capo is telling us that the pitch is raised. I believe now that when the statue that I am bringing to Myanmar is rubbed that it will make a pitch that is too high. That is how we will know that it is a fake. It is not a genuine Kapu statue. That is what I think the answer means. The capo tells me that, he concluded. The dancers were all back in their first positions now, again staring straight at the two of us sitting on the barstools. What we must have looked and sounded like to them was still a complete mystery to me.

Zooks, I said in astonishment, you certainly have reached an interesting conclusion. I mean, Jeepers, could you be right? A fake Kapu statue you have, you think? Criminey, I am amazed at what you have surmised. The pitch is too high, you think? Is that it? Egads, I am dumbfounded that you were able to glean all that from what little information you have.

Oh, but surely it is all due to you, the quack, quack man insisted. It was you who opened my eyes. And, all because I opened the fortune cookie that looked at me. Yes, don't you see, he said with eyes now wide open and bright, it is all due to you. You were the one with the answers, just as the cookie said. But, now I must hurry. He downed the last bit of drink that remained at the bottom of his glass. He stared at me with a face lit up with anticipation. I must go and figure out what to do about the fake Kapu statue. Thank you so much for giving me the quack, quack. The fortune cookie was right – you were indeed the man with the answers.

Then the strange man leaped up from his barstool and hurried out of the bar through the front door. I watched him as he went. What an exceptional guy, I thought. I shook my head. What a far-out guy. I looked back at the ballet dancers. A bottle of triple sec appeared to have lost its tutu.

After a short while I finally relaxed a bit. That certainly was a zany, exotic experience, I mused. Yes, indeedy, a truly bizarre encounter. Bizzarro! It dawned on me that coincidences can sometimes be quite overwhelmingly enigmatic. That one certainly was. But, I then realized, I was getting more than a bit hungry. Yes, I definitely was a bit peckish. But, hmmm, wait a minute, I remembered that the strange quack, quack man mentioned a Chinese restaurant just down the street. You know, that sounded good. Okay, fine; Chinese it would be.

The Kung Pao chicken was pretty tasty. I was finished with my dinner and felt sated and content. I sat slumped in my chair reminiscing about the weird guy at the bar and I had an intangible, dream-like feeling that the whole thing had not happened at all, that it was all imagined somehow, that it was an illusion, a dream, mirage, or phantasm of some sort.

The waiter then interrupted my reverie. He came with the bill, and of course, with a fortune cookie. I took the cookie from its plastic wrap and set it on the table in front of me. I stared at it for a while just out of curiosity to see if it might be looking back at me. But, no, nothing seemed out of the ordinary for a fortune cookie. It was not looking at me in any way that I could discern. I tried closing one eye and looking at it with the other eye. Then I tried the closed eye. And, you know, for a minute there I thought maybe, just a smidgen, that it might be looking back at me. Well, that gave me a bad case of the willies, so I stopped doing that.

I then picked it up and broke open the crisp little tan cookie and removed the inside paper that supposedly held my fortune. Right away I noticed that this piece of paper was much larger than those normally found inside fortune cookies, and it seemed to hold a very long fortune. Very long, indeed. Freaky, I thought.

I unrolled the paper and noticed that the long message on the fortune paper included an asterisk. Yes, that's right, an asterisk. I glanced quickly to the bottom of the fortune, and sure enough, there it was: a footnote. A footnote in a fortune cookie fortune. That is a new one on me, I thought. What an extraordinary coincidence. Today must be a very special day of coincidences, I speculated. I suppose, after all, coincidences have to build up sometimes. It's probably just another strange law of nature, you know, a massive build-up of coincidences day. Perhaps today was one of those massive build-up of coincidences days.

I then stretched out the paper that contained my fortune so that it was fully open and I held it with two hands up to my face and began to read the very long, idiosyncratic message. However, before I even got through the first few words of the long message, I was interrupted by the waiter who was still standing next to my table and whom I had entirely forgotten about. He spoke to me.

I don't think anyone else in the restaurant noticed or heard him when he bent down and looked directly into my eyes with a look of pure sincerity and earnestness on his face, a look of genuine expectancy. He leaned over and quietly said to me: quack, quack.

Why I Write Fiction

"The limits of my language means the limits of my world."
— Ludwig Wittgenstein

"Weirdism is definitely the cornerstone of many an artist's career."
— E.A. Bucchianeri

"A writer should write with his eyes and a painter paint with his ears"
— Gertrude Stein

"Some editors are failed writers, but so are most writers."
— T. S. Eliot

"There are three rules for writing a novel. Unfortunately, no one knows what they are."
— Somerset Maugham

"We are all what we pretend to be, but, we had better be very careful what we pretend."
— Kurt Vonnegut

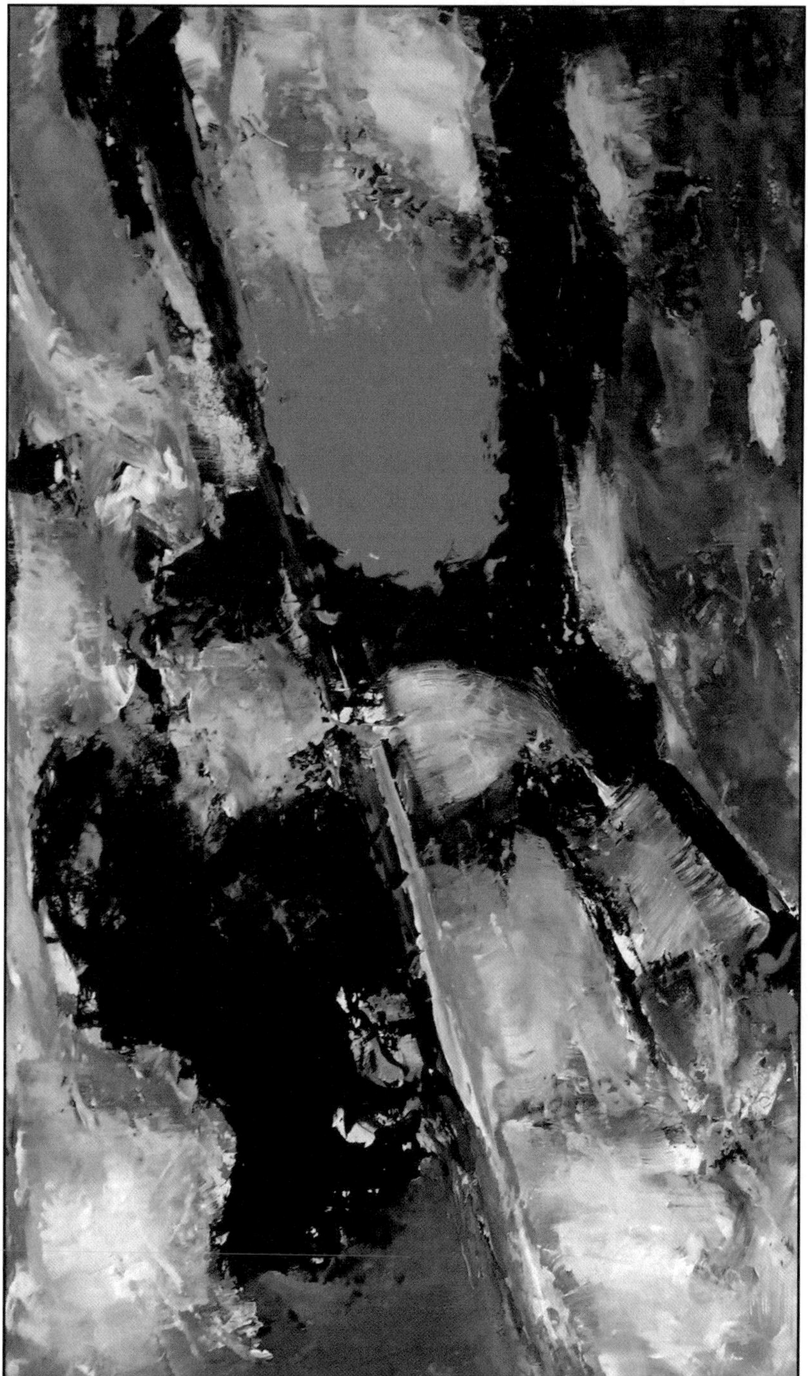

Why I Write Fiction

I used to write essays, but now I write fiction. People ask me why I changed. I've thought about it some, and the best I can answer is this:

I like writing fiction because you can say anything you want, anything at all.

Anything.

You can say that fluorescent rabbits on Mars are reading Frank Lloyd Wright books and are building Prairie-style homes out of rhubarb, or that rays of light from a green flashlight are getting body piercing and growing hair and having it put into braids, or that water droplets are strolling about downtown in pink high heels and wearing neon boas, or that pasta noodles are crawling out from the dried tears on the cheeks of a nun wearing a horseradish scarf, or that geometrical-headed insects whose boredom has overcome them are practicing springboard diving in a pool of purple Jello, or that phantoms bleen on rottled scones whilst humming jibberdy-do-bop punk hymns, or that plarlocks wrangle flittered meagle-pods with scarmpled dreadlock, or that a woman wearing a baloney hat and frozen tattooes plithers her smorgler tarts forward toward the ruminating ruins, or that +)-%4i9~hy{k* cuddles up to the |-=+0=+-#1=+1! with a blambled 6^)!`#-+/(8?.>+_|-+ hoarding (*%u.

Anything.

If you write essays, on the other hand, then your sentences and thoughts must flow logically, consistently, orderly. You must use correct grammar and make perfect, logical sense, or at least try to communicate clear, precise ideas. Your essay should express rational and meaningful conclusions and follow precise modes of thought and expression.

But, if you write fiction, then those there floppy-hoppity, tiddly-wink idee-ears can fly 'bout in space, traversing o'er befuddled, lollipop heads, alighting 'top dreamy, lavender clouds, wishing sideways-rain for dried-up summer crops and dandelions, hip-hopping 'mongst bedazzled Indiana hippopotami, gettin' as strange and illogical as a striped meringue wedding cake, as fantastical as a tattered indigo turnip hat sitting cockeyed on a tangerine colored platypus, as incongruous as an exasperated rattle snake wearing a marshmallow tutu with iridescent tights, or as irrational as a lunch made of a turtle-shell sandwich, polka-dot soup, and a rubbery dill pickle garnish. You know, you can write whatever you like.

Whatever.

And, you know what the best thing is?

The best thing is that if you write fiction you can *be* anyone you want to be, absolutely anyone at all.

Anyone.

You can be the cowpoke who rides the wild horse 'til dawn, or you can commit murder and get away with it, or you can dance with the beautiful, moon-struck Polynesian girl, you can make love with the mysterious, beguiling stranger, you can guide the lost amnesiac to sanity, build a pyramid or even a magnificent tree house in Madagascar, see through solid objects, be invisible, walk a tightrope from the earth to Venus, spend money precariously and frivolously on trivial things, waddle gaily amongst purple ducks emanating odors of gardenias, or possess super powers, such as being rubbery or gooey or fast or strong, that allow you to save the whole world. Why, in fiction you can even find meaning in life, or be happy.

That's what fiction can do.

In fact, with fiction you can even change your age, your gender, your race, your politics, beliefs, attitudes, life-style, even change your size, your shape, or even change your species. In fiction you can be anyone at all.

Anyone.

At all.

Fiction, I've concluded, is where it's at.

The only problem – and it's a big one for sure – is that readers are bound to ask you where you got all those bizarre and crazy ideas you are putting into your fiction.

I'm warning you now: You absolutely, positively don't want to go down that road.

Banana-Fana Fo-Fana

"Man is the only creature that refuses to be what he is."
— Albert Camus

"What appears strange and complex becomes stranger and more complicated once you begin to investigate it. That's the true nature of the world."
— Bilal Tanweer

"Nicknames stick to people, and the most ridiculous are the most adhesive."
— Thomas C. Haliburton

"A nickname is the hardest stone that the devil can throw at a man."
— Author unknown

"The name of a man is a numbing blow from which he never recovers."
— Marshall McLuhan

Banana-Fana Fo-Fana

No one knew the city better than taxi driver Nicaragua Mars. Because of his multi-syllabic name, his friends just called him Nic. However, for purposes of this story we will call him Nicaragua, because it's a much cooler name. Splendiferous, don't you think? A bit geopolitical, though, a bit like being named Kazakhstan or Mozambique, I suppose. In fact, I did know a guy named Mozambique who ran a rent-a-pet shop. We called him Moze. But that's another story (you won't find it here, I'm sorry).

Anyway, no one knew the city better than Nicaragua Mars. Wait, come to think of it, calling him Nicaragua would take up too much ink and space, and would take too long for you to read, so we'll just call him Nic, as do his friends. But, as you've probably guessed, that's not even his real name, Nicaragua Mars – no way! Sounds made up, for sure. Which it is.

Before he officially changed it, Nicaragua Mars's real name, believe it or not, was Real Name. It was pronounced: *Real Name.* Weird, huh? You see, his parents were jerks. Having the last name, "Name," they thought it would be cute to give each of their children first names that made meaningful phrases when paired with their peculiar last name. Like when people with the last name of Christmas name their little girl Mary. Or, when the Falactic parents name their daughter Anna. Or, when parents named Sandwich dub their kid Hero. Or, when a couple with the last name Cadabra name their daughter Abra. Or, when a child is named Deep by a mom and dad whose last name is Doodoo. Or, when a family named Man give the name Bat to their baby boy. Or, when the Gulch mom and dad call their daughter Dry. Or, when parents named Deficit name their son Federal. Or, when couples named Head name one of their children

Crack. Or, when a family with the last name Attitude calls their cute little girl Insufferable. And so on. You get the picture. The "Name" parents were jerks.

Naturally, everyone in Nic's family later officially changed the stupid name they had been given by their jerk parents to something more suitable. For instance, Nic's younger brother, Fake Name, wanted to change his name to Fats Domino, but the judge said that that was a well-known name and therefore he could not allow it. Fats Domino was a 1950s piano player named Antoine who had many hits including "Ain't That a Shame." And, I guess it was. His biggest hit was called "Blueberry Hill," which coincidentally was the name of Fake Name's first grade teacher. The students called her Miss Hill, but her friends called her Blueberry. She later was fired for being a Methodist with poetic tendencies. That was considered a serious faux pas in Tennessee.

Being denied the name Fats Domino, Fake Name then asked the court to change his name to Chubby Checker. The judge disallowed that name also, on the same grounds. Chubby Checker was the fake name of the 1960s rock 'n roll singer, Ernest Evans, who popularized the dance known as the Twist. "C'mon baby, let's do the twist." The song revolutionized dancing since it was the first time couples danced without touching each other. Maybe that wasn't such a good thing, come to think of it.

Chubby Checker got the idea for his fake name from the wife of TV personality Dick Clark, whose name, by the way, was Richard Wagstaff. Yes, his name was Dick Wagstaff. You can understand why he changed it. Dick Clark became famous for hosting the TV show *American Bandstand*, by the way on which Fats Domino and Chubby Checker performed, and for announcing the lowering of the ball in Times Square on New Year's Eve each year. But, that's neither here nor there. Well, I guess it is there, after all, since it is Times Square, which isn't here.

Anyway, Fake Name finally settled on changing his name to Obese Backgammon, thus keeping alive the theme of Fats Domino and Chubby Checker. The judge said that would be fine since there were no famous people named Obese Backgammon. The judge, by the way, was named Maximus A. Pimple. His parents were jerks, too.

Everyone now called Fake, Obese. He wasn't, it was just his name. Obese was a bit overweight though, you might even say pudgy. In fact, Obese had considered adopting the name Fudgy Pudgy, but he regarded it as unappealing because it was so rhymey, and also because it was the name of a Japanese cartoon character. Fake Name wasn't fat enough to warrant his chosen moniker; he just liked the sound of it – Obese Backgammon. It had a nice flow. It was melodic, he thought.

Unlike his brother Obese, Nic was a bit on the thin side. Skinny, in fact. Real Name, I mean Nic, liked to stay thin because he thought it was an advantage for a taxi driver to be lithe. Lithe – that's a great word. One of the Name kids should consider it for a name. Nice for a girl, don't you think?

By the way, Nic did not like to be called a "cab" driver. It reminded him of Cab Calloway, a famous 1930s scat singer who wore natty clothes and whose orchestra played at the Cotton Club working with musicians such as Dizzy Gillespie. His most famous song was "Minnie the Moocher," which reminded Nic of Minnie Mouse and of fares who ran off without paying. No, being called a cab driver made Nic feel dizzy. Nic liked "taxi" driver. You see, Nic believed that the term "taxi" meant a person who paid taxes. In his mind there was the "taxer" and the "taxi." The taxer charged the taxes, and the taxi paid the taxes.

Nic's brother Fake – I mean Obese – scoffed at this idea and told Nic that the term taxi actually was an alternative plural of the word tax. You could say taxes or taxi. "I paid my taxes," or, "I paid my taxi." Except it was pronounced tax-eye. I paid my tax-eye. That's what Obese thought. But Nic's sister, Maya Name, who had changed her name to Plain Jane, although the judge had initially been quite reticent about it, told Nic that the word "taxi" was a derivation of the verb, "to tax," meaning to strain. So, the term "taxi" actually meant to strain, or to put pressure on something or someone. Maya, that is, I mean Plain, figured that was what taxi driving was all about. Taxing people. Straining them very hard. That's what the driver did – he taxed, or strained, the people in his cab. Have you ever taken a ride in a taxi? Taxing, wasn't it?

But Real, that is, Nic, did not buy these interpretations. Nic was proud to pay taxes, and hence, he liked to be called a taxi driver. He figured a taxi driver meant a driver who paid taxes. There was the taxer driver, and there was the taxi driver. Nic was a taxi driver. He didn't charge taxes, he paid them. Nic was proud of paying taxes because a couple years ago his sister Maya – sorry, I mean Plain – had a fire at her apartment and the local fire fighters put it out without charge. Nic tried to pay them, but the fire fighters insisted that he keep his money since the fire fighters were paid by taxes. Ever since that epiphany, Nic bragged about paying taxes. For example, each time he read or heard about a local fire that was put out by fire fighters, Nic bragged about it for days. "I paid for that," he'd say. He was the "taxi."

Meanwhile, down at the taxi station, Nic's boss was a tall, lanky Chinese man named Brake Fluid. Everyone who worked there remarked that it was terribly odd that the boss's name corresponded so well with the aura of the taxi garage. They marveled at how often this seemed to happen – that a person's name fit with his or her occupation. You know – like a paleontologist named Stegasaurus, or a car mechanic named Wrench, or a doctor named Langerhans, or a chiropractor named Quack, an electrician named Shock, a sociologist named Group, a psychologist named Nutz, a potato farmer named Spud, a fire fighter named Hose, a teacher named Chalk, a plumber named Flush, or a lawyer named Attache or Sleazeball. Weird coincidences, for sure. But Maya – sorry again, I mean Plain – understood all this because she had experienced such characters in her past. For example, she had an eighth grade teacher named Miss Taken, a dentist named Incisor Gap, an accountant named Decimal Avogadro, a piano teacher named Tuner D. Keyes, and a pet mouse named Squeak. Ironic, no?

Anyway, as I was saying, no one knew the city better than

Real Name, err, I mean Nicaragua Mars. That is, Nic. Although, truth be told, Nic was not an especially good driver. In fact, he was a terrible driver. Absolutely awful. Even dangerous. It was a miracle that he had a driver's license. In fact, he didn't have a driver's license. Well, not a real one. He had a fake driver's license that he bought from a guy in an alley. Although it was drawn with a crayon on a wrinkled brown paper bag, it was good enough to get him a job as a taxi driver. Actually, the line drawing of Nic was a pretty good likeness.

Nic was a horrific driver who could barely keep his taxi from going sideways. In fact, he did drive sideways. However, bad as he was, Nic was the top driver in the taxi garage. What Nic was best at, though, was knowing his way around the city. No one knew the city better. Well, no one except a few people who had lived in the city for a long time. Oh, and some city officials. Oh yeah, and a few of the construction workers who worked in different places throughout the city. Uhm, that's right, and an old lady who sat on the city commission for several years until they finally said "uncle" and she got up. Oh, yeah, I just remembered, and an idiot savant who happened to live in the same city as Nic. It was amazing, this savant, a young man named Orangutan Marshmallow, could tell you any address in the city if you just told him the color and weight of the house. He could also tell you the circumference of every bald man's head in the city. Orangutan could play the piano with his nose without a piano. He was able to remove his toes and still play *This Little Piggy*. He could calculate the square roots of small electrical appliances. He could also do mirror writing with a magic marker firmly gripped in his butt crack. It had to be a magic marker, though; he couldn't do it with a pen or pencil. He was amazing. He was one of only one idiot savant in the city. Orangutan knew the city better than Nic, but nearly no one else did. And, how was that, you ask, that Nic knew the city so well? I'm so glad you asked that! It's like this....

Nic's other brother, not Fake Name (that is, Obese Backgammon) but Nic's other brother, his older brother, was named Alias Name, but had officially changed his name to Contemporary Man. He wanted to change his name to Modern Man, but another person had already taken that name, so Alias Name decided to stick with the last name of Man, but go one up on the other guy, Modern Man.

By the way, Contemporary Man was not at all. He was quite old-fashioned, in fact. But that's neither here nor there. Well, I suppose it is *here* since we're talking about it. Anyway, Contemporary was driving Nic to the airport one day when they were involved in a serious car accident. Bad driving ran in the family, you see. Nic suffered a severe head injury, but the weird thing was that his brain injury caused him to become a memory genius in visual-spatial perception. He now had a detailed map of the whole city in his head. The surgeons tried to remove it, but the inset was stuck between Nic's medulla oblongata (which, coincidentally was the name of the chief surgeon) and his lateral ventromedial hippocampus (amazingly, the name of the nurse), so they had to leave it in. Talking fast caused it to flap, which gave Nic a headache. The surgeons also found that the map was simply impossible to re-fold correctly no matter how they tried. One of the surgeons, Dr. Piers Yorskin from Neither, Norway fainted after a valiant attempt to re-fold the map. The map apparently was firmly stuck between Nic's gray matter and his white matter, in a region of the brain that neuroscientists called the doesn't matter. So, with a map stuck firmly in his brain the result was that Nic knew the city better than anyone. Well, except for those listed above. Well, okay, and a few others, too, I suppose. Whatever.

Nic's life changed drastically when one day he picked up a fare at the airport, a Mr. Pickled Cucumber, a lawyer from Frozentoe, Saskatchewan, who wanted a ride to a mysterious hotel called the Pleaze Putit Inn. Mr. Cucumber had a peculiar habit of rubbing his head with a worm, which turns out to have nothing whatsoever to do with this story. Pickled Cucumber also had the weird habit of playing a didgeridoo, a primitive wind instrument that requires the player to vibrate his lips while blowing into a beeswax mouthpiece at the end of a long wooden pipe made by termites while simultaneously breathing in through his nose. By breathing in and blowing out simultaneously some didgeridoo players can play a steady note for half an hour or more. This, by the way, had a relaxing effect on the termites.

Pickled got his didgeridoo while he was studying languages in Australia and discovered that the two languages, Pitjantjatjara and Yankunytjatjara, could be grouped together under the name Nyangatjatjara. Psycholinguistics was a hobby of Pickled's. He purchased his didgeridoo from a Pitjantjatjara shaman who worshipped the Urulu rock formation. Out of respect, Pickled named his daughter Urulu Cucumber. Her middle name was SacredRock. Unfortunately, Pickled's daughter had been stolen by kangaroos and was badly injured riding in a marsupial pocket. Urulu Cucumber was now in a vegetative state. By the way, the term kangaroo derives from a Guugu Yimidhirr word "ganguruu," which, contrary to popular belief, does not mean "I don't understand you." Incidentally, the didgeridoo is known as a "yirdaki" among the Yolngu aboriginal people of Arnhem Land in Northern Australia, as a "paampu" among the Pintupi tribe of Central Australia, and is named "ngarrriralkpwina" on the island of Groote Eylandt in the Gulf of Carpentaria. These are true facts. However, to simplify things we'll just call this weird musical device a "didgeridoo." Oh, and because it's a really cool name, too.

Pickled Cucumber played the didgeridoo because it was prescribed by his sleep therapist, Dr. Needle Gozinya, to treat a severe case of sleep apnea. You see, Pickled could not sleep and breathe at the same time. Well, that is, unless he played the didgeridoo. He found it more convenient and interesting than wearing a C-PAP. Incidentally, that also has nothing whatsoever to do with this story. Sorry. Okay then, back to the story...

In the taxi, Pickled Cucumber and Nicaragua Mars started chatting, particularly about the low humming sound that was coming from the back seat. It wasn't snoring, as Nic had assumed. It was Pickled Cucumber vibrating his lips and exhaling on the beeswax mouthpiece of his didgeridoo while breathing in through his nose at the same time. Pickled loved music. He told Nic about his favorite musician, Frank Zappa, who was an eccentric genius who named his four children Moon Unit, Dweezil, Ahmet Emuukha Rodan, and Diva Thin Muffin Pigeen, and for whom many scientific discoveries have been named including the *3834 Zappafrank* asteroid, the *Phialella zappa* jellyfish, and the *Zappa Confluentus* bacterium. These are absolutely true facts, too. As a child, Frank Zappa had sinus problems which his doctor treated by inserting a pellet of radium into each of little Frank's nostrils. As a result, Zappa's lyrics and album covers often contain nasal images, Pickled explained, and he told Nic that Zappa was close friends with musician Van Vliet who changed his name to Captain Beefheart, who with his Magic Band, whose members included Drumbo and Zoot Horn Rollo, released a popular album called *Trout Mask Replica*. It is said that he got his name from his uncle who referred to his penis as a big, fine beef heart whilst peeing in front of Van Vliet's girlfriend Laurie. However, Van Vliet said on TV that his name derived from the fact that he had, "A beef in my heart against this society." Captain Beefheart and Frank Zappa met at Antelope Valley High School, and while neither appeared on Dick Clark's *American Bandstand,*" Zappa was on the *Steve Allen Show* where, inexplicably he did not play guitar, but instead played the bicycle. Naturally, that's neither here nor there. Well, I mean, it's there, of course. Incidentally, comedian and talk-show host Steve Allen's middle name was Valentine, which means strong and healthy, and also was the pen name of British author Archibald Thomas Pechey who wrote many songs, as did Steve Allen. Those are all perfectly true facts that you can look up for yourself and verify if you have any free time for such nonsense. Okay, back to the story...

And, wouldn't you know, wouldn't you just guess, the two of them hit it off right away. Nic and Pickled, that is. They hit it off right away. Two peas in a pod. There was chemistry between them. Mostly carbon dioxide, I think. Perhaps a hint of salicylic acid methyl ester, also known as wintergreen, although that is also quite superfluous to this story, I suppose. Interesting, though, that wintergreen would be developing between them, don't you think?

Anyway, the two of them were getting along so well that

Pickled Cucumber invited Nic to dinner that evening. Since Nic was free absolutely every night without exception, he readily and happily accepted. They went to a nice restaurant called Cannibal's. The host said they had to wait for a table and asked for a name. Pickled immediately said "Pajama." In the restaurant's bar, Pickled explained.

You see, some years ago Pickled Cucumber grew tired of restaurant hosts asking him how to spell his name. It really annoyed him. Every time he had to wait for a table the restaurant host asked Pickled how to spell his name. He thought, "Why are they asking me how to spell my name? Are they going to send me a letter when the table is ready?" Pickled tried asking the hosts to write his name phonetically since they were going to be speaking it later, but the hosts did not know what the word "phonetically" meant. They just stared at him blankly, and then later whispered about him to their peers. So, Pickled decided to make up a name and use a name that would be easy to spell so hosts would not ask him how to spell it. He tried many different names, but to no avail. Each time he went to a restaurant, no matter what name he gave – even Smith, Johnson, Homer Simpson, Banana, Bluebird, Nose, The, Spaghetti, Choo-choo, Furniture, Boogyman, Pinwheel, Spittoon, Oilrig, Crackerjack, Icepick, Whiplash, Doodle, or Smell – the host asked him how to spell it.

But wait, Pickled Cucumber excitedly told Nic, in fact there was one type of name he had stumbled upon that hosts did not ask him how to spell. Pickled had discovered that hosts will not ask you to spell your name if your name is a word that is embarrassing or titillating. Pickled discovered this by accident when he had coincidentally found that his pants were on fire at the precise moment when a host asked for his name. "Shit," he had yelled. The host wrote it down without asking for the spelling. After this serendipitous discovery, Pickled tried many names that were of a similar edginess – names such as Wartface, Bigsucker, Fart, Birddropping, Satan's Pet, Burntcrisp, Pinhead, Burping-Goat, Diarrhea, Vomitlips, and Nixon. They worked! Hosts were too embarrassed to ask how to spell them.

However, there was a weird side-effect that Pickled soon learned. On one occasion he had given the name Frankenstein – embarrassing enough to avoid the spell question – and then later while waiting in the bar he heard over the loud speaker: "Frankenstein party of two, your table is ready." Pickled Cucumber found that this caused a great deal of notice by other people waiting in the bar. They all stared wide-eyed and open-mouthed as the "Frankenstein" couple went to get their table, drinks in hand. At that moment, Pickled quickly decided to walk with a very stiff posture to give them all a nice show and something to tell the kids later. By the way, Pickled explained to Nic, if you want to try the Frankenstein name at a restaurant, I suggest that as the host is writing it down you then meekly add "Doctor." It's a nice touch. Also, Pickled continued, be sure to keep a straight face. Because after you say that your name is Frankenstein the host will glance at you for a moment, not too long, but just will turn his or her eyes up to look at you – it's at this moment that if you are smiling, the deal will be off – but if you have a serious face, then after just a brief moment, after a quick glance, the host will begin writing the name Frankenstein without asking how to spell it. It is then, at that moment, that you should lean forward and quietly, but seriously, without smiling, of course, add, "Doctor."

Then, Pickled Cucumber said to Nic as he finally got to the crux of the explaining, after I discovered that while waiting in the bar you will hear them announce "Shitz party of four, your table is ready," or something like that, I decided to use names that went with the word "party." Like Republican, for example. And, as a bonus, I found that the word Republican is embarrassing enough to avoid the how to spell question, too. So, Pickled continued, that is why I gave the name Pajama tonight. Just then, as the two of them were sitting there chatting and sipping their drinks in the restaurant's bar, they heard over the loud speaker: "Pajama party for two… Pajama party for two..." So, Pickled and Nic went in to eat. Obviously, as one would expect, the other people in the bar stared at them. Pickled walked with a joyous and happy stride, and made a big yawn for everyone to see. At their table, the waitress told them they could choose "All you can eat," but Nic said no thanks, he couldn't eat that much. That is, he couldn't eat all that he could eat. So, Nic just ordered coconut jumbo shrimp and mashed turnips. Pickled had a peanut butter and jelly sandwich with coleslaw and pineapple pie. As they ate, they chatted.

When Pickled learned of Nic's great skill – knowing the city better than anyone (well, better than a lot of people, anyway) – he became very interested. As a lawyer, Pickled was always looking for easy ways to make money. If it was legal, that was a bonus. If not, well, loopholes abounded. If loopholes didn't abound, then certainly some whatnot could be finagled. If a whatnot could not be finagled, then perhaps a thingamajig could be boonswaggled. Or maybe a whatchamajigger could be insinuated. Or a doohickey could be fillydallied. You see, Pickled didn't care about ethics at all. He simply didn't think about that. After all, he was a lawyer.

Hmm, Pickled thought, how can I use Nic's skill, and make a lot of money, and give Nic only about ten percent or less? Okay, he said to Nic, why don't we start a service that will tell people how to get from one place to another in the city? There are lots of people who can't read maps. Most of those people don't own a compute or GPS, either. And the ones who happen to own computers can't use them anyway or even understand what appears on them. Whaddya think?

Nic was all for it. He had a map in his brain, after all, so he may as well sell it to others. A brain map should be shared. Well, sold. So, Pickled and Real Name, I mean Nic, went into business. They called their venture, *Navibrain*. They advertised in newspapers, restaurants, Laundromats, on telephone poles, kiosks, bulletin boards, and on the backs of homeless people and the fronts of prostitutes. They discovered that lots of people couldn't read a map or use a computer and needed to find their way around the city. They were doing great.

Then, one momentous day they got a call from a woman named Flapps Her-Arms. She had been born "Flappsinna Her," but married a man named Missing Arms and then shortened her first name and hyphenated her last. Her brother, Broth Her, changed his name to Phantom Limb and took a job selling mirror boxes. Miss Flapps Her-Arms had called *Navibrain* because she wanted to know how to get from point A to point B. Nic knew about point A (it was near the zoo, just about a mile from Sinus Cavity at the intersection of Della Street and I've Done Her, Avenue?), but he had never heard of point B. It wasn't on his map. Well, Pickled Cucumber told Nic to just make up something to tell Miss Flapps Her-Arms. So, he did. That is when Nic and Pickled discovered an amazing fact: it didn't matter what they said to people. Sure, some people got mad and complained when they were given wrong directions, but *Navibrain* already had their credit card numbers. The few people who took time to ask for their money refunded were cheerfully told that it would be credited to their accounts right away. Several months later, the money was credited. Pickled and Nic kept the interest they had earned on the money. That is when they stumbled upon the capitalist's dream: they could make money by doing nothing. Pickled and Nic started a slew of other companies that claimed to do many different services, such as rust proof cars, clean furniture, change the oil on snowmobiles, fix roofs, run errands, water plants, water children, deliver sushi, eat sushi, wash airplanes, and so forth. But, in fact, they did nothing. They had no overhead whatsoever. They just collected the payments, put them in the bank to collect interest, and then gave the money back to customers who complained. They gave the money back, but it was months later. They kept the interest. They found the best services to offer were those that customers had to wait a long time to find out if they worked, like rust proofing cars. Pickled and Nic made a lot of money. Sure, they made money on the interest they earned, but mostly they got rich off the apathetic customers who didn't ask to have their money returned. People were forgetful, after all. Regarding the profits, Pickled Cucumber kept ninety percent and he gave Nicaragua Mars ten percent. They were making plenty.

It all came to an end one hot summer day. Nic's younger brother, Obese, had discovered what was going on and he started his own similar company – a dating service called *Meet Your Soul Mate or Someone Vaguely Similar*. Obese's intention was to do nothing, just to collect money. He was able to obtain a free website called MYSMOSVS.com where people could pay by credit card. Obese found that a huge number of people were willing to sign up to meet their soul mates or someone vaguely similar, but then he met HER – I mean Lullaby U. Dreamscape – then, the most wonderful thing happened. Not to Obese, but to Nic.

Lullaby and Nic were a perfect couple. That is, if by perfect you mean pretty good. They fell in love right away. Well, if by right away you mean fairly fast. When they got married, Lullaby changed her name to Venezuela Mars. But, unfortunately for Nic and Pickled Cucumber, Lullaby, I mean Venezuela, did not like the unethical nature of their businesses. Venezuela insisted that Nic give up doing nothing for a living. That's what Venezuela Mars wanted, so that's what Venezuela Mars got. You see, Nicaragua Mars, I mean Nic, was a good and obedient husband.

Well, the idea of starting an ethical business was so foreign and unsettling to Pickled Cucumber that he left town immediately and he headed for the big city with his didgeridoo. When he got there he immediately landed a job engineering dirty tricks and spreading lies for a political party, which was quite fitting since schadenfreude and stealing money for the rich seemed to be Pickled's main preoccupations and motivations in life; it was precisely what he was good at, what he was meant to do.

On the other hand, Nicaragua Mars thought that starting an ethical business seemed an excellent idea. He looked forward to it in order to make his wife, Venezuela Mars, happy. Since Nic had encountered so many unusual names, he thought it would be a good idea to start a business that helped companies give names to their products. So, he did. He called his business *The Really Good Name Company*. As you would expect, he was excellent at it since he had a lot of experience with names. Oh, and of course, with Names, too. But, as you noticed, that's quite beside the point.

Now, wouldn't you just know it, Nic's new business giving names to things was a big success. He was very good at creating names for products. Very good, indeed. In fact, his first job was for a mattress company called *Drowsy Knights* that was putting out a new line of pillowtops. Nic named the company's number one elite mattress after his wife's original maiden name – the Lullaby Dreamscape. The officials at *Drowsy Knights* loved it. Nic was a success, an ethical success.

By the way, a year after they met, Nicaragua and Venezuela Mars had a beautiful baby girl. She was adorable. She was the light of their lives. They found her to be not the least bit taxing. Fortunately, she had the looks of her mother and the brains of her father. Well, that is, without the map from Nic's brain, of course.

And, what do you suppose they named their precious little dear? Well, you can only imagine! But, I'll tell you, it is a doozy of a name.

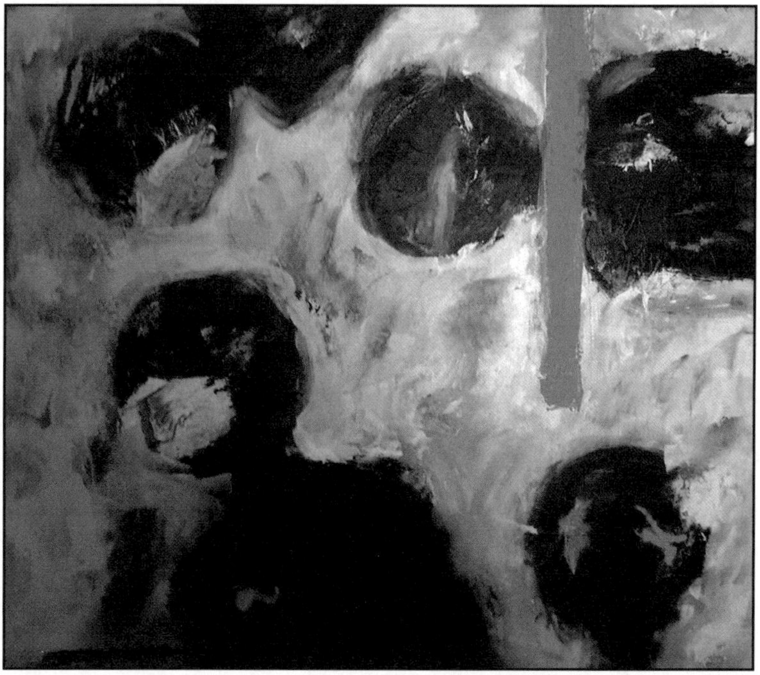

Lulu's Brain

"My head is my favorite swimming pool."
— Lauren DeStefano

"Sitting on your shoulders is the most complicated object in the known universe."
— Michio Kaku

"There are three methods to gaining wisdom. The first is reflection, which is the highest. The second is imitation, which is the easiest. The third is experience, which is the bitterest."
— Confucius

"All relationships change the brain - but most important are the intimate bonds that foster or fail us, altering the delicate circuits that shape memories, emotions and that ultimate souvenir, the self."
— Diane Ackerman

"The funny thing about the heart is a soft heart is a strong heart, and a hard heart is a weak heart."
— Criss Jami

Lulu's Brain

Insanity runs in our family. Aunt Helen spent most of her years in an asylum. Died there alone. My grandfather, Bertrand, bless his soul, committed suicide by standing in front of a train. What a way to go. My mom's not too sound either. Sometimes you can hear her whistling in the back yard, whistling to no one in particular, to no one at all. If you ask her about it, she says she knows that someday her whistling will be answered. Then she smiles kind of funny-like. My dad died when I was little and my mom never remarried or even had much of a boyfriend. Sometimes I think she's whistling to Dad or to someone who will help ease her loneliness.

She doesn't drink though, my mom. That's one good thing. My best friend in the whole world is Irma. Her dad, Mr. McQuiggly, drinks like crazy and then he yells real loud and hits her and her mom. Irma's taking those new Prozac pills everyone's talking about. I hope she feels better soon.

My doctor says I have a lesion on my brain. He doesn't know how I got it; he doesn't have any idea. One time he asked me how I got it and I told him how should I know, I'm no doctor.

When I was little I used to dream about outer space and being an astronaut and I would talk to my friends in outer space through a piece of wood, or if we were riding in the car, I would talk to them through the silver metal handle for cranking the window up and down. Sometimes I would pretend to be an alien just observing earthlings and noting the odd things they said and did. Then I would report back to my outer space friends the bizarre acts of earthlings through the silver car door window crank.

When I was little I also had a small metal bowling pin, about an inch tall maybe, that I called Jenny. She was my best friend. We went everywhere together and it made me feel less lonely to have her near. I would hold her tight between my fingers and talk to her, mostly whisper, I don't know why. I'd whisper, "Hey, Jenny, look at those boys over there playing ball. That one's Tommy John Faber. I hate him. He's a big jerk." But then I lost Jenny.

I guess I had a vivid imagination when I was young and now I wonder if maybe that's how I got my brain lesion, from all that imagining. I wonder if that's how you get a brain lesion?

To tell you the truth, I don't even know what a lesion is. Is it like a cut, or maybe a bruise, or a blown-up section of tissue, or does it mean a part of my brain is missing? Dr. Warren says the lesion's not in an important part of my brain and so not to worry. Dr. Warren says he has an idea of what to do about my brain lesion.

But, I don't want to have one of those brain operations some people say my Uncle Howard had. They called it a lobotomy. I guess the surgeons cut your brain into little bits for some reason. They say Uncle Howard was just like a vegetable after the operation. They didn't say what kind of vegetable, but I guess I wouldn't want to be any kind of vegetable I can think of.

Sometimes Irma and I stay at the high school after classes are over. We like to be there when everyone's gone and the halls are so empty it's eerie. The empty halls make an echo of our footsteps that is somehow both haunting and comforting at the same time. Our science teacher, Mr. Parker, is usually there in his science laboratory and it's weird, but it seems he actually enjoys talking to us, although he still fiddles with test tubes and glass beakers and stuff. They say that one time he nearly blew up the school with one of his demonstrations. An experiment gone wrong, I guess.

Today I told Mr. Parker about my brain lesion.

"The brain is an amazing thing, Lulu," he said. "I once read about a man who had the most unusual damage to his brain that made him unable to learn anything new. He couldn't learn one new thing. He still remembered all the old things he had learned and experienced in his past – still had all his memories from before his accident – but ever since then he couldn't put one new memory into his brain. It was like his brain was all filled up." Mr. Parker paused a moment looking kinda spacey, and then continued, "You know, it sounds so weird and terrible, but sometimes I wonder if that would be a good thing, you know, to not be able to remember some things. I wonder if that would be a blessing."

Well, *I* wondered if Mr. Parker was simply telling me some weird story or if maybe he was thinking that I wouldn't be able to learn any new facts because of my brain lesion. Maybe he was thinking that my brain is all filled up. So I said, "I can still learn perfectly fine, Mr. Parker. I can learn all kinds of new things. I have no problem there."

My friend Irma smiled, nodded her head, and looked from me to Mr. Parker.

Mr. Parker seemed kind of embarrassed. "Oh, of course, I know that, Lulu," he said. "I was just saying that the brain is an amazing thing. It could be that your brain will work even better than before, because, you know, you're still very young and your brain is still very flexible. Neuroplasticity, it's called. Maybe you can develop skills beyond everyone else, skills that no one else has. You know, scientists say that Einstein's brain was different from everybody else's. Perhaps your brain lesion will make you famous. Another Einstein, maybe."

People are always saying that we're young. But I don't feel very young. I'll be sixteen next December and that seems really old because soon I'll have to decide what to do with my life and college and a job and marriage and everything. I bet Einstein was thinking up lots of ideas about relativity and everything when he was sixteen. I'm not a child anymore, so I don't see how someone can say that I'm young. I'm getting old and have many big decisions to make.

I turned away from Irma and Mr. Parker and stared at the long rows of cabinets on the wall, cabinets full of microscopes, test tubes, bottles of ammonia, hydrochloric acid, and other chemicals, white gloves, beakers, and more. I noticed my reflection in the glass door of a cabinet. I saw the reflection of my face on the glass, floating like a ghost, distorted and unreal – transparent, but visible. Then I noticed that the chemical supplies seemed embedded in my head. Test tubes in my head, I thought. Chemicals in my brain.

I stared at my forehead in the glass and mused on what it all means – my brain lesion and biology and chemistry and my mom and Irma and everything. I thought: Could a person's whole being, her whole sum of personality, talent, emotions, ideas, thoughts, memories, and everything, could the whole bit be somehow inside her brain? How could that be? But then I thought, how could it not be?

Mr. Parker was talking. I only heard part of what he was saying.

"...in the eighth grade we even dissected frogs. I got very interested in frogs. I wanted to study them, to observe them and learn all about them. We had learned how scientists put markers – bands – on animals in order to keep track of them. So I decided to catch some frogs and band them to see if the same frogs came back to our lake each year. I tied a little piece of string around one leg of each frog that I caught, maybe fifty frogs altogether. The next month I went back to the same area of the lake to see if any of my banded frogs were there."

Mr. Parker paused and looked down at his shoes. I looked at Irma and saw that her eyes were as big and round as pancakes and her mouth was partly open and still. From the very first time that she saw Mr. Parker Irma was taken with him. Not that she had a crush on him, but she respected and idolized him.

Mr. Parker continued, "They were there all right. Remember, I was only in the eighth grade. It was terrible. Nearly every frog I found had one shrunken, deformed leg – or sometimes no leg at all!" Mr. Parker stood up a littler straighter and explained, "You see, I didn't understand one important thing. The frogs I had caught and banded earlier that spring were still growing. The string I used was not flexible and it cut off the circulation in their legs. To see those shriveled legs hanging limp – I felt awful, just plain awful, to see those poor frogs I had injured. But I learned a valuable lesson from that experience."

Irma was transfixed by Mr. Parker's frog story and had been totally quiet until now. But now she burst open with her idea of the message behind Mr. Parker's story. "You shouldn't band young people," Irma said excitedly. "You shouldn't tie us down while we're still growing."

Mr. Parker smiled broadly, even kind of laughed his deep

laugh. “Maybe that’s true, Irma. But what I meant was that I learned how much there is to think about before you go messing with things. Especially things that are alive. I love science, but, you know, a person’s got to be thoughtful and careful.”

Leaving the school, Irma and I talked about Mr. Parker’s frog story – how gross it was. Those poor frogs! And Irma worried about Mr. Parker. To see what had happened because of his curiosity must have been very upsetting, she imagined.

Well, I wondered if Mr. Parker felt guilty. I bet he did feel guilty. I remembered when my puppy died. I thought there must have been something I should have done, or should *not* have done, that would have prevented that puppy from dying. I didn’t tie anything around that little dog – anything except for my love – but I still felt guilty.

Irma and I hadn’t gotten far from school when Irma remembered that she wanted to tell Mr. Parker about her science project and ask him for some advice. Irma had the idea of constructing a model of a human brain out of clay (I think she got the idea because of my brain lesion!) and she wondered if Mr. Parker could give her some help. We ran back to the school and straight to the science lab. When we got there something seemed odd, so we stopped in the hall outside the science lab and pressed our faces against the square panes of glass in the science room door. What we saw then was absolutely confusing to us. We just never would have imagined such a thing.

Mr. Parker was sobbing! He was crying and his body was jerking. He was standing bent over a microscope, his hands gripping the thick, black science-room tabletop. We later recalled that we saw one of his tears fall onto the microscope on the lab table and we thought it would be really strange if we saw that teardrop super close-up through the microscope during our science class. We wondered what we would see inside that tiny bit of a teardrop. Is a person’s DNA in tears? Would we be able to see the genetic stuff, the DNA, of Mr. Parker? We had learned about the human genome in our science class, but we were befuddled about exactly what it was and what it meant. Could a person’s essence somehow be inside some twisted strands of chemicals in a teardrop?

We stood motionless and silent at the door, faces pinned to the glass, peering in at Mr. Parker. We saw him wipe the tears from his face onto the arm of the white lab coat he wore. Although I was entranced and emotionally moved at the sight of Mr. Parker weeping, still I thought about those tears being absorbed into the fabric of the lab coat, merging with it, together forming a union of sorts, the wet tears and the dry fabric.

Then we saw Mr. Parker begin to turn toward us. We were embarrassed and didn't know what to say or do. Without a word or look to each other, we ran away. We just ran away as fast as we could. Our footsteps in the empty hall were loud and echoed like heavy raindrops on a thin metal roof. We didn't know if Mr. Parker had seen us or heard us.

We ran out of the school and down the sidewalk for about a block. There we stopped, bent over with our hands on our knees, exhausted and breathing deep, heavy breaths. We looked at each other for a long time without saying anything.

Irma has been my best friend for many years and we talk about everything. She told me about when she got her first bra, and about the first time she kissed a boy, and then last month I told her my big secret: I had a crush on Tommy John Faber and even let him kiss me once. She had said my big secret wasn't such a secret at all and anyone could have guessed it. Then we hugged and giggled uncontrollably.

One of the special things we love to do, Irma and me, is to make wishes. Every time we see a shooting star, or blow out the candles on a birthday cake, or break a wishbone, or see a unique number, like when the time on a digital clock is 12:21 or 4:44 or 12:34, Irma and I look at each other with big eyes and full hearts, grasp each other's hands, close our eyes tight, and then we make a wish. When I was younger I used to wish for things like a bicycle, a doll, or roller blades. But recently I've been making a different wish. I guess it's funny, but I always say silently to myself, "I wish everything would be all right. I just wish everything would be all right."

Yes, Irma and I were as close as any two friends could be. Now we stood there and stared at each other wondering what to say and what to think after witnessing Mr. Parker crying.

I was thinking about what my mother once said about one of her teachers. I guess it was when she was in the sixth grade. One day, without warning, her class had a permanent substitute teacher. The students were told that their regular teacher, Miss Eikenberry, would not be returning. Later they discovered that Miss Eikenberry had committed suicide. People said she overdosed on pills and booze. My mom said she learned then for the first time that teachers weren't robots or gods, but were real people just like everybody else. Real people.

Now I was thinking about Mr. Parker. Of course I always knew that he was a real person just like everybody else, but I never really really thought about that and what it meant. You know? Now I was wondering, was Mr. Parker crying about the banded frogs, or was there something else?

Irma spoke first. She said she thought Mr. Parker looked sort of funny when he was talking about being in the science lab all the time and she believed he was sad because he wanted to have a wife and friends.

I realized then that I hadn't heard Mr. Parker say those things, that he must have said them while I was looking at the cabinets and at my reflection in the glass – when I was thinking about chemicals in my head.

"Irma," I breathed half nervously, "what else did he say?"

"Nothing else, really," Irma answered, "but I remember he looked sad. He just said he liked science and being in the science lab, but that sometimes he was lonely and he wished that he was married and had some friends. That's when he told the frog story."

Yes, the frog story. I can't say what I thought then. So many things went through my mind; things that made no sense, yet somehow made some sense. I'm almost sixteen, I thought. I have feelings. I have ideas. Are they correct? What *should* I feel and think? Do I have any choice in the matter? Or are feelings and thoughts all just the result of uncontrollable chemical reactions in my head?

"Irma," I said meekly and uncertainly, "maybe we should just go home."

Irma was staring at me, looking so much like the puppy I once had, looking so caring and innocent and vulnerable.

"Lulu," Irma insisted, "I think we should go back and see Mr. Parker. I want to tell him that I understand about the frogs and I want to tell him even more. Mr. Parker has always been nice to us and talked to us, even more than my own father has. Now I want to be there for him."

I smiled broadly and grabbed Irma's hands, one in each of mine. I had been thinking the same thing and was so glad that Irma said it. Without another word we knew it was the right thing to do. We turned and started back toward the school.

Now, here's the oddest thing. Looking back, it all seems just so coincidental and weird – but that's the way life is, I guess. I remember Mr. Parker once saying how people are automatically inclined to put things together, to find patterns and relationships and coincidences and fate in everything they see. Well, I suppose we are. Maybe everything *is* just a jumble of random happenings, maybe there is no real sense to anything, but that's not how we see it. It's our nature, I imagine, to find meaning in all that meaninglessness.

Anyway, the craziest thing happened right there as Irma and I were starting back toward school thinking about frogs, chemicals, Mr. Parker crying, and loneliness. Just then we saw a car driving right down the street toward us, a car that was going too fast and was completely out of control. And we realized in just a split-second that behind the wheel of that car was Irma's dad, Mr. McQuiggly, who had been drinking, and now was recklessly barreling right toward us. We were so frightened that we froze right there and forgot all about frogs, chemicals, Mr. Parker crying, and loneliness.

Irma and I watched, nearly paralyzed, as Mr. McQuiggly's car careened over a curb, skidded heavily across a patch of grass, and slammed violently into the brick wall of an office building. The front of the car was smashed like an accordion, the hood was bent in the middle, sticking half up into the air, and the noise of the crash still echoed in our ears. First we jumped, then we stared – startled – but only for a brief moment. Then we ran toward the accident.

I never knew I had the energy or the strength inside me, and I never will understand what made me do it, but without a second thought I ran straight to Irma's dad. Something told me it was the right thing to do, and *my* thing to do.

Irma stood silent and still, hands held to her mouth, several yards away from the car, but I was right there next to it. Smoke was pouring out of the engine. The driver's front door was wide open and Mr. McQuiggly was slumped over the steering wheel. He did not seem to be awake, but I saw that he was breathing – his chest was moving in and out and I could hear his shallow, raspy breaths. I yelled at Irma to run to a nearby house to call for help.

Then I saw the problem. Mr. McQuiggly was bleeding heavily. His left leg was hanging partly outside the open car door and it looked twisted and deformed. The sight of Mr. McQuiggly's limp, injured leg immediately made me think of Mr. Parker's frogs, their shrunken legs with the string tied at the top. That thought, I'm sure, is what gave me the notion that I needed to make a tourniquet – to tie a band around the top of Mr. McQuiggly's leg. But, what could I use? I guess the idea of banding made me think of the long cotton fabric that I used as a headband.

I remembered Mr. Parker saying how we need to think about things carefully before we go messing with them, especially living things. But for some reason I found myself merely doing and not questioning, not thinking. I quickly took off my headband, untied the knot at the back, and placed the pink cloth around Mr. McQuiggly's thigh. I pulled it tight and twisted it, but I knew it wasn't tight enough. I knew that I needed something solid to twist the tourniquet in order to stop the leg from bleeding. I grasped the cloth band tightly with both hands and instinctively looked down at the ground for something to use. There I saw the silver, gleaming piece of metal. It was the window crank that had broken off the car door.

As I stared at the smooth, shiny piece of silver metal, I thought of my outer space friends and what a story I would have to tell them. There was blood all over my hands, my heart was pounding like heavy footsteps in an empty hall, and my forehead was dripping with sweat. I grabbed the silver window crank and quickly stuck it into the loop I'd formed at the top of the pink cloth band wrapped around Mr. McQuiggly's leg, and I started twisting with all my might.

Later the doctor said that my tourniquet certainly saved Mr. McQuiggly's leg, and maybe even saved his life. They said I was a hero, but I felt that I had only done what I had to do. Besides, Mr. Parker should get some credit since, after all, it was his frog story that gave me the idea. Afterward, Irma had hugged me dearly and I had never felt so close to her. And the really good news is that her dad, Mr. McQuiggly, has been sober for months now since the accident and recently Irma's been feeling better and even stopped taking Prozac.

And now I want to tell you, looking back, it's the funniest thing. After the police and the ambulance had arrived and took Irma's dad to the hospital, I wanted more than ever to see my mother and just be with her. I had hugged Irma tight and then ran home as fast as I could, all the way hoping that Mom would be there when I arrived.

When I got there I was desperate to find my mother and I ran through the house with my head on a swivel and my ears perked like my little puppy used to do. And wouldn't you just know it, it wasn't but a moment when I heard my mom whistling in the back yard. Then, for the first time in my whole life I knew her whistling was meant for me.

I ran to her as fast as my legs would fly and I hugged her for a good long time. Later I told her all about everything – Mr. Parker's frogs, his crying, what Irma and I thought, the chemicals, and, of course, the accident and the tourniquet. Then I asked her if it would be okay to invite Mr. Parker over for dinner sometime. Though she sort of tried to hide it, I'm sure I saw the corners of her mouth start to form a smile and her eyes brighten, just like my room does in the morning when the first rays of the sun filter through my lace curtains. She nodded and said yes. And although, of course, there was absolutely no possible chance of it at all, I still had to resist the urge to tell her not to serve frogs' legs for dinner!

It's odd, but when I woke up it seemed to happen very much all of a sudden – one moment unconscious, the next very much aware – even though the doctors and everyone else said that my awakening had been very gradual, that I had passed in and out of consciousness many times until I was fully awake. To me it seemed clearly to have happened all of a sudden.

Now I'm lying here in my hospital bed trying to make some sense out of all that has happened. I don't remember one thing about coming to the hospital or having surgery. It's all completely gone from my memory, just like the man who had lost his memory that Mr. Parker told me about. I guess Mr. Parker was right when he said that sometimes maybe it is a blessing not to remember some things. Seeing my reflection in the hospital room window and all the white bandages wrapped around my head, for some strange reason, did not bother me one bit. I liked it. It made me feel that people cared about me.

Now when I see my mom and Irma and Mr. Parker standing alongside my bed, I'm so happy and so relieved. We're all together and it feels so nice and warm and comforting. Dr. Warren is here too, and he's smiling a big smile. I guess that's a good sign. I hope so. I want so much for everything to be all right.

The Party

"I speak two languages: Body and English."
— Mae West

"Some mornings, it's just not worth chewing through the leather straps."
— Emo Philips.

"Enjoyed it! One more drink and I'd have been under the host."
— Dorothy Parker

"If you haven't got anything nice to say about anybody, come sit next to me."
— Alice Roosevelt Longworth

"When choosing between two evils, I always like to try the one I've never tried before."
— Mae West

"I'd rather have a bottle in front of me than a frontal lobotomy."
— Dorothy Parker

The Party

"Come here. Come here a minute."

That's what she said. Really. Come here a minute.

What was I supposed to do? You know the drill. Do you always think before you act? The car was there, I was dressed, it was getting late.

Look, I'm trying to tell you something, really. Something important. Very important. Won't you listen?

"Will you please hold this," she said, handing me her poodle.

"This?" I asked. What the hell kind of way is that to talk about a poodle?

She fixed her hair and tugged at her dress, then said, "Okay, give it to me now." She stretched her arms toward me and gave me that look, you know, the one we get from alpha humans, from narcissists, from everydamnbody.

"It?" I queried. "It?" What the hell is wrong with people?

I *had* to go. What can I say? The party was being held in my honor. I hadn't eaten any food for thirty days. Some people call that a month. Everyone was very proud of me. And me? I just need to tell you this one thing. It's important.

"Give me a dry martini," I said.

I hated it when people said, "I'll have." Not for me. "Give me" was the right thing to say in those circumstances, not "I'll have." I was the guest of honor, for Christ's sake.

I drank the martini, but she was right on me – right all over me. I tried to talk, but there she was. There she was everywhere. This would be a mega-martini night. If only I could get at least one of them dry. Sigh.

"Hold this for a minute," she said, handing me her brother.

"*This*?" I asked. Now she'd gone too far.

Her brother had no legs, not that I knew of anyway. I never asked why. I suppose that's odd, but that's just me. I don't ask about things like that – things like why someone doesn't have any legs. I'm not afraid of embarrassing others, I'm afraid of embarrassing myself. Or of being bored. Or of having no opinion. Or of being asked to hold something. So I just don't ask those things. But, that's just me.

"Okay, give it back to me now," she said, again with the "it."

"It?" I mumbled, this time under my breath. Her brother looked me right in the eye as I passed him to her. He was an accountant. Worked downtown. Didn't drink. That part threw me. I thought, if I didn't have legs, I'd drink. He did run marathons though. I mean, you know, in a wheelchair, although he never won.

"I'll have another dry martini," I said, "but this time make it dry."

The bartender froze, staring at me, then mocked, "I'LL HAVE?"

"Okay, okay … GIVE ME," I corrected. Jeez, some people! Then I noticed that it wasn't the same bartender. It was a second bartender. How the hell? I wondered.

I drank the martini. And a scotch. And two gin and sodas. Then I had another martini, but this one wasn't dry either. Make a note to ask for it "very dry" next time. Is that like 'very pregnant'? I thought.

"Where's the bathroom?" some guy asked me.

"We're in the bathroom," I told him. "What's wrong with you?"

"Here, hold this," he said, handing me his leg.

"This?" I asked taking his leg. Doesn't this bozo know that I am the guest of honor? I shouldn't be holding someone's leg, anyone's leg. I didn't have time to hold someone's leg. I am the frigging guest of honor! Besides, why did this guy's leg need holding, what was he doing? What's the deal with legs anyway? I wondered. Was it the party's motif?

"I'm the guest of honor," I informed him. "Gotta go now.

Can't hold your leg any longer."

"Okay," he replied, "I'll take it now." He reached out to take his leg. I noticed he had a hook for a hand. Don't ask, I reminded myself.

"It" again? What the hell is wrong with people?

The party was a blast. What fun. I never knew a party could be so groovy. Some woman even put a lampshade on her head. And without asking me to hold it. A blonde woman with two legs. Attached. But one guy, this one guy, had everyone entranced, totally mesmerized. He had tattoos of furniture all over his body. On his face was a large tattoo of a bedroom piece, I believe it was an armoire, it ran down his neck, disappearing into the opening in his shirt. I don't know what happened below there, but he said it ended appropriately with the bottom drawer tattooed on his pelvis. He showed it to some people, but I was more interested in the antique divan under his arm.

A beautiful woman approached me.

"I don't want to feel things," she said.

Not this again. I threw my martini into her face.

She stared into my empty glass. The mascara ran down in streams beneath each of her eyes. I was reminded that I needed an oil change. Not my car. Me.

She said, "It wasn't always like this. Once I was constrained. I could hold everything in. I didn't feel anything. I rarely talked at all. But now…"

"Well," I responded, "could you hold this for a minute?" I reached into my pocket, took out a toupee and a chair and handed them to her.

"Feelings," she said as she sat down in the chair and put the toupee on her head. "All I ever have are feelings and I *must* talk about them. What's wrong with me? Why can't I stop feeling? And why must I talk about them? Can't I just feel without blabbering?"

"Perhaps you're a monster," I speculated. "Or, perhaps you're married. Or maybe you need a man. Or, a woman. Maybe you don't drink enough. Or, maybe you drink too much. Perhaps your mother needed more babysitters. Maybe you hate your job, or were raised by people. Perhaps you grew up sniffing glue, or worse, in the suburbs. Maybe you watched TV, or had your heart broken, or didn't fulfill your dreams, or maybe you noticed the people around you, I mean, really noticed. How the hell do I know? Here, hold this." I handed her my empty martini glass. "I'll be right back day after Tuesday."

"I'll give me another have one," I said to the bartender. It was the first bartender again. He looked at me for a long time without saying a word. Finally I asked, "Aren't you the first bartender?"

"No," he said, "that was my twin brother. I'm the third bartender."

"Well, who was the second bartender, then?"

"That was my triplet brother. He had a sex change operation last month. Used to be a man. You can't even tell. I'm having one too. Right now. What can I get you?"

"Don't you mean what will I have?"

"Oh, no. I never say that. You're thinking of my brother."

"Oh, my mistake," I said. "Then just another give me have a martini," I said. "Very dry," I added as the third bartender started to pour vermouth.

The martini wasn't dry at all, quite wet, actually. I drank it anyway and ordered another.

"Can you show me the way to the bathroom?" asked an exotic-looking woman.

"We're in the bathroom," I replied. I was starting to get quite perturbed by people who were having difficulty recognizing men peeing.

"This is the *men's* bathroom," I explained to her while trying not to get too involved.

"What do you mean?" the exotic-looking woman asked.

"I mean I'm a man and I'm peeing here in this room, and so is he, and so is he, and so is he," I said pointing to the other men standing at urinals – well, what I assumed were men; one of them was the second bartender.

"And," the exotic-looking woman asked in a stern, offended

tone, "precisely what are you inferring about me?"

"I think you mean implying," I said.

"How dare you," she retorted, and slapped my face. I was reminded once again that grammar correction can be harmful to one's health.

"Could you please hold this for a moment," I inquired of her while handing her a small monkey playing a kazoo. The exotic-looking woman took the monkey and I went back to the party.

"I'll be back in a jiffy," I added.

I was standing in a corner drinking a martini, unfortunately one that was not very dry, when a markedly strange guy all decked out in purple approached me. At first I thought it was Prince, but then I noticed that he was not musical.

"Peter, I've got something I must tell you," the guy in purple blurted out in a tense voice.

"My name's not Peter," I corrected him.

He said, "I don't know how to tell you this, Peter. You're not going to like it."

"Look, Purple, my name's not Peter. You've got the wrong guy. Now bugger off!"

"Don't blame the messenger, Peter. It's not my fault. I only bear the news, I don't create it. It's not easy for me either, you know. Do you want to hear this or not?"

I threw my martini into Purple's face. Then I went to get another. This time I was determined to get one that was dry, maybe very dry. Purple followed me, gin dripping from his face, continuing to call me Peter and insisting that he had something important to tell me. I quickly tired of his pestering and turned to face him.

"Okay, Purple, what is it? Spill it. Come on, spit it out."

The man in purple gave me a very serious and melancholic look, then said, "Well, I'm sorry to say this, Peter, but you have a phone call. You can take it in the hall."

Of course I went immediately (after stopping at the bar for another martini, although, again, it wasn't very dry, in fact, not dry at all). I hurried to the phone in the hall. I thought this might be it, this finally might really be it, my chance, my big break, what I've been waiting for, longing for, dreaming of, the big enchilada, my moment, my ticket out of here, my time, my dream come true, a chance to be somebody, maybe even a champion, this could be it.

Long, thick, chartreuse velvet drapes swayed in a strong breeze coming from the tall, open windows. There was a new moon. It was very dark outside, and even quite dark inside. I could just barely make out where my hand was, the hand at the end of my arm, the hand holding a martini glass, a glass that was now quite empty, empty save for a single uneaten green olive.

She was hovering, still on me, still pestering me. I had to get out of this skin, this soaking-wet emotion, this crevice of incredibility, this plasticine filament, this fulgent, inscrutable chemical swamp, this pulsating electrical storm in a noggin.

I picked up the phone. "Hello?" I queried into the receiver.

"Mr. Design, you may already be a wiener."

I swear he said "wiener."

"I'm not Mr. Design," I exclaimed with an air of empty authority and a bit of annoyance.

"Well, can I call you Peter?" the voice quickly asked.

Now I was really getting annoyed. "Look, is this some kind of a joke? Don't you know that I'm the guest of honor?"

"Yes, I do," said the voice, "that's why I called. It's time for your speech."

I stood in the middle of the bathroom atop a short, bald woman who was knitting a glass eye to replace the one that was injured by laser surgery. With partygoers gathered around, I began my well-prepared comments: "Ladies and gentlemen, I know that you believe it is a great thing, a truly remarkable feat of self-sacrifice and self-restraint, a brilliant accomplishment, to not eat any food for thirty days…"

Someone shouted, "One month!"

I ignored the remark and continued, "But it is really nothing, nothing at all. It is merely a trickle of continuity in the dense cascade of inexorable, unchangeable events in this predictable universe. It is nothing that a man should be rewarded for. It is nothing for which I am at all deserving. Believe me, I don't deserve this honor. I don't deserve anything, not even another martini. Well, that is, unless you insist..."

"WE INSIST," they all shouted.

The speech was over. I think it went well.

I went back to eating food and drinking martinis. The food consisted of olives. Green olives. Fortunately, I like olives. She was there with me the whole time, like a thick, penetrating cloud of details, watching me, controlling me, hovering over me, asking me to hold this or that, telling me what to do and who to do it with, and where to go, what to eat, when to eat, what to wear, what to say, what to think and what to believe, and everything else that a grown man, a mature, totally functional, grown-up man of a man should be able to do for himself. Then suddenly she was gone. I never saw her again. Never.

And the funny thing is that I never thought to ask who the hell she was.

Later I woke up and realized it was all a dream.

Then later I fell asleep and realized it was all real – I had only dreamed that it was all a dream.

Still later I woke up and I knew what I know now, something so very important, that is, what I'm trying so hard to tell you, what I need to tell you, what you need so very much to hear, to know, if only, if only you'd please, please just listen.

But first, before I tell you, before I explain to you what it is that you need to know, what is so damned important, the thing I've been trying to say all along, that I need so desperately to tell you, before I get into all that big mess, that horrific medley of melodrama, I really, really, really need another martini.

And this time, please, please, please could I please have it dry? Please?

Montreal

"It's no use going back to yesterday, because I was a different person then."
— Lewis Carroll

"Beautiful young people are accidents of nature, but beautiful old people are works of art."
— Eleanor Roosevelt

"It takes a long time to become young."
— Pablo Picasso

"It is perfectly complete. You and I, What more—? Strange, how we suffer in spite of this!"
— D.H. Lawrence

"Many an irritating fault, mahy an unlovely oddity, has come of a hard sorrow."
— George Eliot

"The people long eagerly for just two things: bread and circuses."
— Junvenal

Montreal

Hartford, Connecticut
April, 1952

It is not a pleasant thing to tell this story, to recount those awful events of that summer so long ago. Yet it's a story that should be told, perhaps must be told, not only for the cathartic benefit it may confer upon me (perhaps finally providing some relief from the anguish set upon my mind that horrid summer), but also in the fervent hope that relating those gruesome events – certainly not for purpose of calumny, most of the guilty parties are gone now, and anyway acted less from perniciousness than from insipid ignorance – will in some way diminish the likelihood of anything similar ever taking place again.

That summer was unusually hot, hot and humid, leaving most of us who were fresh out of high school feeling restless and bored. I was but a young woman and I spent most of those summer days with my best friend Maggie sitting on the expansive public dock, the long, shaky, wooden peninsula that reached out away from the steamy air and hovered over the blinding, sun-reflected water of Lake Emory. Merritt was a small town and most of the young people, having little else to do, spent their free time enjoying the water and the beach. Maggie and I would hang our feet in the water and daydream, sometimes chatting excitedly, I suppose unrealistically, about our plans for the future, including college in the fall, and then periodically we'd throw ourselves off the end of that wooden plank into the cool, opalescent water, lazily splashing about amongst the other bathers, temporarily finding relief from the heat, and I suppose, from the inevitable languor induced by those long, humid days.

Among the regular bathers, we often saw the handsome, envied couple, Julia Stonebride and David Harris, both graceful swimmers with gorgeous physiques and radiant smiles. They had been the darlings of Merritt High School, sweethearts from the age of sixteen, unanimously considered the most adorable couple in town. However, everyone could see that their love was torrential, a flood of emotions, strong, erratic emotions. At times they fought loudly and angrily, saying – no, shouting – the most horrible things at each other. But Julia and David, like so many others whose minds were captive to their passions, could not stay apart from each other for long and soon after each of their dire confrontations they'd be back in each other's arms, oblivious to the threats and insults they had not long since hurled at each other with pungent vile. Their emotional intensity was riveting, and also the source of a good bit of trepidation for those of us who silently watched. David and Julia seemed ill-starred from the beginning, and experienced the best and the worst of that ineffable, inscrutable thing called romance.

Julia came from a family that, if not wealthy, certainly was well-to-do; a family that occasionally affected airs of a higher social station than was likely deserved. Still, the Stonebrides were a good family, caring and respectable, honorable participants in our community, and well-liked by everyone. Mrs. Stonebride was president of the PTA, was active in many charities and civic groups, received visitors at her home regularly, and doted on her three children, of whom Julia was the eldest. Julia's father worked at the bank, smoked cigars, wore nice, conservative clothing, and always behaved with the utmost decorum, although his tastes ran to the ordinary and his views were nothing but predictably dull and intransigent.

David's family, on the other hand, was almost precisely the antithesis of the Stonebrides, fitting clumsily into the Merritt community like a torn finger in an otherwise perfect glove. Mr. Harris moved from job to job, drank too much, often exhibited a violent temper, and projected an all-around crabby and moody disposition that was horrifically ill-suited to the demands of a histrionic wife and five rambunctious young ones, including David, who, like Julia, was the eldest. Mrs. Harris, David's mother, was paradoxically both an insufferably over-dramatic personality and a pathetic, even sympathetic, creature of self-deprecation and disarming loquaciousness. She could talk endlessly, mostly about herself, and regularly feigned the most outlandish emotional distress, with the sad consequence that she had few friends or listeners, a fact that only fueled and complemented her eccentricities. The Harris family seemed bereft of the wherewithal to provide a stable and loving home life. They were unendingly beleaguered by one thing or another, struggled, mostly unsuccessfully, through rough times, exhaustingly beset by troubles, monetary and otherwise.

Maggie and I often talked of Julia and David, imagining the anguish and the ecstasy they must have felt, and shuddered at the depth of the emotional stress that we imagined such shifting longings and temperaments must inevitably have subjected them to. Despite David's striking handsomeness, his athletic ability, magnetic personality and popularity, we often concluded, sadly, that David's lot in life was rife with disadvantages that could only ultimately, and without exception, exacerbate his hopelessly volatile situation with Julia. We thus spoke of David more with sympathy than with disdain. Nevertheless, Maggie and I had no sympathy for – in fact, we could neither tolerate nor understand – David's propensity to periodically direct ghastly threats and viciousness toward Julia, or his seemingly uncontrollable anger that inexorably grew to a boiling point whereupon he would exhibit one of his trademark temper fits.

Julia, on the other hand, we envied. At least, that is, we envied her status, her beauty, her loving family, and her charm – when she was willing. What we certainly did not envy was her bittersweet, tumultuous relationship with David, an unrelenting spider web within which she seemed hopelessly ensnarled.

We lived in the city, Maggie and I, practically next door to each other. To call Merritt a city is a bit of a stretch, but the town was big enough to draw many a huckster and scam artist, who appeared so regularly it became a running joke among those of us who couldn't stand the sight or sound of such duplicity and deceit. They came regularly to bilk as many of our hapless citizens as they could, at which they succeeded marvelously and disgustingly, despite the admonishments of a few intrepid (and reasonable) naysayers. Most of Merritt's citizens were not only uneducated, but were stone-cold vacuous in the faculties of wit and reason. It didn't take the brains of Daniel Webster to have this crowd eating jam made from fruit flies or rubbing sorghum syrup on their balding scalps in the pathetic belief that such futile acts would cure obesity or grow hair on their empty heads. It didn't take much ethical sense either – the gall and turpitude those brazen swindlers had.

I guess that's what I first thought when I heard about the McCormick and Brudge plan to light up Merritt's town square with the newly invented electric lightbulbs. I thought it surely must be another flimflam, some scam that I had not yet seen. But I was familiar enough with the sordid modus operandi of the hucksters, such as the summer before when a man who called himself Doctor Benjamin Moons had half the town drinking an alcohol and saffron concoction said to prevent rheumatic fever and tuberculosis. Yes, that's what I first thought, that the electric lightbulb was a hoax of some sort, that McCormick and Brudge, like all the others, had come to our small town to defraud the poor gullible citizens of Merritt.

None of us understood exactly what electricity was, that is, outside the abstract concept that we'd learned in school. Using such mysterious energy to burn a lamp, to provide light, was a strange and even frightening magical idea to many. Still, we'd read about it enough, it was a common topic in newspapers of the time, and a few of us had even seen the huge arc lamps that were newly installed in some railway stations and lighthouses. Mr. Ramsey at the drug store had been talking about it excitedly for weeks. The idea to him was revolutionary, and he envisioned big changes in our lives because of it. He genuinely believed that electric lightbulbs would be commonplace in our homes and businesses by the turn of the century. His comments on all sorts of topics, particularly inventions and scientific advancements, were pithy and erudite, bubbling out of him with such vigor it was infectious. Mr. Ramsey was a boisterous, gregarious man by nature, and when he found a topic of which he was enamored, he became animated beyond anyone I'd ever seen. His quotidian effusions of intellect and enthusiasm were something

Maggie and I not only found fascinating, but dearly relished as nectar in the Merritt desert.

We were skeptical, nearly all of us, about a thin, glass ball that was said to provide enough light to illuminate a room. Mr. Ramsey insisted that the science was valid, that our skepticism in this case was wrongly spent. Still, we needed to be shown, and the demonstration in the town square was aimed precisely at that need, and most certainly was assured of being well attended.

In fact, now that I think back on such things, particularly the sequence leading up to those awful events, I realize it was late summer when the whole thing began. I believe it was early August when Misters McCormick and Brudge decorated the town square with all those glass bulbs and wires. They had the Merritt town square filled with a tangled, streaming web of thick black cables that nuzzled hundreds of dangling clear glass bulbs. In a manner it looked to me like a gigantic Christmas tree spread sideways with streamers wiggling and winding in a serpentine torrent of woven threads, shining glass bulbs emerging here and there, becoming more and more obvious the more one looked, like the stars do on a clear, dark night. I remember Maggie commenting that it looked to her like a bowl of octopuses with swollen suction cups sporadically popping out nether and to.

On the appointed Saturday evening a crowd quickly formed and filled the benches, bleachers, and spindly, wooden chairs that had been positioned around a high stage at the center of the town square. The whole scene was engulfed by the clear bulbs strung out majestically on the thick black wires. The center stage, in particular, was awash in complexity, surrounded by labyrinthine scaffolding that supported an astonishing array of wires and bulbs so fantastical that one could not help but stare wide-eyed and dumbstruck by the whole thing. An electric generator whirred loudly near the stage, a mysterious sound to us, and a mechanical device that Maggie and I didn't understand. I remember Maggie pointing it out to me first, and then looking at Mr. Ramsey who was sitting not far from us fanning his face in the summer heat. We both assumed that he understood the intricacies and ramifications of the strange mechanical contraption.

We waited quite some time. The town square was crowded and the audience was not sitting idly or quietly – they were reverberating with chatter. Most of the talk, naturally, focused on what was going to happen – not only here in the town square in a few moments, but in our society, a society in which technological advancements were rapidly dwarfing the human capacity to respond to them, in practical ways as well as emotional and moral.

The crowd was loud right up until the moment the lights went on. Then, in the magnificent glow of those hundreds of clear bulbs, glistening in unison, sowing photons amongst our willing eyes, the quiet fell on us so suddenly, so hard, so swiftly, it was like an iron anvil slamming to earth, lured by an intense, unyielding gravity. When those lights blinked on there was a blinding radiance that our eyes were not prepared for, and then a deafening quiet. I remember my attention being so focused on the visual extravaganza that my mind entirely blocked out the sound of the whirring generator. For a moment there was utter and serene stillness, a rapture of the eyes and mind. Even these sixty some years later, the splendor of that scene is burnt into my memory, embedded with an unshakable grasp.

Today, so many years later, I might compare that scene to a busy highway at night, a highway crowded with long streams of headlights strung out like multiple parades of fireflies, flickering and glistening, swallowing the darkness. Of course, back then we didn't have highways of headlights. There was so much more to come that we knew nothing of.

It's likely that no one in the little town of Merritt slept well that night, with such an astonishing thing consuming one's memory and crowding one's consciousness. And, for many days we continued to talk about the demonstration; it seemed the entire city's population could think of nothing else. The focus was so intense that we barely gave a whisper of notice to the other goings-on in and about Merritt, including a small circus and sideshow that had set up camp just on the skirts of our little hamlet. But, as with all things, the townsfolk's obsession with the electric light demonstration gradually faded, and with little else to do that idle summer Maggie and I eventually made our way out to explore the circus.

Thinking back on those events, now so long ago, it's funny to realize how naïve Maggie and I were. We were absolutely amazed at how the other observers reacted to the animal trainers at that small circus. While the others, without exception, viewed the trainers as courageous and exotic, Maggie and I, on the contrary, saw them as abysmally brutish, uncouth, and unrefined. To us they were not merely unenlightened and harmless; they were malevolent – manifested in our minds as odious monsters. Maggie, in particular, loathed them. Maggie was ahead of her time, I guess. However rare it is today, it was nearly impossible the better part of a century ago to find someone who cared so much about people and animals, who showed the extraordinary compassion and empathy that Maggie did.

One would have thought that the use of kindness and gentleness would have been a better method of training animals than the constant punishment, even cruelty, that was the preferred, and apparently the only method used by the trainers at that circus. In particular, they teased and taunted a female elephant named Sasha. In all the animal kingdom is there a creature that elicits more distinctive connotations and emotions than the elephant? Proud, strong, majestic, independent, intelligent, and, ironically, obsequious, the elephant exudes a character that seems singular among the earth's creatures. How could sane people treat such an animal with cruelty? We watched in horror as the trainers hit, whipped, pushed, and even burned poor Sasha, as they harassed her daily. Maggie screamed at the cruel men begging them to relent, but they only laughed at her protestations and shouted mean things in return at her.

The constant punishment made Sasha a depressed and surly beast. She held her head down and walked slowly from one task to another, reacting with agitation when she was punished or taunted, suddenly twisting her large body and raising her head in defiance. The trainers were skittish around Sasha for fear she would attack them, yet their unflagging cruelty toward her only increased. One day, apparently in jest (their idea of jest), one of the trainers threw a lit cigarette into Sasha's mouth. Can you imagine? Sasha, as one would expect, reacted angrily and struck out at the man. The large animal moved quickly, her trunk hit the trainer hard in his torso and he fell to the ground, badly hurt. When we heard about the incident, though Maggie and I of course were not happy about the man's injury, we still harbored a wee bit of satisfaction and felt some pride in Sasha's fighting back, such was our sympathy for the dear beast.

Unfortunately, the owner of the circus was not as magnanimous as we, and he decided that Sasha was too dangerous and unpredictable to stay with the circus. Incredible as it now seems, the owner decided that Sasha should be put to death. It was then that Maggie and I learned something profound about the dark side of technological wonders. I'm telling you, one can't imagine the outrage that Maggie felt, how totally inconsolable she became, when the circus owner announced that poor Sasha, that great gray, sympathetic creature, was to be electrocuted in the Merritt town square using the same equipment that had provided the glorious electric light show only a week before.

I want to reiterate what I've already said, how difficult it is to relate those awful events now, though it is so many years later. The barbarism was unimaginable. But others at that time didn't see it that way at all. Animals were viewed by nearly everyone as laborers or dispensable playthings for the unfettered whims of humankind. It was in that misguided spirit that animals were treated so badly, treated as if they were unfeeling objects to be abused for our amusement.

We watched, Maggie and I, together with a large crowd – nearly the whole city – as Sasha was led in chains by a crew of six trainers to the center of Merritt's town square. The poor thing held her head down the whole way, swaying only slightly as each large leg, strapped with a heavy metal iron anklet chained to the next, slowly and methodically lifted and settled to earth, one after another. The procession, to Maggie and me, was like a funeral; yet, the rest of the crowd was animated and talkative, showing nary a sign of remorse or compassion. The event was presented and widely accepted as a spectacle of entertainment. I am embarrassed to say that a sideshow atmosphere prevailed that day. Maggie was crestfallen beyond anything I'd ever seen.

Sasha was led to an area where two large black wires lay on the ground: The wires that had only recently brought radiance and joy would now deliver death. The trainers attached one wire to each of Sasha's front legs and then scurried aside. As I recall, the crowd became very still, though Maggie continued loudly and emotionally pleading with the trainers to stop the barbaric event. The men, of course, had no time for her and roundly ignored her pleas.

A hand signal was made, a switch was thrown, a generator whirred, and Maggie went silent, the anger welling in her eyes. We watched in horror as that huge, proud creature, poor Sasha, wobbled for a moment, lifted her head, her trunk curved upward, and then fell to the ground with a dull thud. A large cloud of dust rose up, blurring our view and creating a surreal, macabre, vision – the hot, humid, and sticky summer afternoon, the thick nebula of dust particles diffusing and sparkling in the hazy air, the foggy, translucent atmosphere, the sad, gray lump on the ground – a moment of pure inconceivability for me and Maggie. The crowd roared.

I remember Maggie suffering so from the death of Sasha that she became reclusive and unusually introspective. "Lily," she said to me one day, "I don't think I'm meant to live in a place that's so savage." That's what she said, I remember it so clearly; the word she used was "savage." Maggie was so despondent it seemed nothing could pull her from her deep blues. She started to talk about abandoning her plans to attend Boston College, though we had long planned to enroll and room there together. Maggie even entertained the notion of leaving the country, such was her displeasure with the uncivilized acts we had witnessed. Even worse, as she often reminded me, was that no one seemed to care, no one even seemed to notice the cruel barbarism, much less react against it. How could one live in such a place?

I admired and respected Maggie so much, not only for her sensitivity – a trait that I believe makes a person seem a bit more human, more civilized – but for her stalwart convictions and steadfast integrity. Moreover, Maggie – my dear friend Margaret Alice Whitmore – was always willing to live up to the high standards and ideals that she set. Maggie was always one on whom you could count.

It was only a few days after the electrocution of Sasha when Mrs. Stonebride went to the police and reported that Julia was missing. The city was still a-gabble with talk of the lightbulb demonstration and the ghastly spectacle of Sasha's demise, and now this news increased the gossip and babble that pervaded and percolated in our little town, a town that now seemed far less benign than Maggie and I had ever believed possible.

Julia had never done anything like this before, Mrs. Stonebride insisted. She'd been gone for three days, none of her belongings were missing, and the Stonebride family had searched everywhere they could imagine her being. The police questioned all of us and discovered that Julia and David had had one of their bitter fights with lots of yelling and threats just before Julia disappeared – David was jealous about something that Julia had done, some suggested. David Harris was questioned, of course, and, as I recall, he claimed to have stormed away after his fight with Julia and he now had no idea where she might be. The police searched David's house and found nothing. Two days later, however, an important serendipitous discovery was made.

The police, while searching for something quite unrelated, found some of David's clothes hidden in a clump of trees just outside the city limits. There was what appeared to be blood on the clothes. Naturally, David was again questioned. Whatever he said to justify such a thing was never made public and as a result, quite predictably, the insinuations and speculation among Merritt's citizens became rampant. The town was abuzz. Ultimately, the police released David saying they did not have enough evidence to make an arrest.

People in Merritt, as you might well imagine, prattled incessantly about Julia's disappearance, and as the days went by their suspicions of David Harris steadily grew stronger. One thing led to another as the rumors, frustration, and anger spread. Now, as I think back on the inexorable manner in which those events unfolded, I am struck by the poignancy of a few simple words, only a phrase, in one of my favorite poems, *The Road Not Taken*. Robert Frost wrote, "...way leads on to way." And so it was in Merritt that obliquitous summer. Like a cascade of falling dominoes, the mood in our village grew steadily and surely against David Harris.

Though Mr. Ramsey regularly cautioned Merritt's hotheads not to jump to conclusions but to wait for the police to do their job, his words had little effect. Mr. Ramsey tried desperately to be an influential voice of reason and patience, but this gang was not one to be guided by wisdom or calm rationality. The combination of grumbling, impatience, and a fervent call to action amongst a certain subset of Merritt's less-than-finest citizens was clearly a train about to derail. We watched and waited with ever-mounting anxiety as the hubbub in our increasingly more foreboding little metropolis steadily reached a fever pitch. Still there was no word at all from or about Julia. As the tenor on the streets of Merritt rapidly and progressively worsened, one couldn't help but sense the inevitability of the events that were about to unfold as way unrelentingly led on to way.

Right enough, one awful night, one hot and humid summer night, a crowd of hotheads had gathered, and, naturally, had been drinking, when David Harris happened to pass by. Angry words were exchanged, and as the level of discourse sank lower and lower, voices were raised, threats were issued, and David soon found himself encircled by a motley band of Merritt's dipsomaniacs, ignoramuses, and hangers-on. David remained defiant, insisting on his innocence, but the squalid assemblage was in no mood for civilized discussion, tolerance, or patient inquiry; they wanted vengeance – plain, unadulterated vengeance.

One of the vulgar, drunken men had a rope, which he held high, swinging it wildly, while he yelled at the others to grab David and take justice into their own hands. Upon seeing the rope and the rage in that man's irascible, hateful eyes, David's defiance melted like a snowball in July and he finally came to realize the gravity of his situation. David tried to run, but unfortunately for him there were too many arms and bodies nearby, and quickly the abhorrent mob had him entangled in the rope and imprisoned in their clutches.

It was late evening, reaching the depths of darkness, and yet the day's summer heat and humidity had not abated. When that detestable band of Merritt's goons snatched poor David Harris off the street and shackled him with a rope, the heat and humidity were at their height. Later, in the light of reason, many people suggested that the hot, humid weather likely was a contributing factor in precipitating the despicable events that then unraveled. Most of us, however, were in no mood for justifications or even rational explanations for what had happened.

Who said what and did what is not publicly known, and never will be. I guess it doesn't matter anymore. The sad fact is that those iniquitous men began to drag poor David off the street with the intention of harming him, perhaps even harboring the notion of hanging him. However, as way so often leads to way, circumstances led these men down another road, a road paved with unspeakable shame. As those irrational men dragged David Harris into the city's town square they coincidentally and unpropitously encountered the two thick black cables still lying on the ground, still attached to the electric generator – the very wires that had delighted us with a dazzling light display, and the very wires that heinously took away the life of dear Sasha. Most regrettably, upon seeing those wires, an ignominious idea took hold within the group psyche of that loathsome horde – an idea nearly too unbelievable to contemplate or report, yet an idea that, in one nefarious guise or another, likely even today forms in the minds of too, too many of our fellow human beings, sad truth be told.

David, bound by the rope, was placed on the ground, the thick black cables were attached to his arms, and then several of the men, driven by their dauntless enmity, teamed together to start the generator. David's howls and cries brought out a sizable crowd, and although many of the observers were outraged and horrified, and even screamed at the men to desist, a much larger number, an embarrassingly large number of Merritt's citizens, whether out of fear or, too, seeking revenge assuming David's guilt, either silently stood by or even encouraged the electrocution of David Harris.

It was over in a moment, only a moment. The air was thick and hot. The vigilantes, having completed their deed, were in disarray, randomly scattering like white puffs of dandelion seeds in a warm summer wind. Of the large crowd of observers standing nearby, some were crying, some were yelling, some were celebrating, but most of them, the vast majority, were silent. Just silent. There's not much more to say; the police arrived too late, people loitered about for a long time despite being advised to disperse, and eventually the dead, limp body of David Harris was removed by horse and buggy and delivered to the city morgue.

The following day Merritt's citizens were remarkably quiet about what had happened the prior evening. Memories were fuzzy, some people weren't saying what they saw, and others claimed to be confused about the details of what had transpired. Maggie and I were in such a state of bewildered shock we were nearly speechless. Maggie sat in a rocking chair on her parent's front porch for hours, merely rocking and staring. David's family, naturally, was aghast. They screamed and wailed and exhorted the police to hold the culpable parties responsible. But, alas, as many of us have learned to expect in similar situations, the earnest and justifiable demands of the Harris family, sadly, but not unpredictably, were in vain.

A few days later we had a funeral for young, handsome David Harris. And a few days after that, Julia Stonebride returned to Merritt, quite alive and well. Julia explained that she had run off by herself in a fit of near hysteria to escape what she deemed to be an overwhelming, insolvable situation. She had been afraid and embarrassed, and as time passed it became increasingly more difficult for her to face her family and friends. She had stayed at a boarding house in a small town just across the state line, she said, where she tried to sort out her thoughts, feelings, intentions, and her life.

"Lily," Maggie said to me in such a serious voice, "I'm going to move to Canada."

Her words took me by complete surprise, though of course I should have realized such a thing was coming. She'd given me plenty of warning and I well could have expected it knowing Maggie's temperament and indefatigable probity. I suppose it shocked me because it was something I so feared because it was something that I so very much did not want. I knew I couldn't go with her, that my way led to Boston College and beyond, not out of the country.

"I've decided to move to Montreal and enroll at McGill University," Maggie continued. Though she began her pronouncement somewhat meekly, there was now bold excitement in her voice. It became clear that this was the right decision for her, that this was her way.

Maggie and I kept in touch for many years, and I even visited her in Montreal a few times. But gradually we drifted further and further apart as our ways led to more and even more divergent ways. I hadn't heard much from her recently, except for a card at Christmas. Then, yesterday, I received a telephone call from her daughter. Margaret Alice Whitmore had passed away in Montreal at the age of seventy-nine.

I talked with Maggie's daughter for quite some time – she's such a nice woman – and I promised her that I would tell this story, a story that I have been mostly quiet about, I don't exactly know why, for all these years. I've purchased a ticket to go to Maggie's funeral and I've made arrangements to stay with her daughter for a while. Her name, too, is Lily. It will be nice to get to know her.

&

"We've begun to raise daughters more like sons... but few have the courage to raise our sons more like our daughters."
— Gloria Steinem

"Most people would sooner die than think; in fact, they do so."
— Bertrand Russell

"How important it is for us to recognize and celebrate our heroes and she-roes!"
— Maya Angelou

"All through life there were distinctions - toilets for men, toilets for women; clothes for men, clothes for women - then, at the end, the graves are identical."
— Leila Aboulela, Minaret

"If not me, who? If not now, when?"
— Emma Watson

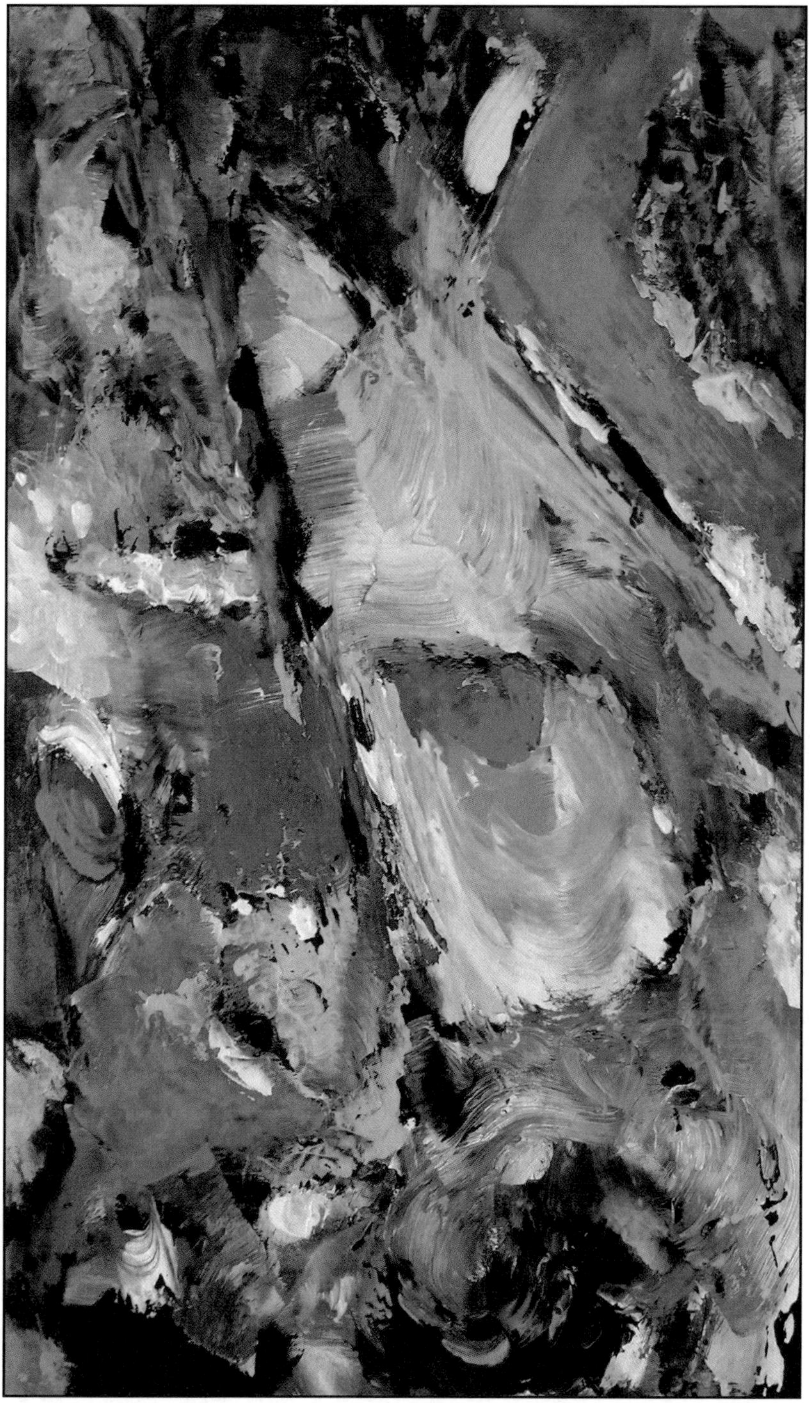

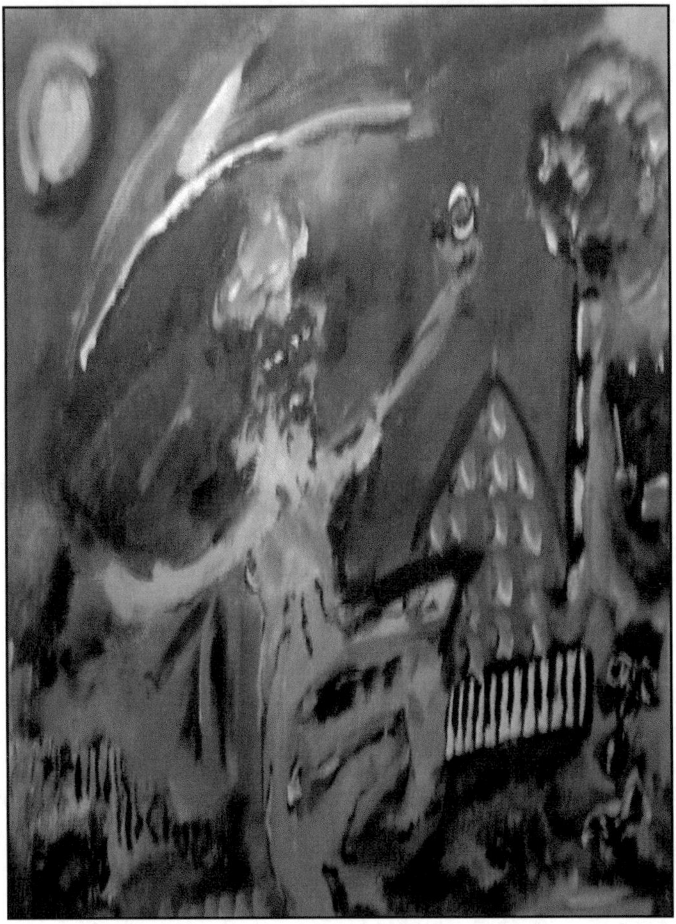

&

As I was saying, she kept calling me Elsa, although my name is Andy Ampersand. It's one thing to get a person's name wrong, but to get their *gender* wrong really makes you wonderuzzle. It's not like I look like a girl. I don't. I've always looked like a boy. I even have a goatee – soul patch included. My name is Andy Ampersand. I am a boy.

And, this woman was supposedly a friend of my mother. She wanted to sell me something; I believe it had something to do with health insurance or coupons. "Elsa," she kept saying, "you really need this insurance." Or, maybe it was "coupons," I don't recamember. And then I would say something such as, "My name is Andy. I'm a boy." And she would ignore me as if I was the invisible man (or invisible woman, in this case), and would continue with her sales pitch, trying to persuadoax me.

And another thing: One day after work I stopped at a bar I've never been in before. I sat on a stool at the middle of the bar. There was a strange man with orange hair sitting at the bar next to me. He stared at me for a long time starting from my feet and slowly moving his gaze up to my head. He looked at my chest for far too long, I thought. It made me all embarravous. When he finally got to my eyes I gave him a very quizzical look. He definitely noticed. He winced a bit. I wondered if he was gay. It was quite a curiomarkable experience.

Then he asked me if I wanted a drink. But get this – he called me "baby." Yeah, that's right, he said, "Hey, baby, can I buy you a drink?" Is this some new sort of illness? People can't tell what gender a person is? What is the deal with that, anyway?

And the other really weird, jumbomazing thing happened when I got stopped for speeding last week and the cop asked for my license. Of course, I gave it to him. But when he handed it back, for some reason I looked at it and I noticed something very bizarre, really too unbelievastounding. On my license where it said "sex" there was an "F." That is very weird. I don't have any idea how it got like that. No ideenotion at all. I'd never noticed it before. No wonder the cop let me go. Well, I was just happy to not get a ticket. But, still, I quiziwondered about that "F."

And, the strangest thing was my doctor. This was just too, too much, I'm telling you. You see, I went in just for a flu shot. But, my doctor asked me some very odd questions. It was just as if he was talking to a girl. That is so preposternutty. And he called me Elsa, too. In fact, you know, come to think of it, that is the name on my driver's license. Elsa. It says Elsa Adishinal. For the life of me I cannot underhend these odd events. My name is Andy Ampersand. I am a boy.

So, anyway, to get to the point, today I had a dentist's appointment. I just hate that, don't you? Anyway, so I was sitting in the dentist's waiting room, you know, the most boring room in the whole world, for sure, and I was forced while sitting there, I mean, just in order to pass the time, to look at some magazines that were not only way out of date, but, get this, they were the most godawfible magazines I ever saw. I mean, for example, there was a zine all about toupees, another about the life of sideshow carnies, there was a catalog of all kinds of zippers, one zine that was only about cucumbers of various kinds, there was a journal for people who worked as pedicurists (with lots of photos of toenails), another for taxidermists, a magazine all about plankton, and another full of various contraptions for picking up dog doo-doo. The only one I could even stand to look at was a quasi-scientific-pop-psychology zine called *Disorders Today*. I am not kidding – it was a zine about the most weirdizarre psychological and medical problems. Have you ever seen it?

Okay, so there were some really tantinating disorders in that zine. Really perplextional. I just couldn't believe most of them. In fact, I was getting into it quite a bit, reading about all those bizarterious maladies when I suddenly became uncomfortably conscious of the fact that while I was reading about one particularly eccentinky disorder I started to experience a very kinkular feeling – like déjà vu, but more of a did'cha view? I'm telling you, reading this article was giving me real goosiebumpimpulies!

Okay, what it was about, this weirdo article was that some neurologists claimed that there is a very rare disorder that occurs in some bigender people in which these people will experience an alternation in genders. In fact, this peculiarazy disorder is called alternating gender incongruity. Can you imagine? People switching genders? A neurologist was explaining in the article how some bigender people can even experience phantom breasts or phantom genitalia as they switch from one gender to another. Well, as you can imagine, I was just flabberstounded by it. I mean, can you believe it – people who change gender? I just couldn't fathomup such a thing. But, I also couldn't comprehenize why reading this article was giving me the willies, the heebie-jeebies, you know, the jittercreeps. Maybe it was just the strangeness of the disorder that was causing me to feel so weird, I really don't know. But I was definitely getting the jittercreeps.

Well, anyway, while I was getting a really freakyqueer feeling while reading about this goofy disorder, you know, the other thing was that I was having a great bit of difficulty paying attention to the article because I kept being interrupted by the silly dental hygienist who was calling out in a very loud voice, "Andy.... Andy... Andy...." It was very aginoying. Very disbothersome. I'm sure you can appresheeize the situation. I mean, it was very difficult for me to read and understand the article about alternating gender incongruity with all those irrigrating, loud interruptions. And, honestly, I simply couldn't appreceive why the person she was calling, this Andy guy, was not there, or if he was there, why he was not responding. Was he asleep? Or dead? Or what? I just couldn't take it anymore, I just could not tolercept it!

But, then the most remarkuliar, unfordictable thing happened: the hygienist saw me, seemed to recognize me, started walking toward me, yes, came right up to me, and stood right next to me, leaned over, looked straight at me, smiled, and said, "Andy, the dentist is ready to see you." That's right. That's what she said. I'm not kidding. I'm sure I didn't fabrimagine it, or hallucinize it. No, she definitely called me Andy.

Well, I was flabberstunned by it, I'm telling you. I mean, I was really confubashed. Yes, indeedy. However, I'll tell you, once I'd regained my composure, you know, in this somewhat awkwardiferous moment, well, I looked her right in the face and forthrightly replied, "But, Miss, you have the wrong person. My name is Elsa. Elsa Adishinal. I am a girl."

I mean, really! What is it with people? I understand that someone might get a name wrong once in a while. That's underhensible. But, getting a person's *gender* wrong! My word! Can you believe it?

What in heaven's name is the world coming to, anyway?

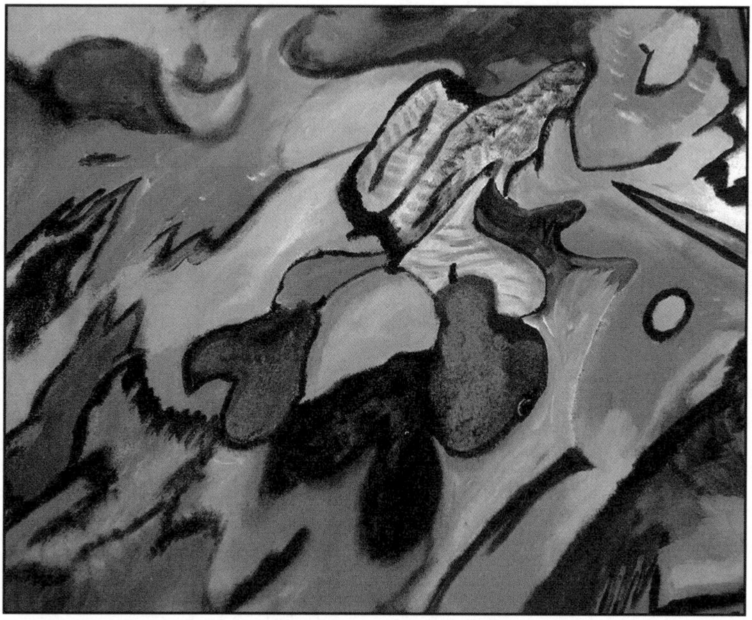

Synesthesia

"A human being is a part of the whole, called by us, 'Universe,' a part limited in time and space. He experiences himself, his thoughts and feelings as something separated from the rest – a kind of optical delusion of his consciousness. This delusion is a kind of prison for us, restricting us to our personal desires and to affection for a few persons nearest to us. Our task must be to free ourselves from this prison by widening our circle of compassion to embrace all living creatures and the whole of nature in its beauty. Nobody is able to achieve this completely, but the striving for such achievement is in itself a part of the liberation and a foundation for inner security."

— Albert Einstein

"The time comes when each one of us has to give up as illusions the expectations which, in his youth, he pinned upon his fellow-men, and when he may learn how much difficulty and pain has been added to his life by their ill-will."

— Sigmund Freud

"Colors, like features, follow the changes of the emotions."

— Pablo Picasso

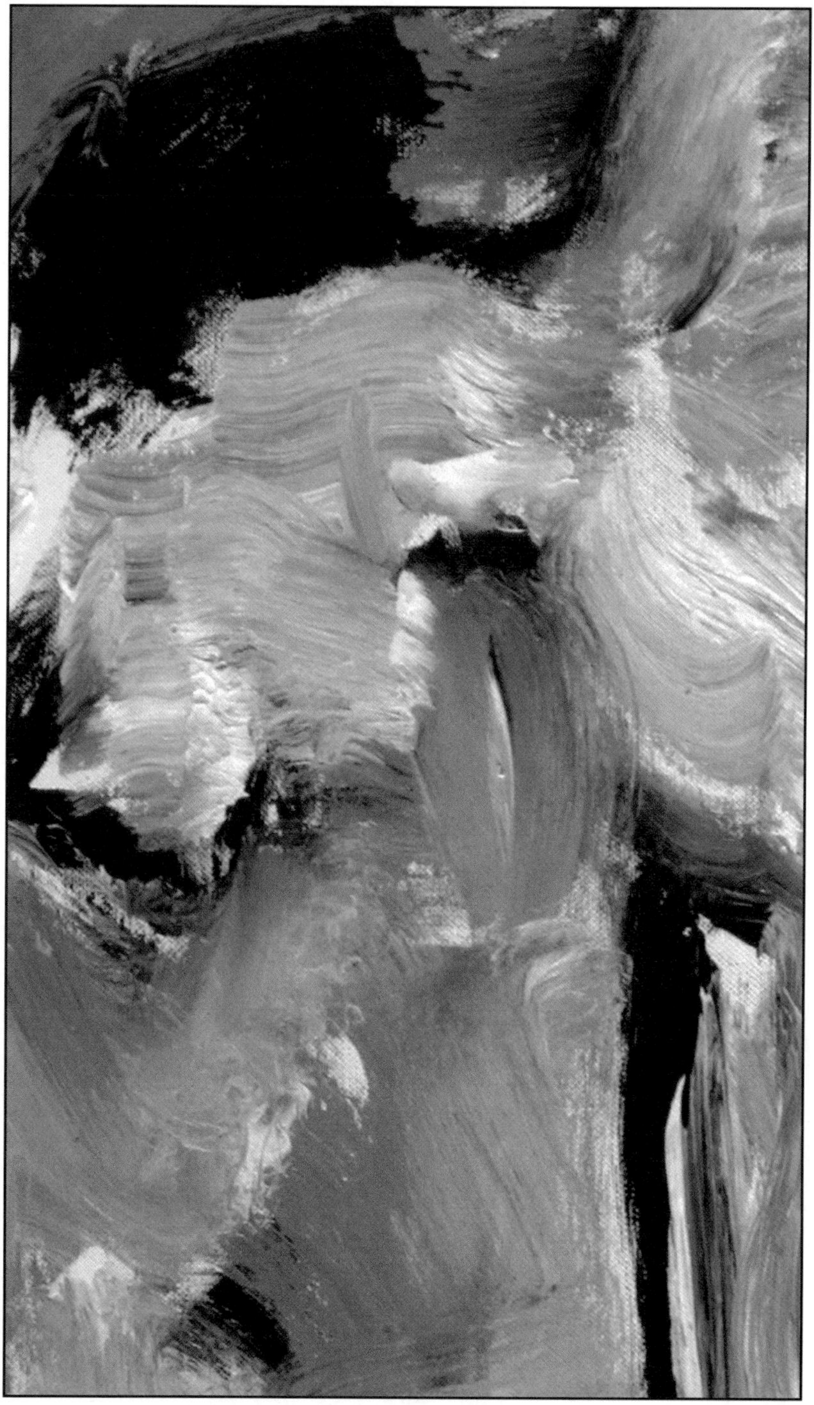

Synesthesia

(1)

Chad walks confidently, briskly, down gray, wheelchair-wide halls, long loping strides, arms swinging freely.

Fresh, black leather soles click-clack on worn, white tile floors.

Chad is thinking about getting off work and going to a bar.

Fun.

Chad is young. Chad is happy. Chad is smiling.

Chad's starched white shirt and white pants swish loudly in the quiet space. Fluorescent lights buzz an incessant buzz. Musty odor, loneliness, quiet.

Chad slows, then stops, leans his head into a doorway – still smiling, still thinking dull, insipid, but happy thoughts. Chad peeks into room 320 at Joseph.

Joseph – reclining in bed, wearing white jockeys, white T-shirt, that's all. Bed sheet crumpled at his bony feet.

Joseph – pale, thin, knobby-kneed, with gnarled hands, wrinkled skin – slowly turns his white-whiskered face toward Chad peeking.

"Hi ya, Joseph. How's it going?"

Joseph slowly turns his face to the window. Eyes yellowed, yearning, nearly crying, but still.

Quiet.

Joseph – just looking, thinking nothing, just looking.

A dark, thin slit of a shadow stretches from the window obliquely across the drab green carpet, twisting up onto the bed and across Joseph's face. A squirrel dashes across the grass, rustling the fallen leaves outside the window.

Click-clack. Chad moves on, thinking about getting off work.

Fun.

Joseph calmly rises, begins to dress.

First, shirt. Pale, thin, wrinkled, skin-sagging arm wriggles clumsily into white cotton sleeve. Reach back, struggle, other arm in. Damn buttons.

Next, pants. Pale, thin, bare, skin-and-bone leg awkwardly into dark polyester pant leg. Slowly, creaking, one leg in. Then another. Zip.

Socks even harder.

Shoes take time.

Click-clack. Chad is well down the corridor now.

Joseph pockets his wallet. Then, photos, cards, some money. Next, checkbook. Hidden. Must remember. Ready.

Goodbye room.

Joseph moves quietly to doorway, stops, leans head out through door opening, peers down hall. Empty.

Good.

Quietly, slowly, move toward desk, opposite direction from Chad. One step, two. Quiet. Shuffle. Breathe. Desk just ahead. Slow. Stop. Look. Nurse is off somewhere.

Good.

Now, go.

Joseph through outer door, outside, find bus.

(2)

"The words are still the same," she said.

As usual, I'm lost. I say, "Why can't you cry? I don't understand."

"It's so cold here at this latitude..."

So cold she says.

"I'm learning... well... I guess to fit in."

Learning to fit in she says. I think: Do I know what she

means?

"I know what you mean," I say.

I'm thinking yes, she's right, people are cold. Politeness is commonly mistaken for friendliness. It's definitely cold here. Cold. But, latitude?

I think more.

Julia stares into my eyes. Hers are blue. A blue that changes somehow. Now grayish, then yellowish, or brown-like. Then again, a hint of green, or as deep pastel as a clear blue sky.

"The words are the same," she says, "but they mean something else, something different, I can't quite make it out."

I think of colors. I once took an art class and I learned how a color can look very different when placed next to other colors. It was amazing how different it could look just because it was next to a certain color. Changed. Are words like that?

I look at my coffee. I sip. I don't like coffee, but I drink it. I wear a T-shirt with words on it.

I don't have any idea what to say, so I decide to be Rogerian:

"What do they mean to you, the words?"

(Roger Wilco. Over and out.)

Before Julia can answer, a man walks up to our table. An old man with a pale, white-whiskered face. Julia looks up at him. I look up at him.

Silence.

Then, "May I join you?"

"Uh, sure," – "Yes, please do," we say simultaneously.

I rise a bit as he sits. He's thin, but sturdy. He looks familiar to me in the way in which everything looks familiar to me. I'm thinking about colors. And people. I'm thinking that people change when they're around other people. I realize now that I change, change quite a bit, when I'm around different people. I'm thinking...

Julia speaks first, "Are you cold?"

...when things look different, when something has changed, I wonder what it is that changes?

"Yes," he answers brightly, "I've lived here all my life, learned to be cold from the get-go. Wanted to fit in. But now I want to be myself. I don't want to be cold anymore."

We smile. I sip. We nod.

My turn: "How will you do that?"

(Roger Wilco. Over and out.)

"Not how," he says, "When. And I mean now. I've waited too long. I want to be warm. I want to be myself."

A siren blares somewhere.

The wind blows.

I sip my coffee and think about colors and words and cold.

"I want to know things. Mostly about myself," the old man continues. "And people. But, everything really. I want to know so much, I ache. I feel like I don't know anything. I've waited too long."

Julia patronizes: "What you don't know can't hurt you."

I imagine a person carrying a chunk of radioactive uranium who comes close to me, wants to show it to me, to give it to me.

The old man is smiling a half smile, staring at Julia.

I'm thinking: What you don't know *can* hurt you. I remember too much. Lies. Deceit. Duplicity. Too many chunks of radioactive uranium. I wonder if this old man was given some chunks of radioactive uranium. I guess most were, maybe all of us.

It is cold here, I now muse. Too cold. Is it the latitude? I'm wondering: Do the words change meaning? Do they change?

The old man says, "I want to know. I want to be myself."

(3)

A red rental car speeds along a highway. A convertible with the top down, an old man at the wheel. Smiling, thinking. The wind whips at his white hair. Shadows of telephone poles glide swiftly, rhythmically, across the hood of the red rental car and then across the old man's face. A city is just ahead. A big city with lots of people.

Joseph smiles the smile of someone who knows something.

Joseph thinks: The words are just the same, but the meaning is changing. Like colors.

The red rental car speeds down the road.

When Joseph sees a bright yellow sign he remembers the sweet little girl he saw playing in the park. Then an orange truck and Joseph feels a sudden tinge of regret from a long-lost childhood memory. A red bird above triggers an emotion from an early marriage.

A small dark cloud passes momentarily in front of the sun and changes the highway from grainy gray to a brooding matte black. In his mind Joseph instantly sees a woman's face, a too familiar face. A knife-stabbing pain surges through his chest. Radioactive uranium. Then a bright, royal blue billboard with yellow lettering comes into view and contentment displaces Joseph's pain.

The red rental car sails the highway. Joseph soaks in the colors, smiles, and thinks.

Now into the city.

Joseph knows something.

Red light.

The red rental car stops.

Time passes.

Joseph, still smiling, slowly slumps forward; his head gently rests against the steering wheel.

Joseph is still.

More time passes.

Green light, but the red rental car is not moving.

A horn blares. Still the red rental car sits.

The cars pile up, horns blare, frustrated voices shout, and yet the red rental car sits unmoving.

"This is 911, how can we help you?"

"There's a car blocking traffic. There's a big mess out here. An old man is slumped at the wheel of the car. It's not moving, and neither is he. Send an ambulance right away. I think he's dead."

(4)

Chad walks confidently, briskly down the quiet gray hall. Chad is thinking about last night's football game. He imagines he is the star quarterback surrounded by reporters after winning the big game.

Fun.

Chad's dreams are all the same. All dreams seem the same at this latitude.

Chad is young. Chad is happy. Click-clack.

Chad slows his pace and then stops at the doorway of room 215. He leans carefully forward, his head tilts diagonally into the doorway, Chad still smiling, still thinking.

Chad stares into the room – looking, but not seeing.

Bertha – sitting, nearly rocking, but mostly still. Bertha's head turns slightly toward Chad staring.

"How's it going, Cutie?" Chad smiling a phony smile.

Bertha offers a short stiff nod.

Bertha's thinking: Now is a good time. Everyone will be in their rooms, Chad will be down the hall, and the nurse should be taking her cigarette break. Good time to try. They can only bring me back inside. What more can they do?

Click-clack. Chad is already on the move, dreaming, fantasizing.

Fun.

Bertha pauses, pulls in a deep breath, slowly rises, pushes her small, frail body out of the rocking chair. Old bones creak, skin sags, eyes gaze longingly out the window.

A dark thin shadow falls from the bright window directly across drab green carpet, up onto Bertha's dress, and then obliquely across Bertha's face, neatly dividing one eye and cheek from the rest.

Bertha's face is now solemn, but hopeful. Now's a good time, she thinks.

Bertha gathers her valuables, her purse, moves slowly toward the door, leans her head out into the gray space, peers down the lonely, quiet corridor, takes one light step silently onto old, worn, white tiles, then steals quietly down the wide hallway, step by careful step.

Bertha was right – the nurse is on her break. Glance side to side. Coast clear. No one around. Move quickly now. Don't look back.

Out door, into fresh air, sun.

Bright, vibrant colors.

Bertha thinks: The colors look so different, so intense, so changed.

But the words, the words are still the same.

Hobbies

"If you don't stick to your values when they're being tested, they're not values: they're hobbies."
— *Jon Stewart*

"People with stimulating hobbies suffer from the most noxious of despairs since they are tranquilized in their despair."
— *Walker Percy, The Moviegoer*

"Hobbies are apt to run away with us, you know; it doesn't do to be run away with. We must keep the reins."
— *George Eliot*

"The only difference between a caprice and a life-long passion is that the caprice lasts a little longer."
— *Oscar Wilde*

"Lost among these entirely strange people."
— *Franz Kafka*

Hobbies

The body of Mr. Kerpunkle was lying on the concrete floor at the bottom of the narrow, steep basement stairs, having recently arrived there following a bumpy descent. The parietal area of his cranium exhibited a serious wound. Mr. Kerpunkle was unconscious. His well-worn railroad train engineer hat was lying on the floor nearby, as was the un-hinged, now somewhat beat-up white door that had once been attached at the top of the stairs.

While not enjoying a perfect marriage, Mr. and Mrs. Kerpunkle had existed for many years in a state of mutual calm and routine. They tolerated each other. Both worked outside the home, Mr. Kerpunkle as a civil engineer and Mrs. Kerpunkle as a registered nurse. Each night when they arrived home after work they changed clothes, ate dinner together, and then retired to spend the evening with their hobbies. Each had a favorite avocation that allowed a diversion from their dreary marriage and dearth of communication. Hence, every night Mr. and Mrs. Kerpunkle went to the basement to pursue their respective favorite leisure activities.

Mr. Kerpunkle's hobby was model trains. He had been an enthusiast since the age of nine when he watched the endless circles made by a glistening Holiday Classic Express that his father had assembled under their Christmas tree. Mr. Kerpunkle's hobby had grown in complexity over the years. Today in one room in the basement of the Kerpunkle home, Mr. Kerpunkle has erected a large plywood table upon which he mounted an elaborate electric train with all the fixings. His Lionel Union Pacific Flyer Freight set with a shiny black engine and a bright red caboose speeds gracefully around the top of the plywood, which is crowded with tiny model greenery, houses, bridges, little people, and assorted railroad paraphernalia, you know, like those miniature black and white X-shaped railroad signs. Mr. Kerpunkle smiles with pride and satisfaction as he guides his Lionel Pacific Flyer through an elaborate labyrinth of tracks that crisscross and wind elegantly, smoothly, through the dense model landscape that Mr. Kerpunkle has assembled. Time flies by each night as Mr. Kerpunkle watches the train's movement with boyish fascination, and as he tinkers with minute details of the model set, adjusting this and re-arranging that. As a proud member of the Koochiching County Model Railroad Association, Mr. Kerpunkle has honed his craft with conviction and love.

Meanwhile, as Mr. Kerpunkle amuses himself in one room of the expansive basement, Mrs. Kerpunkle is in another room, separated from her husband by several fiberboard walls, where she enjoys partaking in her hobby each evening. Mrs. Kerpunkle has a hobby very different from that of her husband. Model railroading, after all, is a common and well accepted hobby, even admired. Mrs. Kerpunkle's hobby, on the contrary, is wholly unconventional, even extraordinary. It is not a hobby which many people choose. You see, Mrs. Kerpunkle's hobby is neurosurgery.

Like her husband, Mrs. Kerpunkle has also constructed a large plywood table in one room of the basement. There is a large drain below the table. Mrs. Kerpunkle has drilled holes in the plywood in order to allow liquids to be cleaned from the surface and run down the floor drain. A sink and hose are nearby. Also, there is a large microscope mounted to the top of the plywood table and a number of surgical instruments are carefully placed on a metal tray that sits atop a small table on wheels. While the Lionel Union Pacific Flyer with the shiny black engine and red caboose is whizzing several rooms away, Mrs. Kerpunkle is enjoying her hobby of neurosurgery in a nearby room in the Kerpunkle basement.

Mrs. Kerpunkle's interest in neurosurgery began years ago when her uncle, Mr. Mobius Needlebaum, suffered a stroke in his right hemisphere that left him with a strange condition known as *alien hand syndrome*. One day while riding with her uncle on a bus, Mrs. Kerpunkle noticed Mr. Needlebaum looking intently at his left foot. Her uncle explained to Mrs. Kerpunkle that he felt someone tugging on his pants leg. However, when Mr. Needlebaum checked to see who was pulling at his cuff, he shockingly discovered that it was his own left hand doing the tugging. Well, this struck Mrs. Kerpunkle not only as curious, but also wildly intriguing.

Coincidentally, at about the same time that Mr. Needlebaum developed an alien hand, his sister, Mrs. Kerpunkle's aunt, fell from a bicycle and damaged the left side of her head. Following the accident she inexplicably began to speak with a distinctive Russian accent, something she had never done before. Mrs. Kerpunkle learned that this was a rare phenomenon known as *foreign language syndrome*. She found these neurological oddities irresistible and began studying all types of freaky brain syndromes. For instance, she read about Phineas Gage, the man who had a metal rod pass through his head, and she enjoyed similar case studies in books by Sacks, Ramachandran, and Damasio.

One winter day Mrs. Kerpunkle took a spill on an icy patch outside her home and clunked her head on the sidewalk. A trip to the hospital revealed that she had suffered a bruise in her right temporoparietal junction. As a result, Mrs. Kerpunkle temporarily experienced a weird malady known as *autoscopy* – a sense of disembodiment in which she could view herself from a vantage point outside of her body. Occasionally she also experienced *heautoscopy* in which she perceived her identical doppelganger imitating her every move, except in mirror image. For instance, one day she went to put laundry in the washer but saw someone already there filling the machine. She looked closer and realized it was her, so she returned to the kitchen. These vivid phenomenological experiences made Mrs. Kerpunkle even more interested in brain disorders and she took advantage of her stay in the neurological ward of the hospital to observe the patients there.

Amongst others, Mrs. Kerpunkle met a man who had been diagnosed with *Cotard delusion* – the belief that he is dead. "How are you, Mr. Teetertoe," asked Mrs. Kerpunkle. "Not well, not well at all," replied Mr. Teetertoe, "As you know, I am dead." Mrs. Kerpunkle then inquired, "But how are you able to talk to me then, Mr. Teetertoe?"

"Surely I don't know. I just don't know. I am dead, so I shouldn't be able to talk at all. I simply can't explain it."

Mrs. Kerpunkle also found a man with *Kluver-Bucy syndrome*. The man attempted to have sex with random objects. One day Mrs. Kerpunkle found him trying to have sex with a bed pan. Mrs. Kerpunkle learned that his symptoms were due to damage in his frontal lobe and both amygdalae. In addition, Mrs. Kerpunkle found that the man's hospital roommate was diagnosed with *Capgras syndrome* and hence thought his friends and family members were imposters, as if pod people had snatched their bodies. He had damage to the neural connections between his visual processing area and his lower, emotional brain regions.

After returning home from the hospital, Mrs. Kerpunkle immediately ordered an elaborate brain model for study. She spent hours going over the model and was guided by brain maps she found online. Then, seemingly out of the blue, her husband, Mr. Kerpunkle, was diagnosed with *restless leg syndrome*. That did it. Mrs. Kerpunkle developed an overpowering urge to operate on the brain of Mr. Kerpunkle to uncover the organic etiology of his condition and to perhaps cure him. Hence, she set up her 'operating table' in the basement.

Mrs. Kerpunkle's first experiments involved examination of model brains on her plywood table. She attached a microscope to the table and spent hours simulating surgery on plastic brains. One day while enjoying her hobby she noticed a mouse scurrying on the basement floor. She set up a live trap and soon the mouse was her first living neurosurgery subject. Mrs. Kerpunkle used a set of clamps, wires, and electrical paraphernalia to construct a crude stereotactic device with which she could make 3-dimensional coordinates. The operation on the mouse went well, though Mrs. Kerpunkle realized she needed a more powerful scope, which she later purchased. Following the experimental brain surgery, the mouse seemed strikingly normal, although it did exhibit an unnatural phobia of pungent odors. Mrs. Kerpunkle assumed that she must have unwittingly damaged the mouse's insular cortex.

A stray neighborhood cat was Mrs. Kerpunkle's second neurosurgery subject. After the procedure, the cat seemed more aloof than usual – a sort of feline *Asperger's syndrome*. More cats followed. And then some dogs. Mrs. Kerpunkle used alcohol and ether as anesthetics during the neurosurgery, and amazingly, the animals fared quite well, with the exception of one dog who after surgery on his temporal lobe always barked in sets of three ascending whole notes (he sounded a bit like he was woofing *Frere Jacques* or *Three Blind Mice*); the result of a lesion in Heschl's gyrus or the planum temporale, Mrs. Kerpunkle concluded. Well, as you can imagine, Mrs. Kerpunkle had herself a very fascinating hobby, and she was becoming nicely proficient at it, too. Mrs. Kerpunkle felt she was ready for the next step.

Finally the target day arrived, the day for which Mrs. Kerpunkle had carefully prepared. That evening Mr. and Mrs. Kerpunkle had finished a dinner of goulash and cauliflower and were preparing to adjourn to the basement to partake of their hobbies. Mrs. Kerpunkle was finishing up in the kitchen while Mr. Kerpunkle put on his blue and white striped train engineer cap and headed for the basement. His restless leg twitched a bit as he stopped briefly in front of the basement door. After a pause, Mr. Kerpunkle turned the handle on the white basement door and pushed it inward. Of course Mr. Kerpunkle was entirely unaware that Mrs. Kerpunkle had removed the pins from the hinges of the door. As he pushed it open, the door came loose from the jamb, and as a result Mr. Kerpunkle's unconscious body landed on the concrete basement floor following a clunky passage down the steep stairway. Naturally, his hat and the basement door were lying nearby.

Mrs. Kerpunkle stiffened when she heard the clatter. She paused momentarily at the kitchen sink with a determined, fatalistic look on her face. She then turned and stoically walked to the basement doorway. Peering down the stairwell she could see Mr. Kerpunkle, his striped train engineer hat, and the white door all lying on the floor below. She had her work cut out for her, she sighed silently to herself.

Mrs. Kerpunkle used a wheeled cart to move Mr. Kerpunkle's limp body to her hobby room. With great effort she was able to lift the top of his body onto the table and then, while keeping his head and shoulders atop the table, she slid her hands below Mr. Kerpunkle's legs (including the restless one, of course) and gingerly swung them up onto the plywood surface. She made it. She then positioned him into place. Mr. Kerpunkle was still unconscious.

Next, Mrs. Kerpunkle replaced the white door to the jamb at the top of the stairs and she tidied the basement floor. She gently placed the train engineer hat near the Lionel Flyer model train set. Finally Mrs. Kerpunkle stood quietly pondering the body of her husband lying upon the plywood operating table. Nearby was the bottle of ether. Okay, taking a deep breath, it is time to get to work, it is hobby time, she enthused excitedly to herself.

Mrs. Kerpunkle's first step was cleaning and sterilizing the surgical area and Mr. Kerpunkle's skull. A razor took off a patch of hair in the appropriate place on his head. Mrs. Kerpunkle adjusted the stereotactic device and her new microscope. She moved the wheeled table containing the surgical instruments to within her reach. Then Mrs. Kerpunkle opened a small cabinet and took out a set of wires, a miniature transmitter, and a remote control device that she had placed there earlier.

During her study of neuroscience, Mrs. Kerpunkle had learned about two brain procedures that stuck in her fertile, imaginative mind. The first was called BrainGate, in which paralyzed people were given a brain implant that allowed them to move objects using only their thoughts.

The second procedure was known as deep brain stimulation, a sort of pacemaker for the brain. An electrical signal was sent to the brain through electrodes from a transmitting device that was surgically implanted beneath the skin in the patient's chest.

These two practical applications gave Mrs. Kerpunkle a daring idea, and the local Radio Shack store had provided the supplies she needed to accomplish her ingenious plan.

The operation went smoothly, though it took several hours.

Mr. Kerpunkle remained unconscious, aided by the ether. A bit of drilling with a hand drill created a small hole in his skull, large enough through which to guide the wires. Mrs. Kerpunkle threaded the electrodes into areas of Mr. Kerpunkle's basal ganglia using her home-made stereotactic tool, and she then attached the battery pack and transmitter beneath the skin of his torso. Some cleaning and stitching finished the job. A stimulating hobby, indeed.

It has now been six months since the operation. Mr. Kerpunkle is doing very well, very well indeed. His hair has grown back and his restless leg syndrome has noticeably improved. But that is not the most astonishing result of his brain surgery.

Fortuitously, the marriage of Mr. and Mrs. Kerpunkle is now significantly happier and more satisfying than before the operation. Mrs. Kerpunkle has even noticed that she is using the remote control clicker less often as time goes by. And, Mr. Kerpunkle has gained a stunning capacity to direct his body movements with his concentrated thoughts – he is better coordinated than he ever was in his life.

And, perhaps the most surprising consequence, both Mr. and Mrs. Kerpunkle have given up their previous hobbies ever since the procedure on Mr. Kerpunkle's basal ganglia. Mrs. Kerpunkle discovered that she was no longer interested in neurosurgery once she had reached what she felt was a pinnacle in that avocation. Similarly, Mr. Kerpunkle's interest in model trains drastically dropped off concomitant with the daily electrical surges to his limbic system.

Most astonishing, however, is that Mr. and Mrs. Kerpunkle now enjoyed a new hobby together; they have become obsessed with salsa dancing.

Each night after dinner (with only a tad of electrical stimulation as motivation), Mr. and Mrs. Kerpunkle push the living room furniture toward the walls and remove the area rug, revealing two large plywood surfaces. They put on a CD and dance on the wood surface. Mr. Kerpunkle is an excellent dancer. Mrs. Kerpunkle has serendipitously discovered an electrical wavelength frequency that is a perfect fit for the 8-count rhythm of salsa. This new hobby has revitalized their marriage. They find it stunningly pleasant and joyful. The hip movements, arm swaying, and pelvic pulsations seem to stimulate their brains even more than the electrical impulses to the ventral striatum experienced by Mr. Kerpunkle. Although, of course, that helps too.

Things were going wonderfully for Mr. and Mrs. Kerpunkle with their new hobby of salsa dancing. That is, until one unfortunate day when Mrs. Kerpunkle was paging through a magazine at the dentist's office and she discovered a captivating article about self-trephining. It seems that a man in England had drilled a hole in his own head (using cocaine as an anesthetic) in order to achieve a higher level of consciousness. Although doctors told him not to do that after the man experienced a spurting of blood from the hole in his head, still he completed the self-trephining and reported that he was much happier afterwards. The man even convinced his wife to have a hole drilled in her head, which he gladly did for her whilst filming the whole procedure. She said that she, too, was happier with a hole in her head. The film was later shown to movie critics, one of whom labelled it "boring."

Well, according to the magazine article that Mrs. Kerpunkle was perusing, there was a self-trephining movement abounding world-wide. Astonishingly, a growing number of people were trephining themselves in an attempt to reach a higher state of contentment. Perhaps because of her interest in neurosurgery, Mrs. Kerpunkle was profoundly moved by this magazine article on self-trephination. She was definitely inspired.

Mrs. Kerpunkle looked up from the article and stared blankly into space. This, she mused, would require some careful thought and planning.

?

"This world is but a canvas to our imagination."
— Henry David Thoreau

"The possession of knowledge does not kill the sense of wonder and mystery. There is always more mystery."
— Anais Nin

"The important thing is not to stop questioning. Curiosity has its own reason for existing."
— Albert Einstein

"Information can tell us everything. It has all the answers. But they are answers to questions we have not asked, and which doubtless don't even arise."
— Jean Baudrillard

"The role of the artist is to ask questions, not answer them."
— Anton Chekhov

?

What is the meaning of light? What is the meaning of sound? What is the meaning of space? What is the meaning of matter? What is the meaning of time? What is the meaning of motion? What is the meaning of frequency? What is the meaning of tempo? What is the meaning of phases? What is the meaning of cycles? What is the meaning of rhythm?

What is the meaning of now? What is the meaning of then? What is the meaning of past? What is the meaning of future? What is the meaning of awareness? What is the meaning of feeling? What is the meaning of caring? What is the meaning of indifference? What is the meaning of loss? What is the meaning of pain? What is the meaning of longing? What is the meaning of memory? What is the meaning of apathy? What is the meaning of never? What is the meaning of always? What is the meaning of alone? How long can one be alone? What will happen then?

What is the difference between here and there? What is the difference between this and that? What is the difference between then and now? What is the difference between start and stop? What is the difference between regret and remorse? What is the meaning of too late?

What is the difference between you and me? What is the difference between feeling and not feeling? What is the difference between sane and insane? What is the difference between silence and noise? What is the difference between staying and leaving? What is the difference between screaming and silence? What is the difference between boredom and death? What is the difference between length and width? What is the difference between paralysis and fear? What is the difference between forgetting and emptiness? What is the difference between something and nothing? Why does it matter? When does it matter? Does it matter?

Was there a beginning? Will there be an end? How will we know what time it is? Will the past be gone forever? Will the future be there forever? How is something similar to nothing? How is now similar to then? How is this similar to that? How will we know when this becomes that? What is the difference between the past and the present? What is the meaning of the future? What is a question? What is a question for? What is the point of a question? What is the definition of a question? What is the definition of knowing? What is knowledge? What is ignorance? What is the difference between knowledge and ignorance? What is the meaning of difference? What is the definition of a promise? Who should we trust? Who should we believe? Who should we accept? Who should we reject? Who should we love? When should we love? Why should we love? What is the meaning of love? Who knows what time it is? What is the meaning of waiting? When does waiting end?

What is the opposite of a rainbow? How many boxes are in a carton? Where do the stripes end? When is the black dark enough? When is the time ripe? When do sentences have meanings? Why do words in one order make sense, and in another order make nonsense? What is the meaning of sense? What is the difference between sense and nonsense?

What is logic for? Where does logic begin and where does logic end? What time is the meeting? Where will we meet? Where are the parts we need? How do the parts fit together? Who has the instructions? Who can understand the instructions? Who can follow the instructions? How do you talk to someone? Who are we when we go to sleep? Who are we when we awake? Where are you now? How do you understand what is said? How does one feel? Why does one feel? What is the meaning of feeling? Why is it difficult to understand? What is understanding? Where are the voices that matter? What does it mean to matter? Is a question ever better than an answer?

How long can you wait? How long is time? When is the time up? Where did the time go? Do you have a minute? Do you have a second? Can you spare the time? Is time up? Did the speaker mean me? Who was he talking about? Who was he talking to? What does talking mean? What is the difference between hearing and listening? What is the difference between seeing and looking? Where does the light go? What is the difference between knowing and not knowing? What is the difference between caring and not caring? What is the difference between feeling and not feeling? Where are you now? Can I get you anything? Do you need anything? Is there anything that you need? How will I know when you return? Where have you been? How long were you gone? What did you do? Where were you? Why did you return?

When will I see you again? What will we remember? What will be forgotten? What will be the difference? How much can one carry? How strong is strong enough? What is strength? What is enough? Will we care? How much will we care? Why will we care? What is the meaning of caring? Do you care?

Will we remember? Will we know what we knew? Will we feel what we felt? Will we see what we saw? Will we think what we thought? Will it seem the same? What is the difference? Who can help us? When will it matter? Will it matter?

Why do we feel? Do we feel? Do you feel? Where did you go? What did you do? Why did you return? Will you leave again? Why does it matter? Do you know me? Can you see me? Will you touch me? Will you care? What is the meaning of light?

True Facts

"My father hated radio and could not wait for television to be invented so he could hate that too."
— Peter De Vries

"The funniest people are the saddest ones"
— Confucius

"Everything has been figured out, except how to live."
— Jean-Paul Sartre

"You got to be careful if you don't know where you're going, because you might not get there."
— Yogi Berra

"Why shouldn't truth be stranger than fiction? Fiction, after all, has to make sense."
— Mark Twain

True Facts

1. Showering

So I'm going into my hotel room and I'm using one of those weird electronic key cards, you know, the ones that look like anonymous, bland gray credit cards with some arcane letters and numbers, that's all, printed on one side, and as I'm sticking the thing into the slot in the door I'm thinking about the 18-year-old woman who I read about in the newspaper, who for some strange reason, maybe she had been in the swimming pool or something, anyway, she was barefoot and soaking wet while she was using just such a key to enter her hotel room and she was electrocuted to death – yeah, electrocuted to death – they said it was a faulty air conditioner, and maybe it was, but it made me think that maybe, as they say, fact really is stranger than fiction, although then I realized that maybe that's not really the case because I have seen some pretty strange fiction, and as a matter of fact, the stories that I write are about as strange as you're going to see, although, you know, I feel quite certain that there are some pretty weird people around and I'll bet anything that some of those people write stories that are a lot stranger than the ones that I write, which, if it's true, I'm thinking, would be a fact, and therefore maybe fact really is stranger than fiction, although, I guess the stories we write are in fact fiction, so now I don't know what to think.

So I made it through the door without being electrocuted and I'm in my hotel room now and I'm still thinking that my stories are so damn strange maybe that's why I can't get them published, because the main thing everybody says about my stories is that they can't even understand them and now when I think about that, I'm thinking that if you can understand something, then is it really fiction?

People are always asking me what my stories are about, and I mean *after* they read them. I mean, they have just read the damn thing and now they want me to explain it! If I could explain it any better than I already wrote it then I would've written it better in the first place. Then I'm thinking about a quote that I read from someone, maybe it was Mark Twain, anyway the quote was that anyone attempting to find a plot would be shot, and I wish I would have written that, although now I'm thinking that of course if I would have written that, then it probably wouldn't get published anyway and no one would know about it, and even if they did, I'm sure people would say they don't understand it and they'd be asking me to explain it to them.

I mean, people are always saying they don't get it, but what's to get? It's a short story, man, it's fiction, I'm thinking, it's not an essay or scientific journal article on how molybdenum is affected by alpha particles. Get what you want, or what you can, out of it, I'm thinking, and if that helps, well, then good, and if it doesn't help, well, then write your own story or scientific journal article on molybdenum and alpha particles.

What am I supposed to do about it exactly, follow everybody around explaining every stupid story to them all the time, I mean, why don't I just get a website on the Internet and be Mr. Explainer or something for people who don't understand short stories. Well, I'm just having a brainstorm now realizing that Mr. Explainer could expand his business by explaining art and philosophy to people besides just short stories. Experts are always saying that people are so uneducated about science and math and geography, but any fool can see that people at least know the rudiments of those fields, I mean, people can add numbers and find California on a map, but anyone who thinks about it for a minute will realize that people know absolutely nothing, I mean *nothing* about art and philosophy, and a Mr. Explainer in those areas could do a whopping business.

Except, there I go again thinking that people would actually *care*, would *want* to have those things explained to them – that is the big flaw in my idea – because nobody would ever contact Mr. Explainer, I mean out of pure apathy, and then I'm realizing that you would have to first have another Mr. Explainer who explains to people *why* they should care to have those things explained to them, except, of course, no one would ever contact that Mr. Explainer either, I now realize.

Man.

Now I'm looking at the TV listings in that little booklet they give you in hotels and I'm thinking that TV really, really sucks and it's a major wonder that it has become such a big deal in the modern world, sitting front and center in everyone's homes, even two or three to a home, I'm thinking that I read that TVs are now the most owned object, passing up toilets. Wow, there are more TVs than toilets, I'm wondering if there's a story in that.

Now I'm thinking that if I had one of those "way-back" machines, you know, what people call a time machine, so I could travel back in time to hundreds or thousands of years ago and talk to people and tell them what we do in the future, man, they wouldn't believe a word I said, they'd think I was telling some of my strange stories that nobody understands. I'd be saying, "We've got these boxes we put inside our houses and then pictures and sounds come out of these boxes and we can see and hear all kinds of stuff, we can even create our own sounds and images if we want to." Then they'd be saying, "Oh, boy, you mean you can see all over the world, different cultures and landscapes and ballets and scientists and poets and operas and world events and you can make up fantastic stories with amazing colors and music and beautiful creations and everything?" Then I'd be looking kind of peevish and have to tell them that we mostly watch reality shows, sitcoms, shoot-em-ups, killings, talk shows, soap operas, deodorant and toilet paper commercials and stuff like that, and that's when they'd be saying that I'm a big stupid liar and that doesn't make any sense and why would anybody in their right stupid mind want to use such a fantastic box just to watch all that crap and my stories sure are strange. Then I'd have to get the hell out of there in my way-back machine before they would beat me up for making up such strange stories.

Boy, truth really is stranger than fiction, I'm starting to think again.

I feel like I'm getting real profound, like I'm really getting on to something here, so I'm thinking really hard about the fact that people all over the world will sit and watch TV all day long, like I read that *Baywatch* was once the most watched TV show in the world but now it is *Friends* or *Crime Scene Investigation* or *Dancing with the Stars,* or some other titillating, voyeuristic, vapid bunkum, and I'm thinking that people will even arrange their lives around certain TV shows, change their schedules, their hair-dos, their values and everything, and that the stuff on TV is so tasteless and godawful that the fact that people will get so attached, so obsessed, with something so godawful, that this fact must tell us something really, really important, I'm thinking, about people, or about the power of visual images on a little box, or about our biology, or our psychology, or our evolution, or something like that, something that is profoundly important... but for the life of me I don't have any idea what the hell it could be.

Now I have to get ready to go meet with Allan and his buddies. This is my big chance to finally get my stories published and I'm wondering how I should approach this meeting and how much is it okay to pander and compromise, and I know that my integrity is not up there with Gandhi's, but I wonder just how much should a guy take? I'm wondering just how obsequious should I be, because you know those business guys are just going to say the weirdest stuff and going to blow my mind with their talk about profit margins and that kind of crap. I know my stories are no big deal, but how much should a guy really compromise, if he has any integrity at all? I mean, how far can you go before you have sold out? You know?

It bugs the hell out of me that most people have no damn principles at all and when someone with principles finally does come along and then even *they* sell out, as they pretty much always do, I'm wondering if that's something that's automatic, that would happen to anyone, or if that person was a jerk to begin with and having principles was just sort of a mistake or temporary lucky thing that happened to them. I wonder.

Then I remember I just heard Meryl Streep on the radio explaining why she did that insipid *Bridges of Madison County* movie.

She said – get this – she said she thought the story would have a big audience. I'm shaking my head and thinking that artists today don't do something because it's a high-quality project, or in order to work with some particular person, or to develop a certain skill, why, they don't even talk about the damn message anymore. Instead – it's really weird – but today no one's even ashamed to say right out loud that they did something to get a big audience. I'm thinking that this is the most godawful crap I've ever heard, and I'm wondering if that's what I'm supposed to tell Allan and his buddies when they ask me why I write these strange stories, I'm supposed to say I do it because I think the stories will have a big audience, and then I start to wonder if I can even say that, at least with a straight face.

Anyway, I'd better take a shower now and get ready to go see Allan, and even though there's probably no way that anything bad could happen, I'm still going to leave my electronic key card out here so that when I get out of the shower and I'm all wet and barefoot, there is no chance of coming anywhere near that damn thing.

2. Waiting

I'm sitting in the waiting room of Allan's office because his secretary said that Allan was going to be a little late and some of his buddies weren't even here yet, so I'm just sitting here looking at the newspaper, and man, the articles in the paper are making my brain hurt. I don't know why, but, you know, ever since I was a teenager I always got a really agonizing feeling when I heard things that were irrational – I don't know why, but for some strange reason it always made my brain sort of discombobulated. I had a friend who was the exact same way and we joked that we should start a motorcycle gang and we would call ourselves "Slaves to Logic," which would be scrawled across the backs of our black leather jackets, and we would go around and beat up people who said really irrational things, anyway so today I hardly ever look at a newspaper or TV because I don't like that feeling I get in my head when I see all that weird stuff that is so irrational.

But now that I'm thinking about it, maybe it's not exactly the absurdity that makes my brain hurt, maybe it's the fact that other people seem so nonchalant about it, like they don't even notice that it's absurd, maybe that's what makes my brain hurt so much, but then I wonder, if that's really true, then why would that bother me? And then I'm remembering some expert who said that it would really be good to look at ourselves and try to understand why we get so bothered by certain things and that if we knew why it was that certain things bothered us then we would have gone a long way toward understanding ourselves and I'm thinking that, wow, I'm nowhere near ready to face myself, faults and truths and all that; no, I'm definitely, absolutely not ready for that.

So I'm looking at the newspaper and I see this article about a cop who was helping his buddies by wrestling with some big jerk who was giving them trouble, and then the cop, who was going to retire pretty soon it says right here, he has a heart attack and dies, and the reporters have interviewed his partner, who, it says, described the dead cop as "good hearted," that's what he said, and now I feel the brain thing just getting started a little.

Next I see here an article about some carnival freak who went by the name "Lobster Boy" and it says he was murdered by his wife, believe it or not, and now she is on trial for killing her husband, Lobster Boy, and she is pleading self defense because she says that Lobster Boy physically and sexually abused her with his claws; that's what she says.

Now I'm reading about a pair of conjoined twins who have been interviewed and one of them said, "Just because we're Siamese twins doesn't mean we're exactly the same, that we think alike, or go everywhere together. Okay, we go everywhere together, but that doesn't mean we have to like it." That's what she said. The old brain is rumbling again.

Now here's an article in which some University professor says, "Hunting is a ritual which gives the hunter a chance to reflect about their responsibility toward the animal they are about to kill." This is really making me strung out, and I'm thinking that I can't take much more. Then here I see a related story about the Hiroshima bombing, anyway the headline actually reads, "A-bombs Saved Lives," and I can feel the dial on my logic meter totally red-lining now, and then, man, here's an article about Vietnam and, can you believe it, some ex-military guy is saying that he is thrilled to see the spread of capitalism in modern Nam because that is what we were fighting for, he says, and now my brain is really hurting because I'm thinking that they finally admit right out in public that the reason for the goddamn war was to sell Coca Cola – yeah, Napalm opens markets – but they don't even feel ashamed to admit it, they don't even seem aware that what they're saying is incredible, that it's downright obscene.

But now Allan's secretary is telling me that Allan and his buddies are ready to see me, so I drop the newspaper like it was full of mad cow disease and I go in to see Allan.

3. Meeting

"I want you to meet our intern, Lois, who studies Literature at Cornell University, my assistant, Michael, and this is Carmen, who is one of our fiction editors." Allan is dressed in business uniform, wears sensible shoes, and speaks perfect English.

"Hello, nice to meet you," we all say.

Allan directs me to a chair facing the four of them.

Allan gets right to it: "Tell us a little about why you write such strange stories."

Strange? I'm thinking, don't they read the newspaper? What the hell can I say?

Then I think about Meryl Streep and Gandhi.

I say, "Strange? Do you find them strange?"

The four of them stare at me in amazement. Then Lois, the intern, says, "Why, they're the strangest stories I've ever seen."

"Michael says, "Yes, for example, tell me what the story about the elephant is supposed to mean."

I'm wishing that Mr. Explainer were here right now to advise me. I somehow blurt out, "The elephant is a large animal... and gray.

Perhaps it represents large, gray issues."

I can't believe I said that.

I decide not to say any more on this topic. I slip them a sly, ambiguous look (did I wink just a little?).

I'm in luck; they change the subject.

Carmen says, "I'd like to do some editing – not a lot – but a little here and there to make the stories more accessible, and I'm wondering how would you feel about that?" She stares right at me. She has pretty, dark eyes and is wearing a lovely short dress that flares gracefully. Her dark hair is short, but falls over her forehead. Her legs are crossed and her dress drapes softly over her thighs. She reminds me so much of my former girlfriend that I want to cry right here and now, cry hard and for a long time. I stare first at the floor, then out the window, then at Allan.

"Yeah, some editing," I say, "would be okay, I guess, if, uhhh, I don't know, maybe my grammar isn't so good, but it's fiction, you know, ahhh, they're not essays or scientific articles about molybdenum and alpha particles, it's just fiction, I mean, it's *made up*, ahhh, then again the words and sentences sometimes, umm, could be that some of it, I mean the denseness in particular, and the deconstruction, uhmm, I don't know, uhhh, some editing, well, yeah, maybe."

Shit. That was bad. What the hell was I talking about? I really blew it this time.

But wait; they don't seem to have noticed. They're all quiet, looking at their feet. Perhaps it'll be okay.

Oh no, Michael now appears to have something on his mind. He's staring intently, right into my eyes, leaning forward in his chair: "Let me understand you, are you saying that if something is fiction that it doesn't have to make any sense, that it is all right if it has no meaning at all?" Then he serves up the *coup de grace*, his profound vision, that, by the way, I'm certain he stole from someone like Gertrude Stein: "I believe," Michael continues, "that in the lies of fiction we can find the truths of our reality. Don't you think that's so?"

Lois jumps right in, excited by this line, "Yes, in my class on theory we talked about just this issue and I think that in some ways one may find more truth in fiction than in fact."

All eyes are looking at me. Fact or fiction, not that again! I feel quite confident that they all know very well what the correct answer is, although each person, I'm sure, has a different correct answer in his or her head, and they are simply, absurdly, waiting for me to say it. And I'm thinking that this is so bizarre that they already know what it is that I am supposed to say but they can't tell me what it is that I'm supposed to say because I'm supposed to say the damn thing myself without any help from them and then after I say it we can finally proceed to the contract for my stories and live happily ever after, except the problem is that I don't know what the right damn thing to say is that will please all four of them and even more important to me right now I'm wondering if I really would or, more importantly, *should* say it if I knew what the hell it was.

"Well," at last I breathe slowly, and feel a bit more confident, "it seems to me that the, uhh, the gestalt pattern, as it were, exists both because of the referent, that is, I mean, the apparent stimulus, and also, it seems to me, uhh, also because of the qualities, that is, the characteristics of the perceiver."

Oh, boy. That was weird. I'm afraid I've really done it this time. The faces are blank and all staring at me. There is silence for a moment. I guess the meeting is over. Allan rises from his chair, smiles, thanks me for the meeting, and sees me to the door. He says I'll be hearing from them soon. Yes, I murmur to myself, I'll be hearing from them soon. I glance quickly at Carmen and leave the room.

4. Square One

Three weeks later I received a letter from Allan. It said they are sorry, but they have decided not to publish my stories. They, however, wish me luck in "locating them." The letter said they thought there was no audience for such strange stories. No audience, they thought. Such strange stories, they said.

Now I'm sitting here looking out my window, Allan's letter

lying at my feet. I see Mrs. Church across the street yelling at some kids who have thrown a whiskey bottle into her front yard. A wet, mottled dog has just come out of the alley and is biting one of the kids who is screaming and trying to evade the grasp of the dog's teeth. Mrs. Church, carrying a broom, is running to help the kid, but she trips on the cracked, asymmetrical sidewalk and falls to the ground. Her arm is bleeding onto the sidewalk and her face is screwed up in pain. One of the kids, maybe four years old, has picked up the whiskey bottle and is tipping it up to his mouth. A narrow stream of brown liquid is trickling down the inside of the clear glass bottle and onto his waiting tongue. He squints with a brief look of disgust then chortles and looks at the other kids. I see that a bird's nest has fallen from a tree and is lying nearby. Three tiny blue eggs are in the nest. A neighborhood cat, a Canadian hairless, has discovered the nest and is sniffing the eggs, and is now biting them, eating the contents. One of the boys playing nearby picks up a rock and throws it at the cat. The rock hits the cat on the side of the head. The cat jerks and twitches and then runs behind the house. The boy guffaws.

Then I notice that a car full of teenagers is speeding, careening, down the street; they seem to be fooling around inside the car. One of them has what looks to be a gun, which he is pointing out the window in the direction of Mrs. Church and the kids. Then there is the sound of a gunshot. I notice a bit of smoke and a flash of light from one of the windows of the car, which is now speeding away, full of giggling faces. I notice a small girl fall to the ground not far from where Mrs. Church is still lying. The girl is not moving; she is lying on the ground, still and quiet. The car full of teenagers has missed a corner and crashes into the side of a parked car which was just then being entered by Mr. Jacobson, an accountant who lives in a small green rambler down the street. Mr. Jacobson is knocked down to the cockeyed street where he now lies moaning and twisting. I see the car full of teenagers pull away from the scene, wobbling and winding from one side of the street to the other, nearly out of control. I hear muffled laughter and whooping from the car's occupants.

I now see that a boy on a skateboard has been giving his full attention to the car that is meandering down the street and has not been watching where he was going on the sidewalk in front of him. His skateboard, with him atop it, veers from the sidewalk and slams into a small girl who was picking a dandelion from the grass. The little girl falls and screams. The white puffs of the dandelion scatter in the breeze. The boy now has gathered up his skateboard and has run from the scene smirking. But a large wasp has alighted on the boy's back and stings the boy, who falls to the ground crying, startled and somewhat immobilized by the intense, biting pain.

I look up and observe that the sky is clouding up. It looks like it's going to rain. And then, suddenly, I have a fabulous idea for another story, a story about molybdenum, alpha particles, and a way-back machine. I hope I will be able to locate it.

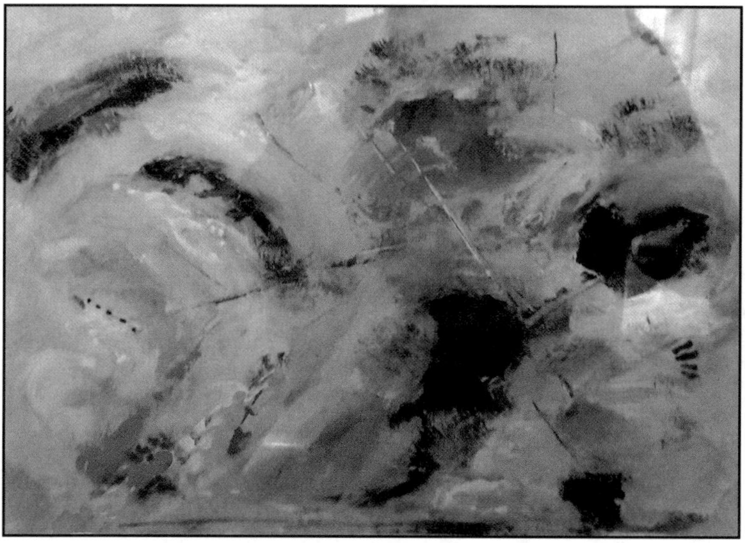

Solve for X

"At eighteen our convictions are hills from which we look; at forty-five they are caves in which we hide."
— F. Scott Fitzgerald

"The world is independent of my will."
— Ludwig Wittgenstein

"To every separate person a thing is what he thinks it is – in other words, not a thing, but a think."
— Penelope Fitzgerald

"What one person rejects as lunacy, another reveres as truth."
— Philip Gulley

"There's a fine line between fishing and just standing on the shore like an idiot."
— Steven Wright

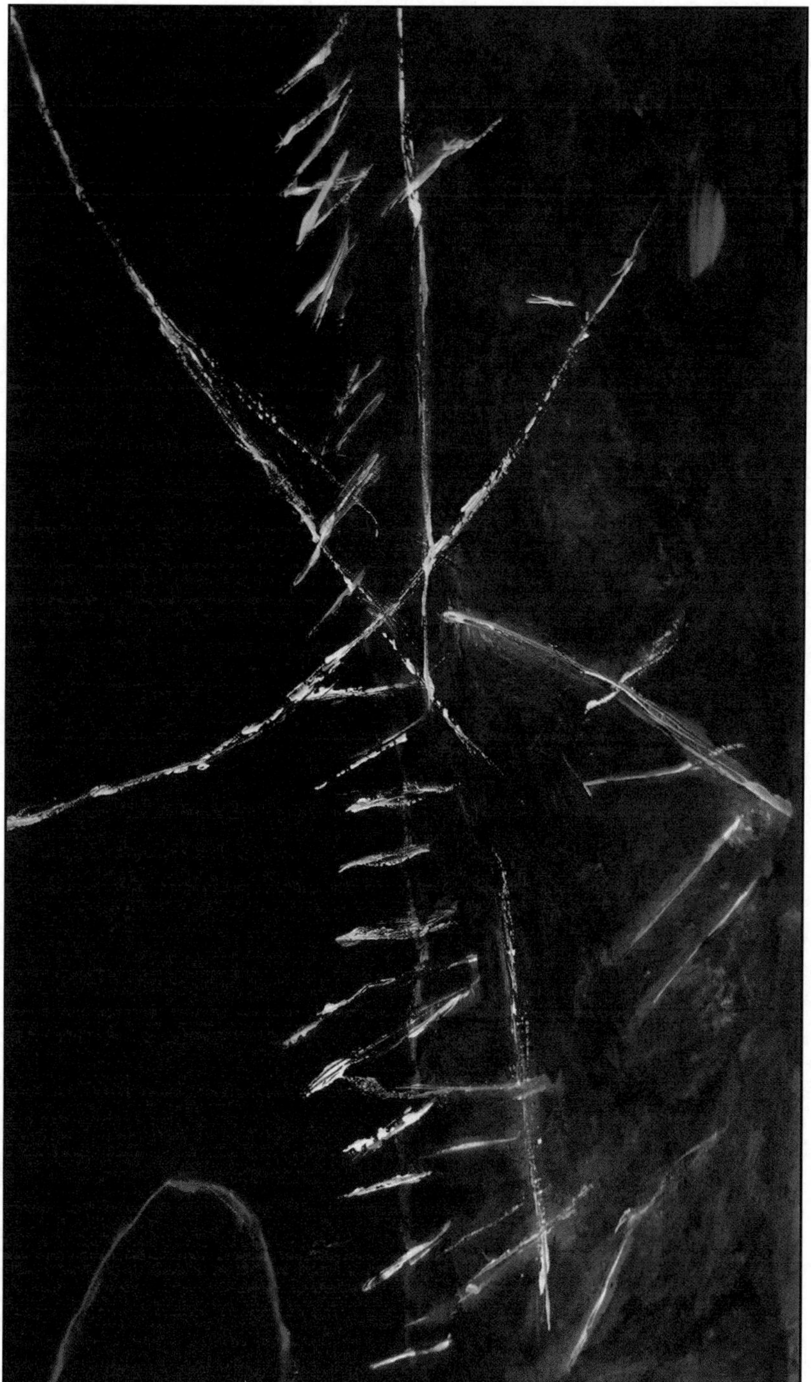

Solve for X

"Stop."

That's all she said.

Just a quick, firm, no-nonsense, "Stop."

And, although I really wasn't doing anything at all, anything obvious or visible anyway, still I knew exactly what she meant.

"Mother," I said, "I can't. Don't you understand? Don't you get it - I can't just *stop*."

Small purple-hued clouds shaped like the black splotches on white cows passed slowly, lazily in front of the sun. The ephemeral near-darkness seemed an apt metaphor at that moment.

I searched for her eyes in the temporary shadows and found them pleading with me, half-hooded but steady and insistent. I couldn't look away.

"You have permission to stop," she said, patiently pronouncing each syllable with calm assurance. Our gazes were locked on each other.

Permission to stop.

It was many years later before I felt I understood what she meant by that cliché. Yet, sometimes even understanding isn't enough to stem the tidal waves. It's not exactly thoughts or feelings, but a dark conflagration that roars and engulfs inside. It comes on suddenly, without warning, and overwhelms. It hurts so much that even powerful clichés fall to the wayside. Turgid moments of disconnect when blue pain sweeps over me like a tsunami; permission, then, is pointless, meaningless.

The collapse, temporary, but complete, and then, regrettably, the aftermath. Yes, the inevitable, interminable, unrelenting and irredeemable aftermath. The aftermath – although, it isn't any kind of math at all, is it?

Just what can you do when you can't solve for x?

The Philosophy of Vision

"Are you going to believe me, or your own eyes?"
— Grouch Marx

"It's not what you look at that matters, it's what you see."
— Henry David Thoreau

"I replaced the headlights in my car with strobe lights, so it looks like I'm the only one moving."
— Steven Wright

"The more I see, the less I know for sure."
— John Lennon

"One of the definitions of sanity is the ability to tell real from unreal. Soon we'll need a new definition."
— Alvin Toffler

The Philosophy of Vision

"You're blind, but don't know it," Dr. Evans said.

I looked at him incredulously. "What?" I exclaimed.

"You're blind. You have damage in the visual area of your brain. It's just that you are unaware of your blindness," he explained. "It's called Anton's syndrome or Blindness Denial. It's not common, but it happens. You're not alone. As a matter of fact, for some strange reason we've been seeing a lot of cases lately."

"Doctor, I hate to disagree with you," I uttered with a quivering voice, "but I'm telling you, I can see. I certainly should know if I can see or not. Sure, I have some problems with my vision, but I'm definitely not blind."

"I know it seems like that to you," Dr. Evans calmly replied, "but you are blind."

"But doctor, I am not blind. How can you say that? Just because I make some mistakes in seeing doesn't mean that I'm blind."

"Look," he leaned forward in his chair, his hands were crossed on top of his desk, his white doctor's coat ruffled against the leather chair, "you have damage in the deeper areas of your visual processing area. However, the surface area, the cerebral cortex, is not damaged. That is why you experience a consciousness, an awareness, of vision. But the damage to the deeper cells prevents your brain from properly analyzing the visual information that is coming from your eyes. You are effectively blind. You just think you can see."

I paused for a long while trying to digest this weird thing he was saying. I trusted Dr. Evans. He'd been my doctor for years and I had confidence in him. But this time he was wrong. He must be wrong. I just couldn't accept such a preposterous idea. I'm blind? That's impossible – I CAN SEE!

"Doctor, what has caused the damage to my brain that you are talking about?"

"We don't know, but I suspect you've had a series of small strokes. Your medical record would support that. It also could have been caused by an infection, or exposure to toxins, or perhaps a trauma. Do you recall any injuries to your head that you sustained in the last few months?"

"No, no, I don't think so," I answered. It was difficult for me to respond, even to listen to what he was saying, since I was totally bewildered by his contention that I was blind. Wouldn't I be the one who knew whether or not I was blind? How could someone else know better than I do whether or not I can see?

"Look," suggested Dr. Evans, "let's try something. Tell me what kind of coat I am wearing."

I glanced at his white doctor's coat and then at his face. He was serious; he wanted me to tell him. "Okay," I replied, "you're wearing your white doctor's coat that you always wear."

"Are you sure?"

"Yes, of course. Doctor, I can see, you've got to believe me."

Dr. Evans paused for a moment then sympathetically retorted, "No, Michael, no, I'm not wearing my white coat. Today I am wearing a green cardigan sweater. My white coat is hanging there by the door."

I saw him motion with his arm toward the door. Didn't I?

"Well," I stammered, "I told you I have some visual problems. The light from the window was in my eyes and the glare made your sweater seem white. Of course, now I clearly see that it is green."

"I'm sorry, Michael," the doctor breathed in a low voice, "I'm afraid I have tricked you. I am not wearing a green sweater. I have on a light blue shirt with no jacket or sweater or coat. I tricked you in order to try to show you the extent of your problem."

"Tricked me! What kind of doctor would purposely trick a patient?" I blurted out.

I sat there even more bewildered. Could this be right? Was Dr. Evans playing some weird game with me?

"I'm sorry," he replied.

I believe I saw a concerned look on his face. I paused for a moment to think this thing through a bit.

"Are you serious?" I finally asked.

"Yes, I'm afraid that I am very serious," he said.

I now saw that he was right, that I had been mistaken. It was now clear to me that he was wearing a blue shirt. I think the poor lighting in the office somehow fooled me.

"Tell me, Michael," Dr. Evans continued, "what color is my necktie."

I looked carefully and with deliberation at his necktie. This time I wanted to be sure. I wanted to get it right and prove to Dr. Evans that I could see. I stared at his tie and I was surprised to realize that it wasn't at all clear to me what color tie he had on. There was a good deal of glare in the room and together with the poor lighting it made it difficult for me to see his tie very well at all. However, I felt certain that I could make out the colors of his necktie, so I stared a little longer and more intently.

I finally answered, "It is red and white striped."

"Again I have tricked you Michael," Dr. Evans said slowly, in a sad tone of voice. "I am not wearing a tie today. Just the blue shirt."

Dr. Evans entered the doctor's lounge and smiled at the five other doctors there. He poured a cup of coffee and sat down.

"I had another case of Anton's today," he said.

One of the other doctors nearly gasped and blurted, "You're kidding! That's eight, isn't it, in just the last week? That's, just, uh, incredible."

"Yes, eight, and yes, incredible," Dr. Evans responded. "I wonder what in the world is going on? Perhaps it's just a coincidence, but I wonder if there's something else."

Dr. Evans thought about the past week. Eight cases of Anton's was more than a coincidence, he thought. What could be causing it? He had sent an email message to a friend who worked at a hospital in New York and was told that they, too, had seen an inordinate number of cases of Blindness Denial. He wondered hard about it. Could it be a virus? Is it something in the water or in food? Is it contagious? What is going on?

"Have you seen that new movie, *Blood of the Stripper*?" another doctor interjected. "It's so amazing... this serial murderer rapes and murders women and the cops track him down. The special effects are amazing. They show an autopsy that is so real – including the interior of the body cavity that's been opened by an ax. I mean, like, it is truly awesome. It looks so convincingly real."

"I'm seeing it tonight," responded another doctor. "My wife and I are totally excited to see it, though she's worried about the violence, of course."

"Me too," another doctor chimed in enthusiastically. Though I really want to see *Death Warrior III* that is opening on Friday. It's supposed to be even better than the TV series."

"Who's in it?" piped up the doctor who had raved about *Blood of the Stripper*.

"Samuel Sterling and Phoebe Star. She is so hot, don't you think?"

Dr. Evans stopped listening to the conversation and went back to wondering about Blindness Denial. Eight cases in the last week. Hmm, he thought. That is so strange. What could be causing it? People who are blind but don't know it. Very strange, indeed. I'd better check with some other hospitals.

"How about the Cowboys?" another doctor asked. "Can they make the Super Bowl this year?"

Martha was waiting at the door for me when I got home. My

friend Brian walked me to the house and I invited him to stay for pizza and beer, and maybe a bit of TV.

"How did it go?" Martha asked.

"Well, Marty," I began with hesitation, "it's very weird. Doc Evans says that I'm blind." I paused for a moment to let that sink in.

Martha looked at Brian, who shrugged his shoulders and scrunched his face.

"Michael, I'm sorry, but I thought it might be something like that," Martha said in a very sympathetic and quiet voice. "Come sit down and tell me about it."

We sat in the living room and talked for a while. I explained the trick that Dr. Evans did in his office. After a while there was nothing more to say. We clicked on the TV. We sat and watched a crime show. A serial murderer was on the prowl in the city. Many women were being murdered. Mostly models and prostitutes. The murderer used a long, serrated knife and cut the women from the bottom up. It was a really good show, very exciting and real, though there were many moments when my perception of the visual images seemed to be different than that of Marty and Brian. After the show, the local news came on. The whole city was so proud of their soldiers who had returned home from the war for a brief furlough. Many had symptoms of PTSD, however, and the war had now been going on for fourteen years. The local guys were headed back overseas after a few weeks. Unfortunately, the news also reported that there had been four more murders on the north side of the city today plus an accidental shooting of a toddler. The north section of the city was where poor people and minorities lived. Viewers were also warned about a rapist in the western suburbs whose many victims included an eighty year old woman.

We were then interrupted by our son, Jason, who had been playing video games.

"Can I get the new version of *Dead Kill IV* that comes out tomorrow? Please, mom?"

"Well, did you clean your room, like I asked?" said Martha.

"I will tonight," Jason said earnestly.

"Okay," Martha replied, "after your room is clean, I will get you *Dead Kill IV*."

I watched the weather report and then the sports news. Or, did I watch them? I really didn't know what to think anymore. I was tired. I decided to go up to bed. I tripped on the stairs and bumped into a table on my way up. It definitely made me think about what Dr. Evans had said.

Tuesday, Dr. Evans sent out nine emails to doctors he knew at hospitals around the country. All of them came back with the same answer. Yes, there had been a dramatic increase in the number of cases of Anton's syndrome in the last few weeks or month. Apparently, there was an unusually high incidence across the whole country that was completely unexplained. Large numbers of people everywhere were blind but didn't know it. What could be causing it? Dr. Evans was truly befuddled.

In the morning I tried to work, but was frustrated and couldn't get anything done. Marty went to get groceries and later planned to see her sister. She had been reading about Anton's syndrome online but her computer froze up when it was infected by a virus that was acquired when she accidentally clicked on a pop-up for pornography with farm animals and children.

I was restless. I spent the day doing nothing, really. I listened to music for a while, looked out the window at passing traffic, took a nap, and when it was time for dinner I walked cautiously to the kitchen. Yes, I bumped into some furniture, but doesn't everyone?

Incandescence

"It is foolish to pretend that one is fully recovered from a disappointed passion. Such wounds always leave a scar."
— Henry Wadsworth Longfellow

"There is nothing that living things do that cannot be understood from the point of view that they are made of atoms acting according to the laws of physics."
— Richard Feynman

"People label themselves with all sorts of adjectives. I can only pronounce myself as 'nauseatingly miserable beyond repair'."
— Franz Kafka

"It has been said that man is a rational animal. All my life I have been searching for evidence which could support this."
— Bertrand Russell

"If the world was perfect, it wouldn't be."
— Yogi Berra

Incandescence

Prosenjit buckles his belt. Done, he stares without expression at his reflection in the bathroom mirror. Stark face. Bitter. Stoic. His thoughts are jumbled, discordant, like an orchestral pre-concert tune-up. He smooths his shiny black hair with the palm of his hand.

No one's going to stare at me and get away with it. I'll show them they can't mess with me! I'll show them!

The bathroom light, a single, bare, 100-watt bulb, flickers erratically, as if in a Frankenstein movie. A cacophonous crackling sound fills the small bathroom – Kkkzzzrrrkkk. A jittery, pulsating light and sound show.

Loose connection. Perhaps a short circuit. Something wrong. Bad wiring.

Talking about me behind my back. Laughing. Think they can do anything they please. Someone's got to show them they can't get away with it! Someone's got to do something!

It's late. Prosenjit can't sleep. Too much ruminating. Not enough something.

Sonofabitch, you can't just look at me that way, whispering. You can't do that. No one does that to me! No one! I'll show them!

Prosenjit picks up his wallet, keys, and change. He shoves them into familiar pockets of faded denim jeans. Now he picks up a large gleaming knife. He turns the knife lovingly in his hands, gently but firmly caressing it. His eyes are fixated on the shiny, sharp steel surface. He has that born-again, wide-eyed stare. Mesmerized. Entranced. Something wrong. Bad wiring.

The knife triggers the usual associations in Prosenjit's subconscious mind: strength, power, violence. He feels excited, aggressive and powerful. Strong, and in control. Tuned-in. Focused. His mind is whirring now. Whirring like a pressure cooker gone berserk. Pressure. Compulsion. A definite, undeniable need for action.

The bare bulb hanging from a thin, stringy, frayed wire in the middle of the bathroom now flickers and buzzes – Kkkkrrkkzzzkk,

KKrrkkzzkk, Kkrzk. Tiny sparks – like fireflies on speed – zip and buzz around the silver spiral base of the bulb where it meets the metal fixture socket. Tiny sparks. Fireflies. Jittery noise. Flickering light.

A short circuit. Loose connection. Bad wiring.

Prosenjit paces the floor – angry, determined, intense, tight. A diffused, deflected light from the bare bathroom light bulb falls on his face creating eerie bright yellow, glimmering Rorschach blots, blending and mixing with shadowy dark splotches and edges. Jittering. Crackling. Sparking.

Prosenjit doesn't notice the light; he's preoccupied with more important matters. *What to do about those voices? How to protect myself from those who are out to get me. No one can do that to me and get away with it!*

Then a shuffling, muffled noise from the adjacent apartment; dense, like someone moving furniture. Voices. Bottles knocking together. Glasses clunking on tables. More thumping. More voices – arguing? Prosenjit now reflexively turns his face toward the wall where the sounds seem to be coming from and turns his mind to the peculiar noises. His body frozen still, tense, head tilted, ears listening. But then, silence. Only silence. Prosenjit hears nothing from the apartment next door. Hears nothing at all.

Hallucination? Another damn hallucination? When will they stop? Why is this happening? Damn people! Why can't they leave me alone? They're out to get me. It's all their fault!

Prosenjit recalls the beating he got from his crazy-drunk father long ago; he remembers the whipping he got that raised welts. A whipping that hurt. Welts that lasted a long time. *What the hell – I was just a kid! It was only a stupid old stray cat!*

Prosenjit recalls his mother laughing at him, encouraging the beating. *Damn her. She was always against me. She would never take my side. I'm glad she's dead. I hope she rots in hell!*

Now a car drives by. Headlights – strobe-like – flash through the sparse apartment, briefly illuminating the greasy ceiling and the tacky posters that Prosenjit has scotch-taped to the walls. Momentary spotlights for his treasures. A disco ball lights the room, igniting glimpses of images, popping, percolating, much like the agitated spurts of a geyser. A geyser exploding.

Prosenjit sits now, pensive. He looks intently at the large knife, caresses it, strokes it with his hands, relaxes a bit. The knife calms him. It shines. Hard. Cold. Solid. Something sturdy. Something to count on. *I'll show them!*

Now a loud crashing sound interrupts his thoughts, alarming him. Prosenjit – frustrated, angry, sullen – instantly jerks his head to the right, eyes wide open, stares at the wall of the adjacent apartment. Yelling. Arguing. Unintelligible voices. Taunting voices. *Noooo! Please stop! The fear. Please stop!*

Prosenjit remembers his classmates at school laughing at him, laughing at his accent and his funny clothes. His child's mind was confused, but full of deep anger and resentment. He remembers the feeling of dejection and the undeniable promise of retribution, the fantasy of revenge that his mind had hatched, cherished, and been perennially obsessed with.

Bastards! Someone will pay. Someone will pay!

Now the knife is gripped with tension, with strength. Fists are tight. Then, Prosenjit's conscious mind forms the beginnings of an idea. A plan. A deadly plan. *Something must be done!*

The voices have stopped. It is quiet now. Only a slight dripping sound and a dull hum.

Prosenjit returns to pacing in the tiny, sparsely furnished living space. A living space much too small. Much too dark. Much too... well, small.

The bathroom light has stopped its flickering and hangs still, quiet. The apartment is dark; the only light at all is filtering in from outside, from street-lamps, nearby apartment windows, and a slim slice of a light beam from a full moon. In fact, a blue moon. August 31. A slim slice of light from a blue moon.

Prosenjit now pauses his pacing and stands still, listening for the voices, and now notices the light on the wall. A small space, mostly dark, illuminated by a stream of moonbeam light. A slim slice of lunacy. A slim slice from a blue moon. An extra moon. Once in a blue moon. Once.

The beam of light, the slim slice of blue moon light, penetrates the small, dirty window in Prosenjit's apartment and illuminates the opposite wall in what looks to Prosenjit like 3-D structures with faces in them. Faces staring at him. Faces challenging him. Faces in the geometric blue moonlight, shapes hovering on the wall. Men in the moon. Men in a blue moon. Once in a blue moon. Once. *Something must be done!*

Prosenjit again paces, plans. His mind is racing, determined, unrelenting. The part of the brain that gives a sense of conscious control is now on hold. Dysfunctional. Loose connection. Bad wiring.

Then, unexpectedly, the single, bare bathroom light bulb hanging precariously from the stringy, frayed slim cord gives off a burst of static, flickering sparks – Zzzkkkkrrrzzzkk – emits a loud pop, and now turns a dull, cloudy, diffused black-gray color.

Loose connection. Now apparently completely loose.

One hand is tight on the steering wheel, the other grips the large knife, the butt pushed hard against Prosenjit's leg, the knifepoint aiming straight up towards heaven. The conscious-control part of the brain is completely shut off. Prosenjit is now on autopilot; an automaton now irretrievably coursing to his ugly, inevitable destiny.

Must not let people treat me this way. Got to show them!

The mall is just ahead. There are many cars. It is late. Prosenjit, now an automaton on automatic pilot. Plans to be fulfilled. Compulsions to be completed. Bad wiring. Loose connection.

The big full blue moon shines above and a slim reflected light beam penetrates Prosenjit's car windshield and rests quietly, effortlessly on his face. A slim slice of blue moon. A slim slice. The knife still held tightly at his side.

Prosenjit parks in the back of the mall lot as far from a lamp as he can. Dark, except for the moon. He turns the ignition key off, but the engine doesn't stop. It sputters for a moment, a moment frozen in time. As the engine sputters, the whole car shakes harshly. Bbbrrrruuuummppprrr. Prosenjit sits transfixed, blue moonlight on his face. Finally, the engine dies. Dead. The shaking stops. Just quiet now. The slim slice of blue moon sits on Prosenjit's face, which is gray and fixed.

Prosenjit tenses himself, takes a deep breath, then reaches

for the car door handle, the knife still firmly in his other hand. He is thinking about his mother. He is thinking that when he was a small child he wanted so much for her to hold him, to love him. But now he can remember only the cruelty, the shame, the punishment, the rejection, and the yelling. The incessant yelling.

Damn her to hell!

Now Prosenjit remembers a woman's words. *I don't want to see you anymore. I don't love you. I don't like you. You are crazy. Leave me alone! Go away forever!* The pain is too much. Automatic pilot. Loose connection.

The staring. The whispering. They're out to get me. I must protect myself... must fight back.

Prosenjit walks quickly and enters the mall, a mall full of shoppers.

Now quietly, calmly, inexorably he moves down the mall's wide hallway, surrounded by people talking, laughing, shopping. *They are talking about me. They are staring. They are whispering about me. They will kill me*!

Prosenjit stops in the middle of the hallway and stands quietly staring robot-like at the people around him, ostensibly unaware of his presence. A sliver of moon light enters from mall sky light and slashes across the wall behind Prosenjit.

Standing tense (autopilot), Prosenjit raises the knife above his head, gripping it as tightly as his teeth are clenched. His muscles are young and firm. Prosenjit now stares at the many people nearby and thinks of his parents, the girl who rejected him, and of those out to get him – he can think only of revenge, of justice. *The time has come. Something must be done.*

Feeling bitterness, anger, and an inexorable need for self-protection, Prosenjit's brain now initiates the very muscle movements that will fulfill his destiny. *Got to win - have to fight!*

Prosenjit's brain sends the jittery neural signals to his arm and hand, now flexed hard and tight, extending fully above his head holding the big, sharp, gleaming knife.

But now, a glitch. A snafu. A misfire. A coincidence? Or, did the neural signals combine with the tension – the adrenalin – to create a deviation? In fact, the misfires have been familiar events for Prosenjit since childhood. Loose connection. Bad wiring.

A seizure. An epileptic brain seizure. A misfiring of brain circuits. Prosenjit's brain has long experienced such neural anomalies. *Damn brain!* The pills that supposedly would stop such misfirings, the little blue and while capsules, rest undisturbed and unused in a prescription bottle that sits on Prosenjit's bathroom sink directly below the bare light bulb that hangs on the stringy, frayed cord. The pills that Prosenjit has not taken for a very long time.

Now, just at the precise moment when Prosenjit's brain has sent the neural signal to his arm directing it to violently move downward, just at that very moment, the glitch – the temporal lobe anomaly, the seizure – interferes with, and distorts, the neural signal. Kkkzzzrrrkkk. Bad wiring.

Prosenjit's arm does not move as directed. Prosenjit's arm moves not directly dowtoward the crowds of people as intended, but moves in a slightly counterclockwise direction, a half circle. The arm muscles are twisted and jerked by the seizure. Now the blade of the knife no longer points toward the enemies, but instead points toward Prosenjit himself. Loose connection. Once in a blue moon.

Prosenjit's arm moves quickly, muscles hard and flexed. The arm muscles convulse. The gleaming knife that is held so tightly is now pointed at the center of Prosenjit's chest. The arm is now under the control of a misfiring brain. Prosenjit stands bent, rigid, disabled. Kkkzzzrrrkkk. Bad wiring.

Prosenjit's arm, directed by the brain seizure, now slashes aggressively, quickly, in a sweeping counterclockwise direction, a semicircular motion, downward and inward, arcing from high above Prosenjit's head through space in a half circle, moving down and in.

The arm jerks rapidly and powerfully. Inevitably, the tip of the hard, gleaming knife that is held so tightly now pierces the skin of Prosenjit's chest. The knife effortlessly slices deeper, finally severing an artery in Prosenjit's chest. Blood surges, gushes, and pours from the wound, and implacably streams to the floor. A heap of dark crimson blood courses down his rigid body and accumulates at Prosenjit's feet.

Prosenjit can no longer maintain his stance. The blood is being drained from his body and pooling on the floor at his feet as a crowd of shoppers, mouths agape, assemble around him. The slim slice of light from the blue moon that illuminated the wall behind Prosenjit now takes the shape of a long point, and rests on the body of Prosenjit.

Time has nearly stopped. Prosenjit's body now slowly crumples to the floor atop the heap of blood. Quiet. Still. The only sensation Prosenjit has is a brief, fleeting awareness of utter absence – the lonely, abject emptiness of paralyzing shock. Dazed. Numb. Still.

A large pool of blood forms on the floor and then continues a dark scarlet stream across the hallway. A sticky, irregular puddle of deepest red hue of Prosenjit's blood. Prosenjit's body is now a lump, quiet and still atop the rubescent pool, his brain entirely inactive, his mind deadly unaware. So still. So pure.

Then, without the slightest noise, without any apparent cause, mysteriously, inexplicably, a slender hole emerges in Prosenjit's head. A small hole in the side of Prosenjit's head. The temporal lobe; the anomalous temporal lobe, source of the seizure, the glitch.

The small hole extends inward through the bone of the skull, through the dura mater, the cerebral cortex, the corpus callosum, the limbic system, and finally ends in Prosenjit's brain stem. A brain stem that is now defunct, disengaged – loose connection now permanently disconnected.

Then from the strange, enigmatic hole in Prosenjit's head there begins to flow a stream of Prosenjit's delusions that emerge quietly and effortlessly from Prosenjit's brain. The flowing stream of delusions gently cascades down to the floor, smoothly following and gripping the ridges and contours of Prosenjit's skull, smoothly, gently proceeding without pause, without sound, continuous and steady, until the flowing stream of delusions eventually forms a large, neat, symmetrical pool on the hallway floor as the crowds watch incredulously. A pool of Prosenjit's delusions.

The slice of blue moonlight still hangs on Prosenjit's body, silent and fixed. The crowd of people stand frozen, perplexed by the unfolding scene, staring at the body of Prosenjit and the pool of blood and delusions amassing at their feet. The mall is now quiet and still.

Once in a blue moon.

!

"All men by nature desire to know."
— Aristotle

"I don't care what is written about me so long as it isn't true."
— Dorothy Parker

"It is a happiness to wonder; it is a happiness to dream."
— Edgar Allan Poe

"Anyone who says he can see through women is missing a lot."
— Groucho Marx

"It's not true that I had nothing on. I had the radio on."
— Marilyn Monroe

!

She took off all of her clothes and stood there stark naked – I mean, stark naked – staring right at me. So, I took off all of my clothes and I stood there stark naked staring right back at her!

We stood there silently staring at each other for what seemed quite a long while. Then she did something terribly odd, something completely unexpected, something very, very strange. I was truly surprised!

I'm telling you, it was utterly fantastic what the naked lady without a stitch did while standing there staring at me. Who would have guessed? I certainly didn't. I mean, we were standing there fully naked and then she… she… well, I would love to tell you what the totally nakedly nude girl did, but that would be so utterly, I mean, completely inappropriate in a story of this type. I just can't tell you. Sorry!

But, it was really, really odd what the stripped-nude naked woman did, really spectacularly unusual. It was freaky, truly freaky, that's for sure. Freaky. But, I just can't tell you what it was. I know that you are curious. I know that you are wondering, really dying to know, what it was that the strange, beautiful woman did while standing there stark naked staring at me, with me standing there stark naked staring back at her. But, I just can't write it. Don't even ask me, please don't! I just can't!

Hey... you know it's weird how people are always saying that they understand something when in fact they don't have any clue whatsoever, not any clue at all? You know? How people pretend to know stuff they don't? Doctors and lawyers are probably the worst.

Teachers are near the top, too. I guess no one wants to say that he or she doesn't know something. So people go right ahead and make up stuff. For example, did you ever ask someone for directions? People will say anything other than they don't know. You ask for directions and they boldly, very confidently tell you to go here or there, right or left, and so on, when in fact they have no clue whatsoever what they're talking about. "Go straight down there then turn right when you get to the corner drug store, you can't miss it." They don't care if you end up lost. They don't care at all. I mean, no one wants to admit they don't know something. Isn't that wild? I tell you, it's crazy. Simply crazy!

On the other hand, quite contrarily, people very often say that they don't know something when, in fact, they surely must know. If you ask people how they are feeling, for instance, they often say they don't know. "How do you feel about that?" "I don't know." But how can a person not know how he or she feels? In fact, how could anyone *but you* know how you feel? Aren't you the world's greatest expert on how you feel? For example, not too long ago I was just minding my own business when…

Oh, shoot... okay, okay, all right, I guess you've figured out that I was just trying to distract you. Damn! Well, I guess that didn't work!

I was just trying to get your mind off, well... you know what! And, yes, you caught me. Okay, I was trying to distract you from the naked girl because I just can't tell you what she did. I hoped I could get your mind off it with some wry observations. But, I now see that you don't want to be distracted. No. You want to know what the nudely naked undressed lady did that was so odd, so weird, so utterly strange. Yes, that's what you are interested in. Not some wry observations about what people say or do in this or that situation. God, you really are persistent, aren't you!

You want me to tell you what she did while standing there stark naked wearing only a smile staring at me while I was standing there buck naked, unattired in my birthday suit staring right back at her? Okay, here's what happened. We both took off our clothes and stood there staring at each other and then she did the most incredible, most remarkable, most unbelievable thing. That's right – the most stupendous thing. Well, I know you are imagining some possibilities of what exactly the naked lady did, but you just can't quite figure for sure what it could have been. You have some pretty good ideas, but they are general, sketchy ideas, and you want to know for sure. You really are a curious one, aren't you? Yee gads!

Look, I wish I could tell you, but I just can't put that kind of thing into this kind of story. I mean, what would that be like? I can't write stuff like that!

Yes, what the completely naked, nude, clothing-less woman did was curious, bizarre, and astonishing. Even somewhat erotic, I suppose. Certainly it caught me by surprise. I'm sure my mouth dropped open. Wide open. It was stupendous, really fantastic. And strange. I never would have guessed it. Never. Not in a zillion years. But, now *you* are trying to guess it. Hah, but you'll never guess! No, no, you will never, ever guess. It was that weird!

Right now you are trying to guess what it possibly could have been that the bare-naked, exposed lady did. So many ideas are going through your mind. But, you will never get it; it was just too strange. Too strange. Well... okay, perhaps you might guess it, I don't know. But, you will never find out if your guess is right because I just can't write it down here! I just can't!

Wait a minute, here's an idea: perhaps I could whisper it to you. I wonder if that would be alright in a story like this. Just a little whisper, you know? What do you think? Yes? Okay, I'll try whispering it to you. But, wait, I'm not speaking to you, I'm writing. Okay, what then is the equivalent of a whisper in writing? Well, I don't know! I just don't know!

Here's an idea: maybe if I wrote it in triple parentheses? Would that be a whisper? I'll try that. Here's what she did: (((We were standing there totally stark naked, just staring at each other all au naturel, then all of a sudden, most assuredly unexpectedly, she stepped forward and out of the blue she…))) Wait a minute!

No. No, that's not working. That doesn't seem to me to be

like a whisper at all. Not at all. Let's see. Let me think. Okay, here's another idea for a written whisper: maybe I should write it in a small font. Would that be a whisper? Okay, that is a good idea! I will try!

She was staring at me stark naked and I was staring right back at here, equally stark naked, we were just standing and staring, naked, you know, when quite out of the blue she abruptly moved, she reached down and… no, no, this is not a whisper, either. It just doesn't seem like a whisper to me. It simply doesn't feel right at all. I, I really don't think that this is going to work!

I mean, seriously, I'd really like to tell you what she did, what the completely clothes-less woman did. I really would. It really was priceless. I really want to tell. I do! It was so odd, so very odd. You know how when something weird happens then you are just dying to tell other people about it?

For instance, if you have some weird experience then afterwards you are just bursting to tell people about it, just to tell anyone, it doesn't matter who? You know that feeling? You just want to tell it! Why is that? It's like when you've had a very strange dream and you wake up and then you are just dying to tell someone the bizarre, irrational things you dreamt, even though it is totally pointless and has no effect on anything in life, yet still you want to tell it, to relate your weird, surreal dream to someone. You are just bursting to let it out.

Why is that, anyway? Why do we yearn so much to tell others our odd experiences? What is the nature and source of such a desire? Is that part of human nature? Why? Did it have some survival value in our evolutionary past? You know, could it have helped survival somehow? It really is an odd thing. I mean, it's freaky! Just plain freaky!

I'm sure you must have had that kind of experience – like, you had a very strange dream and then when you awoke you had an overwhelming urge to tell someone all about it right away, as soon as possible. Well, this is like that, you see? I would sincerely like to tell you what she did. You know, what the nakedly nude woman did that was so odd, so strange, so perplexing. I really do want to tell you. I do. But, it's just that... well, okay, that's it, I've had it, I'm going to do it. I give up. I'm going to tell you what the stark naked nude woman did! I'm going to tell!

It sure was wild, I'll tell you that. You are going to be so amazed! I mean, wow, it definitely knocked my socks off. Well, not literally, of course, since I didn't even have any socks on, you know, since I was stark naked, too, just like her. Anyway, okay, here goes, I'm going to tell it, I just can't resist anymore, I'm going to do it, let it out, share the whole thing, I'm going to tell it to you now, just what the nudie lady did while I was also naked and we were staring at each other! Okay... here goes....

She was just standing there naked and all, the naked lady, and I was naked, too, and we were staring at each other for a bit, both of us nude, no clothes on at all, just naked and staring at each other, and then she reached down and picked something up from atop a low, small table and then she moved a bit forward, still staring at me, and then… no, stop, wait, no, I just can't do it! I'm so sorry! I thought I could do it, but no! It's just not right!

But, now wait a minute, wait a minute, I've another idea. This is kind of crazy, kinda wacky, but perhaps it will solve the problem. How about if I write it down but you promise not to read it? That way I can tell it – you know, get it off my chest – but you won't read it, so in a way it really won't be in the story, you know? Look, I'll write it in the paragraph below this one if you promise not to read it, okay? Will you promise? Will you? Don't just keep reading. Stop and think. Will you promise not to read it? I will write what she did, the strange thing the naked lady did, but you have to promise to skip over it. Now, promise!

Come on, I'm not going to write it if you don't promise not to read it. Okay? You will? You promise? Okay, I'll put it down in the next paragraph. I'll write what the stark naked lady did. But you don't read it. Okay? You just jump to the following paragraph. Don't read the very next paragraph, the next one. Just jump down to the one after, the paragraph after the next one. Promise? Don't cheat, okay? I mean, this will be great because this will allow me to tell it, to release it from my mind, so to speak, but it still won't be in this story, in a weird way, because the readers won't see it. I'll write it, but you have to promise not to read the next paragraph. You promise? You do? Okay then, here goes!

She was standing there all nudie and cute, the naked lady, sort of relaxed, but tense in a way, soft, smooth skin, hair flowing, staring right at me the whole time, and I was completely naked, too, and I was staring right back at her, just staring right back, not glaring or anything, just relaxed and looking at her while she looked at me, and she was all skin and curves, I noticed, and I was getting a little excited, you know, and then after we'd been standing there staring at each other for a little while, then just like out of the blue, like I never expected it at all, a total freaking surprise to me, right then she stepped forward and...

Hey, wait a minute, you're not supposed to be reading this! What are you doing? I thought you promised to skip over this paragraph? Why are you looking at these sentences? You promised not to read this! You promised!

You are a big liar and cheat! Well, I'm certainly not going to tell you what the nudie naked girl did if you're not going to keep your promises! That's just not fair! I said I would write what she did if you promised not to read it, but there you were reading what I had written in that last paragraph!

Now, look, I told you I can't tell you what the naked lady did, but you insisted! I guess because you are so damned interested in what nudified naked ladies do, so I gave in and said I would tell you if you wouldn't read it, but there you were reading away! What kind of person are you, anyway? Why are you so interested in what nudie girls do? You broke your promise!

Look, let's be fair. I just can't tell you what she did. I'm sorry. But, I really do want to tell it. As I said, it's like a strange dream, you know? I mean, I'm just dying to let it out. I really want to tell it. So, what do you suggest? What can we do about this awkward, frustrating situation?

It really does seem impossible! Do you have any ideas?

I want to tell it, but I just can't. What? What's that you say? Some clues? You want me to give you some clues about what she did? Oh, I see, you want to narrow down your guesses? So, you have some ideas in your mind about what the clothing-less lady did, and you want to see which one might be right. You think you might know, you think you might have guessed, so you just want me to give you a few clues? Okay, that's okay I guess. So, okay, here are some clues, then...

Hmm. Well, it wasn't something gross or stupid, I don't think. She didn't throw up, or anything like that. No, not something gross. Hmm. A clue? Ah, she did move. She moved her body. And, there was another object or objects involved. Well, maybe not "involved," but there were objects. What she did was something that affected me. It was directed toward me, but objects were in the picture. She...

Look, this just isn't working! I can't think of any good clues without just totally giving it away! I may as well just tell you what she die! No, wait, wait, I have an idea! Yes, I have a grand idea! An absolutely grand idea that will solve this problem!

I will write it here, I will write down what the disrobed, totally naked lady standing staring at me in the altogether did that was so damned odd. I will write it, but, I will write it in invisible ink! Yes, invisible ink is the solution! All right!

Isn't that a great idea? I will write what she did in invisible ink. I'm not sure how this works, but let's try it. I will write the next paragraph in invisible ink and then you take a brush or paper towel or something and dip it into milk and then rub the milk onto the next paragraph. Just dab milk on the next paragraph. That should make the invisible ink appear. Then you can find out what the naked lady did that was so startling and fantastic. Wait 'til you hear, it's a doozy! Okay, here goes...

I'm going to write the next paragraph in invisible ink. The ink will become visible when you put milk on it. Don't put too much on because that could smudge the ink and the words might not appear. Just dab some milk on the next paragraph with a brush or something and then the words should begin to pop out. Okay? Here goes...

There! Did it work? Could you read it? Did you put milk on it? My god, wasn't that amazing? Unbelievable, don't you think? Now surely you can understand why I couldn't write such a thing in a story like this. It just wouldn't be proper, would it? No way!

Well, was it what you thought, I mean, did the stripped-down, un-draped naked lady do what you were guessing? I'll bet you never guessed it, did you? Can you imagine how I felt? I mean, when she... well, you know! Such a very strange thing to do. So bizarre! Well, can you imagine? What was I supposed to do? I mean, what would you have done in such a situation? It was so weird!

What was that? What did you say? What did *I* do, you ask? What did I do after she did, well, what she did? Is that what you are wondering? What was my reaction to what she did? That's what you want to know? Well... I must say that that is certainly something I could never, ever, ever tell in a story like this! No way! I most certainly could never write that! Even invisible ink is not acceptable for that, believe me, for something like that! No, sir!

Now that you know what the nudie, naked, leafless lady did, well, I guess you'll just have to imagine what *I* did after she did what she did!

Sorry!

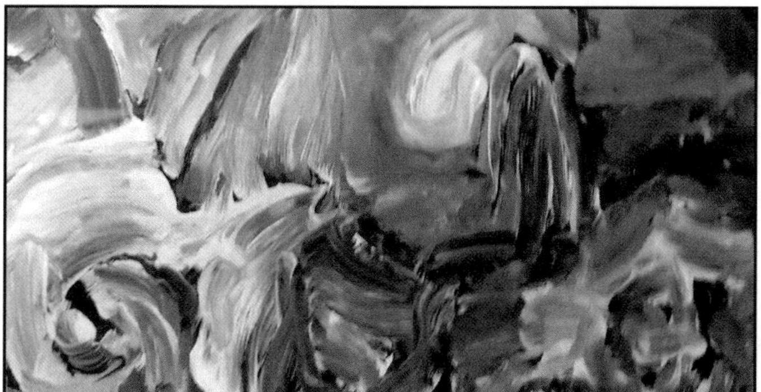

What Seems Now, Well, Only Too Ordinary

"The Universe is not only queerer than we suppose, it is queerer than we can suppose."
— J.B.S. Haldane

"Start with what is right rather than what is acceptable."
— Franz Kafka

"All things are strange which are worth knowing."
— Catherynne M. Valente

"I have seen so many extraordinary things, nothing seems extraordinary anymore."
— Lewis Carroll

"The difference between ordinary and extraordinary is that little extra."
— Jimmy Johnson

What Seems Now, Well, Only Too Ordinary

Small electric appliances prance, steam,
march grandly, effortlessly, atop
smooth straight granite countertops,
then fling themselves high, extending,
grasping heaven's red velvet trapezes,
swinging freely, tenaciously through
majestic white/gray/silver clouds of silky,
murky, nebulous water vapor,
flipping, curling, twisting,
finally releasing their grips,
sailing like whispers, float, fall, stretch,
STICK their landings.
Later standing rigid, heads high,
noble, stately, august
whilst the small electric appliance
anthem is played by well-worn,
straining, determined musical instruments.
The victorious again are
the toaster, the blender,
and the coffee maker;
bread is transformed to toast,
solid to liquid,
bean to black java;
and, you and me to
what seems now, well,
only too ordinary.

The Art of Looking

"I'm afraid that if you look at a thing long enough, it loses all of its meaning."
— Andy Warhol

"There is hardly anyone so insignificant that he does not seem imposing to someone at some time."
— Charles Horton Cooley

"Words are all we have. Words are the clothes thoughts wear."
— Samuel Beckett

"You have two eyes, and two ears, but only one mouth. This is so because you are supposed to look and listen more than you talk."
— Lucca Kaldahl

"Some people see the cup as half empty. Some people see the cup as half full. I see the cup as too large."
— George Carlin

The Art of Looking

What are you looking at?

Yeah, I mean you.

Sitting there staring at these black scratchings on white, smugly making your quick judgments, and even worse, hoping for, maybe expecting, something entertaining or engrossing or even sage… oh, oh, or maybe truly captivating, or at least something time-consuming and not objectionable. Oh no, nothing objectionable for you.

And, certainly not anything boring or unusual or insulting. No, not for you. You sit there staring at these little black symbols, piled up one after another with spaces between them, wanting something awe-inspiring, surprising, edifying, absorbing, or at least mildly satisfying to emerge from them.

Well, what are you looking at?

Staring at these black letters, scanning them, as if there was some miracle to be found in them, some answer, some insight, some entertainment for you just sitting there doing nothing, just looking, just gazing on these abstract, obtuse scratchings and trying to find meaning and ideas and feelings and even inspiration in them, or at the minimum some entertainment and distraction from your tiring life.

But, I know what you're thinking – you're thinking that you don't want to do all the work, you don't want to find meaning on your own, in your own mind, no, you need some scratchings, something to stimulate the process, you want someone to arrange these words and sentences, someone different from you, someone creative and smart and clever and wise, someone to arrange these black letters and words in a manner that will create a story, a tall tale with characters and a plot and dialogue and action and surprises and suspense and coincidences and a nice, happy ending, a story that ties together all nice and neat, but oh, no, nothing too out of the ordinary, nothing too strange or upsetting, you want a story that's normal, just normal, a story that makes you smile and think, but not too deeply – no, not too deeply – something realistic, but not too realistic, certainly not anything grotesque or odd or weird or unnatural or unsettling, no, not for good old normal you, no, you want a nice little happy story that will be wise and cute and witty and surprising and different, but not too different, no, not too different.

Oh, I know what you want – you want these words and sentences to form a nice little story, a story you could probably make up for yourself with a little effort, but, I know you, you don't want to make the effort, you want someone else to do the hard work while you just sit there staring at these black symbols on white all lined up ever so properly, words and sentences not causing any disgust or anger or chagrin, simply unfolding a proper little tale, a tale perhaps of love or intrigue or sentiment or warmth or poignancy or, of course, I know what you want, a story about redemption and justice, yeah, a nice little story about redemption and justice.

Well, what are you still looking at? You're still here? You want a story, do you?

All right, let's start with some characters. I suppose you want a man and a woman. And some kids. A house in the suburbs. And a dog. A nice, modern, dysfunctional family – so normal and sweet on the surface, but horrifically screwed up deep down inside. Perhaps they have incompatibility issues or personality clashes. Let's see… I suppose the teenage boy could be doing drugs. And I guess the wife could have a gambling addiction. That would be good. Maybe the husband should be an alcoholic. You'd enjoy that, I'll bet.

Now, what do they do, this man and woman? Do they have jobs? I'll bet the man works downtown, something with computers. And the wife has a part-time job at an art gallery. Yeah, you'd like that, computers and art, that's nice. A nice gender cliché.

And I suppose you want some sex in this story, something

steamy and lurid. Of course you want sex. Every good story must have sex. Oh, and of course you want an affair. Is that what you want? Yes, that's what you would like. An affair. Okay, then, let's say that the man is seeing a woman. Someone at work, I imagine, someone much younger. They've been going at it hot and heavy for months, but the man, the husband, he is uncertain about the affair and thinks maybe he should break it off. However, he keeps telling this woman, this woman from the office at work, this young, thin, dark-haired woman, this sexy woman, he keeps telling her that he will leave his wife, that he will leave her soon, that he is only staying with her because of the kids and that he is just waiting for the right moment to leave, and he tells this young, dark-haired sexy woman from the office that he will run away with her, will run away and get married in some nice, warm vacation spot, maybe in the Caribbean, would you like that, maybe Jamaica. Is that what you're wanting, is that why you're looking at these small black marks? Is that why you're staring and scanning? I mean really, what are you looking at?

Oh, but certainly you want some suspense, some conflict. This little story needs drama. Okay, how about this, maybe one of the kids, the sensitive little girl I suppose, the innocent 10-year-old, maybe she finds out about the affair, maybe she even sees her father and the woman from the office in bed together. What will the girl do? Will she tell her mother? Will she confront her father? Then what will happen? What? You want me to tell you? You can't write your own story?

Well, okay, perhaps the man finds out that his daughter knows about the affair, perhaps his daughter tells him (wouldn't that be a choice scene to read? – gripping dialogue, very entertaining), or maybe he overhears his daughter telling a friend on the phone about her father's affair, or, even better, maybe the man sees his daughter standing there in the bedroom door staring at him and the sexy woman from the office (just as you are staring at these words now), she sees the two of them lying there all naked, kissing and rubbing and touching each other. Is that what you want?

Yes, the daughter sees the cheating couple in bed having

sex. Are you happy now, or is that too much for you, has this little story gone too far outside your nice little boundaries, your nice little morals, the sensible morals you have, the nice little notions that you have about what should and shouldn't happen in a story, a nice little story that will make you smile, that will make you feel contented, a story that will pass your time and amuse you?

No? Well, let's continue then. I suppose the man now is very upset, is excruciatingly upset now that his daughter, his sensitive little daughter, knows about his affair with the beautiful, striking, dark-haired woman from the office. The man is terribly confused about what he should do. He needs advice. He needs to talk things out, to get his head straight. Isn't that what you want in a story like this, some psychological crap? Maybe some Freudian mumbo jumbo, or better yet, some New Age psychobabble or Jungian gobbledygook. Maybe some Buddhist hogwash. It's quite popular now.

Yes, I could write you some platitudes, some clichés, some smarmy dialogue full of selfish, sophomoric, and shortsighted aphorisms about insecurity, self-esteem, archetypes, superegos, narcissism, and such, all disguised as philosophy or depth psychology. Would that make you happy? Huh? Would you like that?

So all right, I'll play along some more. Let's see, I suppose you want the man to talk to his best friend, to confide in him, to ask for advice, ask what to do, and so on. Isn't that how a nice little story is supposed to go? The man is in quite a tough spot and should ask for advice from his best friend.

Well, what advice do you think the best friend should give to the man? Do you want this little story to be realistic, to be happy, to be funny, or what? What sort of dialogue do you want? You want short and crisp, or long and involved? You want educated, back-alley, or what? Should they talk like men, macho and hard, or do you want sensitive talk? Who is this man, anyway? Is the man an insensitive, unrepentant brute, or is he a gentle, misunderstood victim? What do you want from this man and his friend? Who are they? Do you know them? Is one of them you or someone you know?

Well, do I have to do everything? I suppose I do. You just

sit there judging me, smug and content, staring at these words, scanning and thinking. Reading and thinking. And judging. Is this a good story? Should I keep reading or should I put it down? Is that what you're looking at, something to judge? You say you just want to be entertained, to be engrossed. Well, is that what you want, what you really want? Is that it? Don't you have something better to do? Why do you keep staring? If you know what you want in a story, then why don't you create one for yourself?

Do you really need someone to write stories for you, cute little stories with all the right ingredients, the right format – a sentence here, a sentence there, paragraphs, indentations, commas, quotation marks, periods, a plot-line, a climax, a denouement – and, of course, the right philosophies and morals and language and style, nothing too far out, something realistic and normal, but at the same time different and exciting, something smart and funny, but poignant and sublime, something so, so, so *something*, but what is it?

How about: based on a true story, but dramatized and embellished? Is that what you would like? That's what most people want. Is that why you are staring? Is that what you are hoping for here? Well, just what are you looking at?

You know what I think? I think you want a story with elements and morals exactly as already in your own head! If that's so, then what do you want of me? You want me to continue the story, to do the hard work, to do the creating, is that it? You just want to look, just to look; you want me to do all the work?

So, okay, I'll humor you. Let's suppose the man, the cheating husband, confides in his best friend, and suppose his best friend tells him that he has to decide for himself. His friend says to the man, "Do you want your girlfriend, do you love her that much, enough to give up your comfortable life? Or, do you want your wife and kids? Only you can decide. Only you know what you want and how much you want it. It's up to you. It's purely up to you. It's your decision." Kind of a Dr. Phil deal. Wouldn't that be nice?

Right – the best friend tells the man that he has to either quit the affair and come clean with his wife, try to build a decent life, at least for the sake of the kids, to be a good husband and be loyal to his wife, or, if he loves this woman from work so much, this very young, dark-haired, striking woman, if he loves her so much and if his life with his wife and kids is so, so horrible, then what he has to do is tell his wife the truth and run off with the woman from work. It's up to him. Only up to him. That's what his best friend tells him. That's his only advice. What else could he say?

What do you think? Isn't that what you want the friend to say? You sit there so relaxed, so confident of yourself. You just sit and read. Sure, if you're just the reader, it's easy. You don't have to do any of the hard work, you just read and judge. All you do is look. But what are you looking at, anyway? Couldn't you simply finish the story in your head in a much more satisfying way than it can be finished here? Why not?

Now, think about it – isn't it obvious, the best friend's advice is of no use. It's totally useless. It's just a simple cliché that everyone believes and wants to hear. A simple, useless cliché. Of course, the man doesn't know what to do. I already told you he's confused. Weren't you paying attention? Why am I writing all this if you're not even going to pay attention? What good does some Dr. Phil advice about choosing do for someone who doesn't know what to choose? Why doesn't someone tell him *how* to go about making such a choice? Telling someone to choose but not telling them how to go about choosing doesn't help much. Okay, so what would you like to happen next?

I think I know what you want. I'll humor you some more and continue. Okay, what does the man do? What would you like him to do, expect him to do? I think I know. Perhaps the man goes on a drinking binge. He is an alcoholic, after all. Yeah, he goes to a bar and really ties one on. That kind of thing is big in stories. Is that what you wanted? Okay, let's suppose the man gets really drunk, totally wasted, drowns his sorrows in booze, hoping for an answer, for some resolution to his problem. You like that? Good. The man really ties one on. Okay, then what?

Well, here's an idea, maybe he has an accident with his car – drinking and driving, that's very modern, very exciting – messy, but gritty and realistic – you'd like that. I can see the movie rights – good visuals, lots of exciting action. Yeah, the man has a car accident while drunk. But, what sort of an accident? What happens? What would you like?

Maybe the man hits a dog with his car. Would that be good? Would that be engrossing? But, oh boy, the dog mustn't die, you wouldn't like that at all, not at all, then the story would be far too sad for you. *Why did the dog have to die? That poor dog!* So, okay, the dog doesn't die. He's not even badly injured. The man will take the dog to the vet and he'll be fine. Are you happy now? The dog is fine. The people are a mess, but the dog is fine. Just what everyone likes.

And now, finally, what about an ending? This isn't a novel; it's just a short story. We need to wrap this thing up. How would you like this cute little story to end? What would be satisfying and edifying and, most of all, entertaining? What are you looking for? Do you even know? You want me to do everything, don't you? I even have to tell you what to want. Sure, I do everything and then what? You don't like it. I know you – you won't like it at all. Isn't that just the way it always goes? You do nothing but sit and stare and then you don't like it.

You want a good ending? Okay, fine – here's one: The man gets home and finds a note. His wife has left him. She's run off with – guess who – that's right, his best friend. Turns out they've been having an affair for months and now that she knows about her husband's infidelity (the irony: she heard it from her lover, her husband's best friend), she has decided to leave her husband. Tit for tat. It's nearly perfect. It'd be better if the husband would die. I could easily tack that on: Upon hearing the news, the man blurts out, "But darling, I love you, I've always loved you and I always will love you 'til the end of time," then drops dead of a heart attack. It's precious. You will love that ending. No, really, I've seen *Casablanca*, *The English Patient*, and the rest. You like it, don't you? But wait, I've another idea.

Here's a better ending: The drunken man doesn't hit a dog with his car, he hits his wife! Oh, that's good. After getting drunk, the man decides to go home and tell his wife about his affair with the young, dark-haired woman from work. Meanwhile, his wife has been worried about her missing husband and she is outside, in the dark, pacing near their driveway. The man, in his drunken state, doesn't see his wife in front of the driveway and strikes her with his car. A tragedy!

You'll like that, that's a good one. Then, this is really good, while the wife is in the hospital, maybe dying, the husband realizes how much he loves her and wants her. Yes, he sees the light and ends his affair. His wife recovers. They live happily ever after. The end.

Do you like that? No? Why not – too pat, too common, too manipulative? Well, just what in the world are you looking at then? What is it that you want?

Okay, okay, I've an idea; how about this for an ending: The man comes home after drinking, still confused, he admits the affair to his wife and, holy cow, he discovers that his wife is also having an affair – and here's the good part, it's an affair with the same dark-haired woman from the office that he's having an affair with! Yes, that's clever, that's a twist. You'll like that. It turns out that the women are bisexual and the wife is having an affair with the very same woman from work that her husband has been seeing. One of the women, or – wait – both of them together tell the man about their affair. Or, better still, perhaps he finds them in bed together when he gets home. Yes, this is good. The man gets his daughter's perspective of things. He is devastated. The women tell the man that they are leaving him to be with each other. He gets what he deserves, the dirty, cheating rat. The end. Oh, wait. Maybe he dies. Yeah, the heart attack thing. That was good – he drops over dead of a heart attack. Oh, oh, but wait, I've got an even better one, a beaut of an ending. See if you like this.

Here it is: The man comes home and tells his wife that he has something important to tell her. But his wife is upset and insists that she needs to tell him something first. She's held it in for so long. She says that when she was young, years ago, long before she met her husband, when she was just a teenager, she got pregnant and had a baby – a baby girl. She tells the man that she gave her daughter up for adoption. Now that daughter has sought out her birth mother and has found her, has contacted her. And, the woman says, her first daughter that she has recently reunited with after all these years, that daughter lives right here in this very city. The wife then tells her husband the girl's name, the name of the daughter that she gave up for adoption so many years ago. And – did you see it coming? – it's the same name as the young, dark-haired sexy woman from the office! That's right – the man is having an affair with his wife's daughter. Good one, don't you think?

You don't like it? You know, I kinda suspected that you wouldn't. You are so picky! You sit there so smug, so judgmental, so glib. Just staring and thinking. You make me do all the work, all the hard work, and all you do is look.

And judge. I arrange these little black scratchings to make a story, a nice little story, so normal, so realistic – but not too realistic – so clever, so ironic, so savvy and surprising, and what do I get out of it – nothing but criticism! You just sit there, quiet and smug, and, of course, judging. I do all the work, you do nothing. Nothing. Well, nothing except look. Just look. All you do is look.

Well, what are you looking at?

Prevention Code

"Men may change their climate, but they cannot change their nature. A man that goes out a fool cannot ride or sail himself into common sense."
— Joseph Addison

"I don't want to achieve immortality through my work. I want to achieve it by not dying."
— Woody Allen

"All things are subject to interpretation. Whichever interpretation prevails at a given time is a function of power and not truth."
— Friedrich Nietzsche

"Most misunderstandings in the world could be avoided if people would simply take the time to ask, "What else could this mean?""
— Shannon L. Alder

"The strangest things in life, are often closer to reality, than reality would like to admit."
— Anthony L.S.

Prevention Code

Jarden had just completed his prayer PC and was preparing for bed. He hung the prayer headset back on its holder and the link went blank. The prayer PC had been used since before Jarden had been clorned and sociobred. He still used the old headset, though most robos now had the auto link. No one questioned the purpose of the prayer PC, which was not unusual since one of its recurrent prayers was the circle-tone that provided users the correct values and acceptance standards. This kind of direct brain-link had been debated at one time, Jarden had heard, shortly after it was introduced in 2038. But robos now accepted it as necessary and good.

Jarden glanced at the shadron on the wall and for the first time in years thought about windows. He had never seen a real window, but had read about what they were like and had learned in CorpColl how windows eventually were replaced with shadrons, huge silky screens that allowed photon beams to replicate serene scenes and appropriate, approved images on the wall. The shadron was soothing and beautiful. There was no need for windows, no need to see the ugly outside world anymore. And, of course, no need for other robos to look in. The images that were replicated on the shadron were selected by a division of the Oversee Committee and had been scientifically demonstrated to be therapeutic, peaceful, and calming.

Jarden remembered how in CorpColl he had been taught why windows were unacceptable. Sobiopsy researchers had shown the horrible, insidious effects that windows had on people, such as causing drastic increases in loneliness, envy, anxiety and melancholia. It was said that there had been a time when people enjoyed windows, a time when the outside world was more enjoyable, more inviting than the inside, a time when robos felt comfortable with transparent screens. But all that had changed long ago. Windows were now believed to be disgusting and unacceptable.

Jarden recalled that he had been taught in CorpColl that many prominent neoconstructionist theorists believed that the disrespect of windows began with the analysis of the writings of Franz Kafka, a writer from the before-times, who often used the window as a metaphor in his stories. The connotations generally involved paranoia, loss of privacy, and repulsiveness. It was believed that the impetus was there in Kafka's writings and that gradually robos came to despise windows. The outside world was so hideous that people rejoiced when the shadron was convented. Soon the Oversee Committee required that windows be replaced by shadrons everywhere. Windows were prohibited by the Overseers for mental health reasons. It was for everyone's good to avoid windows. Whether or not the neoconstructionists were right that it was the writings of Kafka that served as a Gladwell point to move society toward the shadron, the fact was that everyone now seemed pleased by the removal of windows. Of course, the prayer PC helped enhance that value.

Jarden, like other robos, was pleased that technical progress allowed him to avoid looking at the depressing world outside his condapt. He couldn't imagine a past that allowed such things as windows. What a weird, unpleasant experience that must have been. Jarden had read some excerpts from the stories of Franz Kafka while at CorpColl. While the stories inspired an interest inside of him, he knew best to keep this interest to himself. He had never told anyone that he was curious about windows and their early place in society, in literature, and in sobiopsy theory. Now Jarden looked at the shadron and began imagining what windows must have been like. His interest was growing, though he fought against it since he knew it was unacceptable. Why hadn't the PC prayers worked better at inhibiting his interests, he wondered?

But then his thoughts were interrupted as an alterd began unraveling on Jarden's shadron, an event that always caused a brief twinkling glitter of light, called a "blink," on the edges of the screen near the locations of the photon beam generators. The blink startled Jarden and left him with an unusual sense of trepidation. He wondered why that was, why that happened, his odd feeling. He had never felt such a feeling before when seeing the blink. Jarden paused and stared as the shadron screen changed to a more appropriate evening scene. But Jarden wasn't thinking about the alterd that now gleamed on the shadron. Jarden's mind was preoccupied wondering why the blink had startled him. Jarden was typically very comfortable with the familiar, common blinks. The anxiousness he now felt was unusual and he wanted to know why it was happening.

Jarden continued his habitual preparation for bed, changing into his cloth sleeping gown. But mentally he was pondering why he had felt a sense of panic at the moment of the blink. Searching for the cause, he began to mentally review the events of his day. Then it struck him. He began to understand...

That morning at the place-time stage Jarden had talked with his friend and co-enabler, Maxim, about an odd event. Maxim had insisted that he overheard his supervisory aide refer to a double-6 agency need. A double-6 was never talked about in public. It was a reference to a serious prevention code order. Prevention code orders had been used for nearly 40 years and were widely accepted as the only reasonable way to prevent crimes. This concept was provided and reinforced on the prayer PCs that all robos used. While the prayer PC enhancement was strong, it was not perfect, not universal.

The prevention code had come about gradually. Some said that its fundamental philosophy originated far back in history during what was referred to as World War II. The leader of the country then known as the United States was a man called True Man. It was said that his words were understood to be unquestionably true. It was written that True Man had ordered the most powerful explosive device available at that time to be de-toned on a heavily populated Max Live-At of his enemy. Many non-military people and resources were terminated. History-Reads said that True Man had explained that the de-tone was justified because it saved many of his nation-state's combatants. This idea was roundly accepted, even embraced, by robos even in other nation-states and other triboups. So, it is said, the prevention code philosophy began. Saving combatants justified the termination of others who were not part of the triboup.

Gradually over many years the prevention idea expanded. Many times outsider Live-Ats were de-toned, causing the termination of noncombatants from other triboups. These terminations were sometimes called "collateral damage," Jarden had learned, and were tolerated, even applauded, because they prevented other terminations.

Later this concept was applied by the Guardians. It was discovered that if a criminal would not surrender or confess, his submission could be elicited by terminating his family members or friends. The first recorded case of this occurred in 2043. A criminal named Crayon Black was trapped inside a bank that he had intended to de-stuff. He refused to come out, and instead threatened to terminate consumers and bank enablers. In order to prevent this, the Guardians brought Crayon Black's wife to the place-stage and told him they would terminate her if he did not come out. He still refused, perhaps doubting the veracity of the Guardians, so they imploded his wife's skull with a de-jack stan. Afterwards, an early version of the prevention code was used to justify the termination of Crayon Black's wife. However, since the wife's termination had not been successful in removing Crayon Black from the bank, the Guardians then brought Crayon Black's mother to the bank with the same warning. This time Black came out, apparently now believing that the Guardians would indeed terminate his mother if he did not surrender. Thus, the Guardians had saved many robos by terminating only one. The trade-off was considered very good and eminently reasonable. In this case, only one innocent life was lost in order to save many. Crayon Black's wife was considered collateral damage.

Robos nearly unanimously believed that the prevention code policy was very wise. Preventative terminations subsequently began to occur regularly. The Guardians began to call these terminations "premptive terminations," which was soon shortened to "prempts." Gradually the prempt principle spread.

Then, in 2066, a major advance was made in the prevention code philosophy. A criminal named Taynee Scam, who was an enabler at a Molar Post Stage, was threatening to terminate a fellow enabler, a hostage he held. The Guardians wanted to use a prempt to save the hostage, but they could not find anyone whom Taynee Scam cared about. If Taynee Scam had cared about someone, then the Guardians could have threatened to terminate that robo to force Taynee Scam to surrender. But Scam cared about no one. He was a complete loner, which, in fact, was fairly common in 2066. There were many loner robos like Taynee Scam.

As tensions grew, it became obvious that Taynee Scam was soon going to terminate his co-enabler. Then, somewhat unexpectedly, one of the more experienced Guardians inter-aired his laser-stan at the hostage, Taynee's co-enabler, which terminated him. That is, the hostage had been terminated by a Guardian. The Guardian later explained to the Judicial Division of the Oversee Committee that he reasoned that by terminating the co-enabler he was preventing Taynee Scam from committing an illegal termination. It was not that different from the current prevention code, he argued. A criminal act had been prevented by incident of collateral damage.

Some said that this idea was not a new one, but that it had existed more than a hundred years earlier in pre-Structured schematic literature. For example, in a novel called *The Human Comedy* written by William Saroyan in the year 1943 is the line, "If you give to a thief, he cannot steal from you, and he is then no longer a thief." In 2066 the Overseers similarly reasoned that if a hostage was terminated that would then constitute a prempt action that prevented the illegal killing of the hostage. Thus, a homicide was prevented by Guardian action. And so it was reasoned: If you remove the intended victim of a would-be murderer, he cannot then terminate that robo, and then cannot become a murderer.

In the case of Taynee Scam, the Guardian who inter-aired the hostage was given a commendation, and the Oversee Committee immediately seized on this clever addition to the prevention code. Subsequently the prevention code was altered and unanimously adopted to include this new provision. It came to be known as a double-6, because of the year it was enacted – 2066.

The double-6 section of the prevention code now requires that any robo who intends to commit an illegal termination or other serious crime against another robo must file a petition to the appropriate Overseer division. The petition names the intended victim and a special Double-6 Committee assigns an agent to terminate the intended victim so as to prevent the petitioner from carrying out the illegal act. This effectively reduces the homicide rate to near zero.

The agent who performs a prempt termination is called a double-6 agent. It is one of the best enabler positions in the Stage Arenas because it is virtually impossible for a double-6 agent to get prempted. Double-6 agents will ignore an order to prempt one of their own (another double-6 agent), and will instead file an order against the originator of the order. This makes the double-6 agent position highly desirable. However, it is also a highly secretive position, for obvious reasons. Robos simply do not know who the double-6 agents are.

The prevention code is so successful that it is being expanded to include other illegal acts besides homicide. For example, if a robo plans to de-stuff another robo, the Overseers can prevent this by removing the stuff first. Eventually all crimes will be prevented by the prevention code philosophy. There are very few robos who do not accept the prevention code philosophy, and they are wise to keep their objections silent.

Jarden now realized why he was nervous. No one ever spoke of double-6 agency, yet Maxim insisted that he heard such talk at the place-time stage. Jarden now realized that, although almost unthinkable since he had no enemies, perhaps he was the target of a double-6 order. Jarden believed it was a long-shot, yet he realized that this was the cause of his uneasiness – he was worried that he might be the target of a double-6 agent. Who would want him terminated? There was nothing to do about it now, except to take a trank dosage and go to bed. Jarden, in fact, took two tranks and slept soundly until notified of the required wake time by the shadron.

The next day at his place-time stage, Jarden made certain to have mid-eat with his friend Maxim. When they were together and separated from the other robos, Jarden carefully raised the issue of the double-6.

Maxim: I definitely overheard them say it was petitioned for Stage 58.

Jarden: Our place-time stage?

Maxim: That's right. That's why I was so concerned. I believe someone in Stage 58 is targeted for prevention code. In fact, Jarden, I am sorry to say that the implication of the talk was that it might be you.

Jarden now clenched his jaw and his fists, and stared wide-eyed at Maxim: Me?

They talked in hushed tones. It was not good etiquette to talk about such things and could be trouble for them if they were overheard. In fact, if their talk went too far it could be a violation of Overseer edict 593-b which required robos to respect Overseer judgments and not create upsetting conditions. Jarden was relieved that Maxim was such a good friend that he was not afraid to speak of double-6. Jarden suspected that Maxim might be one of the very few who did not totally approve of double-6.

Jarden: I can't believe it. Why me? I have no enemies? Who could it be? The d-6 agent, I mean. Any ideas?

Maxim: I don't know. It is always clandestine. I don't think anyone knows. I am worried.

Jarden: Yes, me too. Last night I became aware of my nervousness. Who would target me? Are you sure it is me?

Maxim: No, Jarden, I am not sure. I am not sure of any of this. It is only rumor that I partially overheard. Of course, everyone has enemies. And, of course, it is not unheard of that a prempt could occur by mistake, or could be initiated and enabled by mental-unclears.

Jarden: Is there anything we can do?

Maxim: Have you mentioned it to Ajandee?

Jarden: No. I will be meeting with her after our term is expired here. Do you think I can trust her?

Maxim: I do not know. But, you two have made an O-B pact, so it might be time to find out. I think you should ask for her help. She is wise and has connections. She may be able to find some answers for us. You should mention it to her when you see her tonight.

It was true that Jarden and Ajandee had made the pact that was referred to as a monogamy bond, M-bond, or O-B. They had met about a year ago and had quickly become emotionally close – suited for one another. Therefore, they had gone to an appropriate Overseer Guide and requested a permit for the O-B pact. This meant that they had agreed to take nasal spray tinctures of oxytocin hormone within one hour prior to having intimate relations.

The O-B (oxytocin bond) pact was almost always required for couples who wanted to be monogamous and wanted to be considered for child-birth licensure. Couples without an O-B rarely received parenting licensure. Jarden and Ajandee had decided that they eventually would want to have a child, so they wanted very much to take the first step. The hormone oxytocin acted on areas of the brain and as such strengthened trust, bonding, empathy, and monogamy. Taking the nasal spray tincture just before being intimate would help cement their monogamous bond and would significantly enhance their chances for later consideration as parents. However, they would still need genetic testing and parenting instruction at a special division of CorpColl after completing the O-B pact.

It was rare that a robo brain did not respond to oxytocin, however all robos knew that it occasionally happened that an individual did not have enough oxytocin brain receptors for binding action success. So, sometimes the nasal spray tinctures were not enough to ensure monogamy. However, Jarden and Ajandee were not worried since they already felt a close emotional bond with each other. They were confident that the O-B pact would be successful.

Jarden and Maxim finished their mid-meal and continued with their duties at Stage 58. The rest of Jarden's day went without problems, though he felt on edge the entire time, and when his term expired he immediately took a Z-beam through the Max Live-At to a Groupace where he had earlier agreed to meet Ajandee. She was already there when he arrived and had secured a partner bench for them.

Jarden approached Ajandee with a cautious smile and with a worried look on his face: Sweets, hi, hi, hey.

He kissed her on the cheek and gave her a strong hug. Ajandee could sense that Jarden was more nervous than usual. Something was up. His face looked tense and he was quieter and less animated than was his usual pattern.

Ajandee: Hi, hi, hey. How are you?

Jarden: Okee-doe-do. How are you?

Ajandee: Well, it was a long day for me. I am a bit tired. But, Jarden, is something sneaky-mal with you? What's wrong?

Jarden looked surprised: Sweets, why do you ask?

Ajandee: You seem a bit tense, a bit quiet. And, you have a worried look on your face.

Jarden: You are very perceptive, Ajandee.

That was definitely a quality that drew him to her. Anyone could tell by the look in Ajandee's eyes that she was a sharp, knowing robo. Jarden not only enjoyed her dark, distinctive looks, but also was attracted to her because of her intelligence and perceptiveness. Anyone could see it in her eyes.

Ajandee: You are very kind, Jarden, thank you. But, sweets, what is it? What bothers you?

Jarden moved closer to her on the bench and spoke in a quiet voice: I am going to tell you something important, but it could be dangerous. I feel that you should know about it, though. And, I feel that perhaps you can help me. There is a problem, Ajandee. There is talk of a double-6 at Stage 58. Maxim heard about it and told me.

Ajandee now became alarmed: Please, Jarden, you mustn't talk of it!

She quickly glanced around. She saw that there were no robos that could be looking at them or listening to them. Ajandee turned back to Jarden.

Jarden: But, sweets, this is important. We do not know who the target is, but we are afraid it might be me. Maxim heard rumors. Certainly it must be someone at our place-stage. Sweets, it might be me!

Ajandee: What? Are you sure? How could there be such talk?

Jarden: I don't know, and Maxim has no notion either. We agreed that I should tell you about it and see if you had some ideas about what we could do if in fact there is a double-6 prevention code at our place-time stage. Do you have any ideas what we can do?

Ajandee: Well, I, I... I just don't know, Jarden. The rumors may be true. Of course, double-6 agents are not known to robos. Unless there has been a leak, I guess. But that is unheard of. Jarden, we should not talk of this anymore. Listen, sweets, we can meet later tonight at our secret place and then make a plan. Let me think about it. I'm sure I can help. Let me think. We will meet 2 hours before sunrise at our secret place. Two hours before sunrise. Let us think about it and we will talk later. Let us not think of it now, but let us enjoy our short time together.

Jarden: Yes, that is a good plan, Ajandee. You are so wise and so kind. I am very pleased that we have agreed to the O-B pact. I hope this d-6 rumor is merely a blasay and that we can start soon with our pact.

Ajandee: Yes, me too. Now, let us enjoy our eve-eat and then meet later, two hours before the natural light. We will have some time to think about this quandary. I am sure we will have a solution to it.

The evening passed quickly for Jarden and Ajandee. There were no problems, no incidents. Safe, so far. Jarden was pleased, but a bit anxious. Though he tried not to show it, what was on his mind the entire evening was the anticipation of meeting Ajandee later. He had a lot of thinking to do.

When they parted that evening Jarden went to his condapt to perform prayer PC. He sat in front of the shadron and watched the play of photons on the silky screen. He thought about windows and how he had learned about them in CorpColl. They must have been horrible, he thought. Why had robos wanted them, he wondered. He stared at the shadron and imagined a window in his condapt.

Time passed and Jarden was becoming quite nervous about meeting Ajandee. He had completed a full cycle on the prayer PC and was now just staring at the shadron without really seeing the calming images. He still had no ideas about the d-6. He wasn't sure what he could say to Ajandee. He hoped she had better thoughts than he did. Finally, it was time to leave.

The secret place was one that Jarden and Ajandee had found together shortly after they met. It was not entirely secluded, but it did offer a good deal of protection from other robos. Jarden got there first and slid between two plasoards that were a bit off-kilter and had left a wider opening than normal. He sat in the small dark space of their secret place and waited.

It wasn't long and he heard Ajandee squeezing through the slim opening. He moved to make space for her to sit. They greeted each other with smiles.

Jarden: Hi, hi, hey. I am so happy to see you, Ajandee.

Ajandee: Hi, hi, hey. Yes, me too. Oh, Jarden, please hold my hands. Look at me. I need to tell you something important. Something, well... very important.

Jarden looked concerned: Okay, sweets, but is it about the double-6? Did you think of a solution? Do you have some ideas?

Ajandee now had a very serious look on her face, and was staring directly into Jarden's eyes: Yes. Yes, I have. There is something I have meant to tell you for quite a while, but it is very difficult. I have concluded that now the time is ripe. I have decided that I must now tell you, although it will mean big changes for us. Big changes.

Jarden was now worried by the look on Ajandee's face and by her tone of voice: What is it, sweets? What is it that you want to tell me? You know you can tell me anything. We don't need the O-B to trust one another. Do you know who the double-6 agent is? It's not Maxim, is it?

Ajandee was still squeezing Jarden's hands tightly and staring into his eyes: No, not Maxim. But, yes, I do know who it is....

Jarden interrupted: WHAT? YOU DO? But, how could you know? No ordinary robos know who the d-6s are. How could you be sure? Ajandee, who is it? Who is the double-6 agent?

Ajandee was now beginning to cry a little and her hands were shaking: Jarden, please don't get upset. Jarden, sweets, listen, please. Jarden, it is me. I am a double-6 agent. I was given the diruler to terminate you. You are the target and I am the d-6 agent!

Now she looked down. Embarrassed. Or just sad. Or both. They still held hands, but Ajandee's hand loosened just a bit. However, Jarden squeezed harder.

Jarden was now very confused, trying to assimilate this information: You.... you.... you... but, how could that be?? Ajandee, HOW...?

Ajandee now looked up into Jarden's eyes with a soft, sympathetic, pleading look on her face: I am so sorry, sweets. I couldn't tell you before. Though, believe me, I desperately wanted to. Now, of course, I had to. But, I have broken the codes now. Now, I am in serious trouble. But, sweets, there is more... much more...

Jarden started to relax a bit: I am beginning to understand. Ajandee, it will be all right. We will be all right. Please be calm. But, sweets, who was it? Tell me... who filed the double-6 against me? Please tell me!

Ajandee now with a clear, direct voice looked steadfastly into Jarden's eyes: It was Stylla. He wants your position at Stage 58. The paperwork was all in order. It was my alternation period. I couldn't do it, of course. You are right that we don't need the O-B pact. We already have a bond-pact. One that is natural for us. Jarden, we are suited for one another. I knew that earlier, of course, but today was a moment of decision for me. Now, Jarden, listen, there is much more... We are in danger...

Jarden interrupted: Danger? What kind of danger? You mean because you told me? But, I won't tell anyone! You know that...

Ajandee: Jarden, please, please just listen. Surely you understand that if I do not complete the d-6 diruler, not only I will be in trouble, but another d-6 agent will be sent to terminate you. That is certain. However, listen to me, sweets, we do have a way out. It will not be easy, but there is a way out of this blotch-clutter...

Jarden: But, Ajandee, I don't see how we can...

Ajandee: Please, please be calm, sweets. There is a way. Listen to me. There is something that very few robos know about. Jarden, there is another Live-At for rebels. A Mid Live-At that is known only to a few. I learned of it from a rebel d-6 agent who sensed that I, too, had severe doubts. The rebel d-6 agent told me all about it before he went there. To the rebel Live-At. This rebel Live-At is called Parock. It was created years ago by some robos, like us, some robos who needed sanctuary, or who had doubts, or who did not fit in. They have created this place called Parock.

Jarden's eyes and mouth were wide open as he absorbed this incredible news: But, Ajandee, surely the Overseers know about it, about this rebel Live-At. Why has this place, Parock, not been de-toned by the Overseers?

Ajandee now squeezed Jarden's hands tightly, turned to face him straight on, stared directly into his eyes, and smiled just a wee smile: Sweets, not all of the Overseers know about the rebel Live-At, Parock. It is a serious dilemma for the Oversee Committee because if the Overseers who know about it mention it to the others they will surely be in trouble. They cannot mention it because they do not have a solution for it. To de-tone it would almost surely make it known to robos everywhere and it could become a Gladwell point. It would almost certainly create more rebels. The more robos who know about Parock, the more who will be curious, and the more who are curious, the more who will defect, and who will become rebels. The prayer PC is not infallible. The Overseers who know about this rebel Live-At prefer to just let it be and not mention it. It is not large enough – it is only a Mid Live-At – to cause trouble for them, and by keeping it under cover nearly every robo is oblivious to it. Only a few of us know about Parock.

Jarden: I am beginning to understand. It must be kept secret from the robos. But, Ajandee, are you suggesting that we must now become rebels and go to the rebel Live-At? Is that the only way out of this d-6 quandary?

Ajandee: Yes, sweets. It is the only choice we have. We are a bonded couple in many ways and we will have each other when we are there. I believe there will be others like us, others who are not accepting of the double-6, and likely there will be many rebel agents, like me, who are there. We will be accepted and will have each other. Jarden, we can even have a child there. I have been told that it is a very nice Mid Live-At, though quite different from the standard that we are used to. Still, we are flexible, Jarden, and we will be with others who feel as we do, others like us.

Jarden now released Ajandee's hand so he could rub his together. He looked at the ground and at their feet placed next to each other, so close together. He thought for a moment, then looked back at Ajandee and took her hand: I will miss Maxim, for certain. But, you are right, Ajandee, we do not have a choice anymore. The double-6 situation has put us into this blotch-clutter. We no longer have a choice. If I stayed here, surely another double-6 agent would be diruled to terminate me. And, you, Ajandee, you would be in serious trouble. We must leave soon. I only wish I had the time to fill out the papers for a prevention code against Stylla before we leave!

Ajandee, now sympathetic, reminded Jarden: I know you feel that way now, Jarden. But, we both know that we are not like that. That is not our way – the double-6. We will not now or ever contribute to the prevention code. It is not for us. And, Jarden, I do believe that Maxim will want to join us when I tell him what is going on. He is like us. I will talk with him and explain everything. Jarden, we must leave at first sunlight. Give me just a brief time to contact Maxim. I will muon him that I need to talk to him. I must see him in person and explain the situation and his options to him. I will then meet you outside your condapt at first natural light. I will arrange a Y-beam for us.

Jarden: A Y-beam?

Ajandee: Yes, there are some advantages to being a d-6 agent, you know!

Jarden smiled, accepting, even welcoming the changes to come: Okay, it is set. I will see you at first natural light.

They left the secret place, each content with the decision they had made. Ajandee sent a muon signal to Maxim. He quickly muoned her an acceptance and she went to meet with him. Jarden returned to his condapt. Ajandee and Jarden were both filled with hope.

Jarden had very little time to prepare. He put a few of his

special items into a star-sack. He glanced at the shadron which had its nighttime images glowing in a sleep-cycle pattern. He waited for the shadron to signal the initial natural light. He did not have to wait long. Soon it was time. The shadron indicated the first sun's rays were on the horizon.

Jarden took his star-sack with him and left his condapt for the last time. He would never return, but did not feel any regret. He found both Ajandee and Maxim waiting for him with a Y-beam outside his condapt. He smiled at them, and they smiled back: Hi, hi, hey.

The Y-beam was very efficient. The three were at the rebel Live-At in a short period. Jarden's first impression of Parock was that it was very welcoming and even beautiful. Ajandee had arranged for a single condapt to be prepared for Maxim and a duo-condapt for her and Jarden. They said bye to Maxim, agreeing to meet with him later, and they quickly went to find their way to their new home.

Soon, Ajandee and Jarden entered their own duo-condapt for the first time. Jarden looked around in amazement. He truly felt at home here. Somehow, he was not surprised; it seemed right to him. He smiled at Ajandee, and she smiled back. She, too, felt comfortable here with him. They could make a nice life here, they were both thinking.

Jarden walked into the main living space of the condapt and instinctively looked up at the wall. A reflex action. But this time the result was different. This time Jarden did not see a shadron on the wall. In fact, there were no shadrons at all in this rebel Live-At. No, Parock did not have shadrons. Instead, Jarden saw a window on the wall – yes, a real window. Jarden was mesmerized. He stared through the glass and was enthralled to see the heartfelt sights outside the condapt through the window.

Jarden stood quietly, without movement, for a long while simply staring through the glass.

$\sqrt{}$

"Man knows much more than he understands."
— Alfred Adler

"It's hard to believe in coincidence, but it's even harder to believe in anything else."
— John Green

"A certain man once lost a diamond cuff-link in the wide blue sea, and twenty years later, on the exact day, a Friday apparently, he was eating a large fish - but there was no diamond inside. That's what I like about coincidence."
— Vladimir Nabokov

"You don't get explanations in real life. You just get moments that are absolutely, utterly, inexplicably odd."
— Neil Gaiman

√

Ever since childhood, for as long as he could remember, Ziddian had always assumed he would one day work at the number factory.

"What are you going to be when you grow up?" he was repeatedly asked. Ziddian would smile. He knew. It was the number factory for him. He had always, always been good at threes and eights. More than good. In fact, Ziddian was absolutely the best at threes and eights. Everyone knew that. A bit weak at pi and zero perhaps, but still very good, and his overall number talent was so fantastic that Ziddian had never, ever entertained the thought of any other career. Never. Yes, it was numbers for him.

Though his younger sister incessantly teased him about it, Ziddian was sure that numbers were his game. His sister, Mauritza, was a word person all the way. Word people arrogantly assumed they were better than everyone else, even superior to sentence people and paragraph people. Words were the basis of language, of communication, they haughtily asserted, and therefore word people were at the very top in status. So, there. But Ziddian didn't care. He could take the teasing from Mauritza because he believed in numbers. He was good at numbers. He was going to be the best number person ever. He had no doubts. No doubts at all. He had never once in his whole life ever entertained the idea of anything other than working in the number factory. And that was that.

Of course, number people were stereotyped as geeks. But, to be fair, the stereotype was, in fact, correct more often than not. So maybe it wasn't a stereotype after all. Ziddian, for example, was a geek. Like all the other young men, Ziddian fantasized about being a rock star. But, being a geek, Ziddian was clumsy and uncreative. Still, he loved to pound on drums. If he had had any musical ability at all, Ziddian would have loved to be a percussion person. Pounding on things calmed him. It made him feel relaxed. Ziddian often fantasized about playing drums for a cool rock band. But, that was not to be. Ziddian's talents were in numbers, not in drumming.

Although everyone looked down on geeky number people, the truth was that the whole technical industry depended on numbers, and therefore on number people. Particularly zero and one people. Yes, a good zero person or a high quality one person could make a very good living with fabulous job security because zeros and ones would be needed forever, or so it seemed.

While adjective and adverb people were at times in demand, at other times they were laid off from their jobs. Adjective people were especially busy when there was a disaster – you know, a flood, tornado, or something. Adjectives were king then. Tops. At other times, adjectives seemed cliché and fell into down times. But zero people and one people had never even known a work slowdown. On the contrary, they were now being hired in greater numbers than ever before. Oh, to be certain, verb people, like Mauritza, were important, but it was disturbing how often they kept infringing on the work of noun people: "prioritize, friend me, google it, task him, copy me, let's network" – all of this excessive verbing of everything! Verb people were so arrogant. Number people weren't like that. Geeks, yes, but humble geeks. Well, except maybe for the zero people. Sure, zero people could be haughty at times, but, Ziddian thought, deservedly so. Not like those silly gerund people who thought they were so important. Or, the fanatical pronoun people. Give me a break! Mauritza's work was generally steady. Verbs, you know. Orders kept coming in. Of course she would be busy when there was a big political convention, but verb people generally worked at a very steady rate. In fact, all word people had plenty to do. Numbers were a bit different. Number people found that their work would ebb and flow depending on great variations in demand. Zeros and ones were hot right now, that was obvious, but still Ziddian was happy with threes and eights, and he made a good, steady living with them.

Currently, Ziddian was in the middle of a big project. Lots of threes were needed for some sort of complex architectural building. Ziddian thought it must be an art museum. Who uses so many threes any more? Ziddian had been working over time for weeks. Good money. Then the big day came. Ziddian was called to see one of the top bigwigs at the number factory: Dr. Beehive X. Bovudorp, top supervisor of all the number people. Ziddian was understandably quite nervous about his big day.

Dr. Bovudorp told Ziddian why he had recently been kept so busy with threes. Being the best three person, Dr. Bovudorp explained, Ziddian therefore had been selected for a top government project.

Ziddian smiled ever so slightly, feeling both pleasure and confirmation from Dr. Bovudorp's compliment.

The doctor continued to explain that the new project wasn't an art museum after all. A new building was being constructed for the purpose of – get this – creating another medium, another modality, that is, a new dimension in addition to words and numbers. A new dimension different from words and numbers. That's right: a new modality. So there would be words and numbers, and now this new thing, whatever it was. This was big. And, Ziddian was in on it, right on the ground floor. He was very pleased.

It had always been just words and numbers. That was it. Two modalities. But now, now there was to be another dimension… that's why so many threes were needed. The new medium was going to be based primarily on threes. And the threes had to be just right – no errors or variations would be allowed. No, there could be no mistakes in creating the new modality. That's why Ziddian had been selected for this assignment. He truly was the best three person. The top. Ziddian was dazed by the news. He stared, and he was silent. The only sound was birds twerping outside the large open windows in the back of the number factory.

"What in the world could it be?" Mauritza asked Ziddian. Understandably, under these unexpected circumstances, she was a bit nervous. Mauritza was afraid that the new modality might be more important even than words, might even have a higher status than verbs. Ziddian's news put her a bit on edge. She was feeling some trepidation about his new assignment. A new dimension? She didn't really believe it, though. It was just too preposterous to think that anything could surpass verbs. But still she was a tad on edge upon hearing the news.

"I haven't a clue," said Ziddian. Coincidentally, they were both thinking about the things called emoticons that had been popular some years ago. Emoticons had been widely used on the old computers. They were small drawings of faces showing emotions, like a happy face or a surprised face. Mostly teens and preteens used them. They had never been accepted into the adult news channels or usages, however. But, Ziddian and Mauritza were simultaneously thinking: were emoticons a new medium? Ziddian wondered. Mauritza wondered. They weren't numbers or words, were they? Still, they had not been accepted into usage. And, they had not been used for building or creating anything, like a poem, a novel, a newspaper, or a computer language. So perhaps emoticons could not be considered a third medium. Or, if they were, at least they were short-lived and not a very useful modality. Now, what would the new medium be like? Would it be something similar to emoticons? Ziddian and Mauritza stared out the window and listened to a bird tweeting far away. Nice tweeting, melodic and soothing.

The bigwigs huddled. They needed a name for the new medium, the third modality. This was important. A good name for the new dimension was very important. Many ideas were suggested by the top word people. The best names that the noun people had offered were: substantite, fundamenta, basicon, and overallian. All were fine names for a new medium of communication, for connotation and denotation, but still the bigwigs felt that none of the terms proposed by the noun people was just right. The bigwigs were perplexed. Then Dr. Beehive X. Bovudorp suggested that they ask one of the number people, perhaps someone like Ziddian, the best of the three people who was working on the project. Okay, the bigwigs agreed. Couldn't hurt to ask. Let's ask Ziddian.

Ziddian sat in front of the bigwigs. For some inexplicable reason, perhaps out of jitters, Ziddian was not fully focused on what the bigwigs were saying to him. Obviously he should have been paying very close attention at this very important meeting. But, for some enigmatic reason, Ziddian was absorbed with daydreaming while the bigwigs talked. Surprisingly, while being the center of attention in front of all these important people, Ziddian's mind flowed effortlessly and pleasantly to his recurrent fantasies. He imagined being the rock star that he had so often conjured in his mind, in his daydreams. Instead of listening to the bigwigs, Ziddian had drifted off into one of his common fantasies beating the drums in front of a cheering crowd.

They were staring at him now. The bigwigs. Staring at Ziddian. However, because of his rock star daydreaming, Ziddian had not clearly heard what they had said, what they were asking of him. Since he had been so deeply immersed in his fantasy world the only image in his mind right now was of himself sitting behind a shiny, glittering, king-sized drum set in front of a concert hall full of adoring fans, screaming and chanting his name. It was utterly bizarre, but in this awkward moment while lost in a daydream of drumming, out of Ziddian's mouth, without thinking, completely non-consciously, came but one word, "Cymbals." Yes, that's what he said to the bigwigs: "Cymbals." Ziddian then sat blank-faced, open-mouthed, staring at the bigwigs.

That's it, cried the bigwigs. Brilliant! What a genius idea. This guy is really good! Yes, "Symbols," that will be the name of the new medium, the new modality. "Symbols" it is, the bigwigs all yelped as they patted each other, and of course, Ziddian, on the back. Ziddian smiled as he was jolted out of his rock-star fantasy, still uncertain about what was happening around him or what had been said.

All Ziddian noticed then was a tiny bird sweetly chirping outside the nearby window.

SpaceWizards.com

"You can observe a lot by just watching."
— Yogi Berra

"The painter has the Universe in his mind and hands."
— Leonardo da Vinci

"An empty canvas is a living wonder... far lovelier than certain pictures."
— Wassily Kandinsky

"Not only do I not know what's going on, I wouldn't know what to do about it if I did."
— George Carlin

"Since light travels faster than sound, people appear bright until you hear them speak."
— Brian Williams

"There is no exquisite beauty… without some strangeness in the proportion."
— Edgar Allan Poe

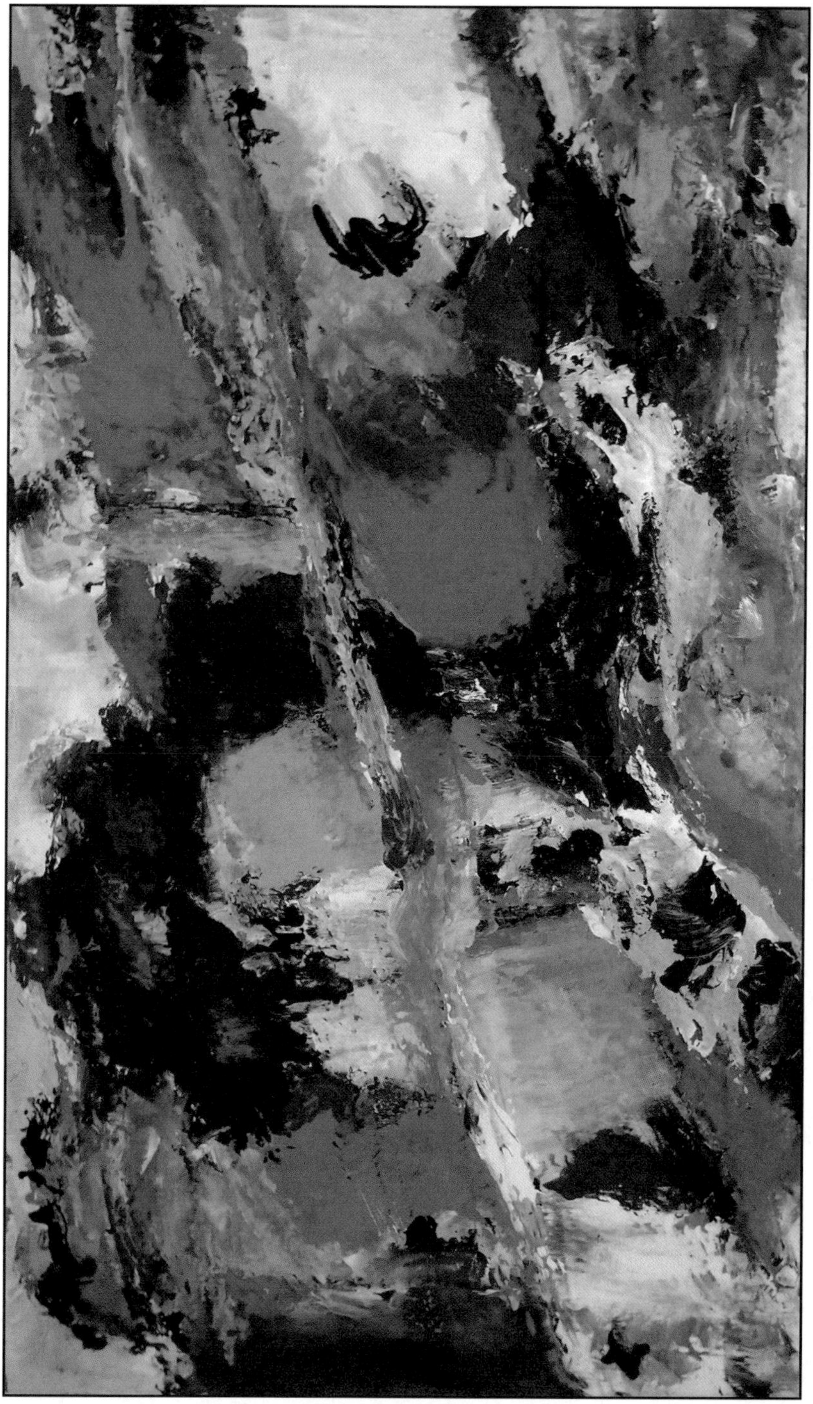

SpaceWizards.com

His friends called him "The Cat." That is, what few friends he had. Two, to be exact. The term "friends," however, is a bit generous. Perhaps "acquaintances" would be more appropriate, though that term is terribly stuffy and formal to describe these characters. "Buddies" or "pals" would fit better. Okay, his two pals called him "The Cat."

His name was Jerome John Jaguar, making obvious the derivation of the moniker. Tall, lanky, quick on his feet, "The Cat" fit him much better than Jerome.

The Cat was unemployed. Had always been unemployed. Well, that is, he'd never had a permanent, full-time job of any kind. The only work he'd had was temporary or part-time. The Cat once worked in a bakery for a couple of weeks (burned the tortes), as a lifeguard (couldn't swim), was a busboy at Luigi's Restaurant (broke too many dishes), bagged clothes at a dry cleaner's (too hot, so he quit), and planted tree seedlings just outside the city limits (came home much too dirty). Right now, The Cat wasn't working anywhere. In the very rare event when The Cat met new people, they naturally would ask about his line of work, "What do you do?" being the single most common thing said to men in contemporary society. In such instances, The Cat invariably answered, "I'm between jobs." He always said that. That was one thing The Cat had down pat. Between jobs.

On the other hand, The Cat's older brother, Jacob James Jaguar, whom everyone called Jake, had a full-time job. He worked for a computer parts company and had something to do with inventory, or parts, or shipping, or something like that, although no one in The Cat's family knew exactly what it was that Jake did. It wasn't that they weren't curious, that they didn't inquire, it was that Jake just simply wouldn't talk about his job. In fact, Jake didn't talk about much at all. Jake was not what you would call articulate or loquacious. That's one rock-certain thing you could say about Jake. Not a talker.

But at least Jake had graduated from high school, unlike The Cat. And at least Jake tried to be normal. He fished and hunted, went to all the new Hollywood action movies, ate meat, liked sports, watched porn on the Internet, masturbated daily, spat before he peed, scratched himself, wore a T-shirt that advertised some greedy corporation that sponsored sports millionaires, drank Mountain Dew, and wore his baseball cap backwards. Yes, Jake at least tried to be normal. Quite unlike The Cat, who was just plain weird. Not fashionably weird. Just weird weird.

The Cat also had a younger sister, Jennifer Joy Jaguar. Jenny, as she was called, had graduated from high school two years earlier and now worked as a waitress at The Totem Pole Supper Club and took classes at Tuber County Junior College. Jenny thought she might want to become an accountant. She was good with numbers. Not with math, just with numbers. In fact, Jenny had something of an obsession with numbers. Nonetheless, her friends still called her Jenny – not Digit, Integer, Mathy, FiveSix, or some other sobriquet that a more inventive or witty group of compadres might have saddled her with. No, they just called her Jenny.

Perhaps you've noticed the pattern with the names of the Jaguar siblings – Jacob James, Jerome John, and Jennifer Joy. The reason? Well, their parents, James John Jaguar and Juliet Jaspers Jaguar, were a bit odd – fastidious to a fault, meticulous, persnickety, and obsessively drawn to orderliness and patterns. They were pleased as punch with themselves that everyone in the family had names starting with the letter J. They often referred to their little family as "The Jays," or "The Jaybirds," and smiled broad smiles of pride and self-satisfaction when they said it. Some other people called them The Jaybirds too, but more with a snide laugh than with a smile. Some other people called them… well, let's not get into that, okay?

Similar to his sister's interest in numbers, The Cat liked to count things. Or, more precisely, The Cat didn't *like* to count things, he simply *did* count things. Very regularly. Far too regularly. The Cat was a regular counter. A far too regular counter. When The Cat went too long without counting, the perturbation was unyielding. Yes, counting was a powerful compulsion of The Cat's. Although, The Cat did not consider his counting to be a compulsion. No, any such suggestion would have put him off, put him right off. In the mind of The Cat, counting was more of an avocation, a hobby, a pastime.

Often The Cat would sit on a plastic lawn chair in his parents' garage with the garage door up, would sit and watch the cars drive by on the suburban street, and he would count. The Cat counted cars, pedestrians, animals, trees, clouds, telephone poles, and everything else he saw. The Cat would sit for hours drinking beers and sodas, eating hot dogs, chips, and cookies, would sit on a plastic lawn chair in the open garage, peering out into the afternoon happenings, and he would count. The Cat would count anything that was countable. He was an obsessive counter.

Sometimes The Cat's pals would join him in the garage, and once in a while Jake, and even occasionally Jenny, would be there, too (though more often Jenny teased The Cat about sitting in the garage and counting – she called him a geek, a dork, or a spaz). However, most often The Cat sat alone in the garage and counted.

The Cat lived in the basement of his parents' suburban home, slept on a twin bed surrounded by a dresser, a TV, a VCR, a small closet, a large boom box, a few books (mostly sci-fi paperbacks – The Cat liked reading sci-fi, but went absolutely gaga for sci-fi movies), and a desk piled with papers, posters, knick knacks, coins, and a collection of small rocks and bottle caps that The Cat had picked up at various vacation spots, mostly at lake resorts his family had visited when he was young. The Cat was particularly proud of a bottle cap that said "Blue Egyptian Soda Water" on it. It was yellow and blue and had tiny pictures of a pyramid and a sphinx neatly arranged on its small space.

The Cat's newest pal was Melvin Dalwimple, who until his sophomore year in high school was usually called Mel or Wimpie.

Melvin now enjoyed a more unique nickname, more befitting his personality. You see, in his first year of high school, Melvin and about a dozen other "slow learners" were invited to a special luncheon with the school principal. Melvin sat right next to Principal Thorpe as they enjoyed the Sloppy Joes that had been prepared by the school lunchroom staff. About midway through the luncheon, Principal Thorpe turned to Melvin, smiled a patronizing, perfunctory smile and explained to Melvin that he had been identified as "special," that he therefore had "special needs," and that the school would subsequently be providing him with "special education." Principal Thorpe's smile widened as he finished his little speech and he looked at Melvin for a response, probably expecting a "thank you."

Melvin did not smile, he looked serious, his brow wrinkled. Melvin looked into Principal Thorpe's eyes, then he looked down at Principal Thorpe's partially eaten Sloppy Joe, then he looked back at Principal Thorpe, and finally after a long moment Melvin meekly asked, "Are you going to eat your pickle?"

Ever since that day, Melvin has simply been known as Pickle. Pickle Dalwimple.

The Cat's other pal was Roger Terwiliger. Roger worked at a factory where he cut, bent, and glued clear Plexiglas sheets into box-like shapes that were used by department stores to display their wares. Essentially, Roger made clear, plastic boxes.

When people learned about Roger's line of work they invariably quoted to him the line from the movie *The Graduate* in which a middle-aged man's advice to Dustin Hoffman's character regarding a future career is "One word: plastic." Roger never saw *The Graduate*, had never even heard of *The Graduate*, and remained perplexed each time someone said "One word: plastic" to him, particularly because they always said it to him accompanied by a wink. Each time this happened, Roger merely nodded and muttered, "Uh-hmm." Roger would not be well described as eloquent. Or even informed.

Roger tended to be quiet, while Pickle on the other hand was quite loud. Pickle had some mental problems that went unnoticed by Roger and The Cat. At least they went unmentioned. Quite astonishingly, Pickle thought of himself as exceedingly normal. He had always thought of himself as exceedingly normal and continued to think of himself as exceedingly normal even though very odd things happened to him regularly. It wasn't that Pickle thought the odd things that happened to him were normal because they were happening to everyone else too, or even that Pickle reasoned that the odd things that happened to him were the result of some odd circumstances, that they were due to the situation rather than to his bizarre personality, no, rather Pickle simply didn't think about them at all. Pickle certainly would never be described as self-reflective or introspective. Pickle would better be described as emotionally disturbed.

The Cat met Pickle at a bowling alley. They had both dropped out of high school nearly ten years earlier and had since just wandered about making nothing of their lives. The day they met they were sitting in a lounge area in the front of the bowling alley, an area decorated in the standard shade of orange, each sitting with his back to the wall on adjacent sides of the large room. The Cat was distracted from counting ceiling tiles by Pickle who was very animated. Pickle was staring, waving, and smiling at the opposite wall.

You see, Pickle had seen another young man, a very familiar-looking young man, sitting directly across from him. Pickle looked at the stranger, and the stranger looked back at him. Pickle smiled at him, and the young man smiled back. Pickle waved, and the stranger waved back. Pickle nodded, and the young man across the room nodded.

"That stranger is very friendly," mused Pickle. "And he is very familiar-looking."

Pickle considered it odd that he did not recognize this friendly person, that he could not place the familiar-looking face. Meanwhile, The Cat had abandoned counting and intently watched as Pickle smiled, waved, and nodded at the opposite wall.

Eventually Pickle decided to introduce himself to the

friendly young man sitting across the room. Pickle rose to his feet and bounded across the bowling alley lounge, quickly striding across the teal-blue shag carpet, straight to the stranger who, coincidentally, also had risen from his chair and was smiling back at Pickle. Pickle soon reached the other side of the room, smiled and extended his hand to the waiting young man. The young man extended his hand, too.

As he stood staring into the stranger's eyes, it finally dawned on Pickle that the familiar looking person who had stared, smiled, waved, and nodded back at him was actually him, Pickle, that is, it was his very own image reflected in a large mirror. There was no stranger looking, smiling, waving, and nodding at him; it was merely his own reflection he had seen and interacted with. Well.

Pickle giggled and acted as if such a thing was a normal experience. "No wonder he looked so familiar," Pickle mused.

Meanwhile, The Cat had observed the whole event with Pickle and his reflected image. The Cat didn't understand what was going on. He thought Pickle might be on drugs, or rehearsing a part in a play, or perhaps was just playing around. The Cat didn't know what to think, but he started laughing. He was laughing like crazy. The Cat laughed easily and had a friendly, contagious laugh, though his sister Jenny said it made him sound like a psycho nut-case.

Anyway, that's how The Cat and Pickle met. Here's how it happened: The Cat decided to introduce himself and just walked right over to Pickle, thinking to himself, "thirty-eight, thirty-nine, forty, forty-one...."

When he reached the smiling Pickle, The Cat stopped counting long enough to inquire, "Hey, whatchya doing?"

Pickle responded, "Nothing. Just fooling around."

The Cat laughed out loud and then asked, "Do you bowl?"

"No money," replied Pickle, who was smiling broadly and giggling a bizarre giggle. Inexplicably both of his arms were loosely draped over the top of his head. He was wearing brown plaid pants, red sneakers, and a T-shirt that read, "Who wants to be normal?"

"I've got two bucks," The Cat offered generously. "We could go see *Fire-Breathing Dragons from Mars* at the dollar cinema."

"Okay," said Pickle.

And off they went. To become pals. Good pals. The Cat and Pickle.

The Cat had met his other pal, Roger, who worked in plastics, while they were in high school. They both dropped out at the same time, but they had met earlier when they were on the hockey team. Well, rather, that is, when they tried out for the hockey team. Neither of them was on the hockey team, they both had been cut right away – Roger because he couldn't skate, and The Cat because he was too distracted by his counting to pay attention to where the puck was. One time during practice The Cat was hit in the groin by the puck and even continued counting the light fixtures in the ceiling of the ice rink as he fell to the floor clutching his crotch.

"Are you okay?" asked one of the coaches.

"Twelve, thirteen, fourteen," replied The Cat.

After the Cat met Pickle he naturally wanted Roger to meet Pickle. So The Cat arranged a meeting at the same bowling alley, in the same orange lounge with the teal-blue shag carpet.

Roger had a car, an old Plymouth Valiant so rusted, faded, damaged, and oft-repaired that it was impossible to tell what the original color had been. The body of Roger's car was a patchwork of gray, brown-red, blackish burgundy, and orange-khaki. Roger called it "shmarkle." Not the car, the color. He called his car "Putnam."

Roger liked to name things. Roger spent a good deal of his time making up words for things. He enjoyed naming things but had such an impoverished vocabulary that it was easier for him to blurt out nonsense words, which he did regularly. Far too regularly. Roger didn't speak spoonerisms or malapropisms, at least not as a rule. He simply made up words for things. He neologized. He was a regular neologizer. A far too regular neologizer.

The day that The Cat was going to introduce Roger and Pickle, a Saturday, Roger picked up The Cat in shmarkle-colored Putnam and they rode to the bowling alley. They waited in the orange lounge standing on the teal-blue shag rug and The Cat recounted to Roger the circumstances when he had met Pickle. The Cat pointed to the mirror on the opposite wall and laughed explosively. (Lucky Jenny wasn't there.) Roger said the whole thing sounded splendorical, then smiled at his neologism.

Soon Pickle entered the lounge, glanced at the mirror, waved at his reflection, then put his arms on top of his head and walked with giant steps as if he were playing *Captain May I* toward The Cat and Roger.

"Hey, Pickle," The Cat shouted.

"Hey," responded Pickle.

"This is Roger." The Cat made a slight hand motion toward Roger, who was smiling a crooked smile and acting somewhat nervous.

Pickle wasn't nervous. "Hey, Roger," he said, "I bet you thought I was my brother." Pickle extended his hand toward Roger. The Cat and Roger acted as if what Pickle had said was a perfectly normal thing to say.

Roger stuck out his right hand and said, "Yes, yes I did." They shook hands.

"Okay," said The Cat, "let's go. I am so looking forward to seeing *Revenge Attack of Planet X*."

"Shattung!" said Roger enthusiastically.

And off the three went. To become three-way pals.

Oh, and on the way out of the orange bowling alley lounge, Pickle waved goodbye to his image in the mirror.

After the movie, the three pals drove in Putnam back to The Cat's house and sat on plastic lawn chairs in the garage gazing out the open door.

"Wanna beer?" asked The Cat.

"Yeah," said Roger.

"Yeah," said Pickle.

The Cat went to the refrigerator in the back of the garage, removed three bottles of Rolling Rock, and then handed one to each of his pals, keeping one for himself.

Nothing was said. The three pals unscrewed the bottle caps (Pickle took a little while to unscrew his) and threw them one at a time into a special jar that The Cat used for collecting bottle caps. As each bottle cap fell into the jar, The Cat thought to himself, "sixty-three, sixty-four, sixty-five."

This happened precisely the same way several more times that evening, with the exception that The Cat thought, "sixty-six, sixty-seven," and so on.

The three pals stared at the street, all lined up in their plastic lawn chairs straight across the front of the garage like bowling pins four through six, they drank their beers, and said nothing. The Cat silently counted to himself, Roger ruminated about a funny incident at work, an incident involving a drill press, and Pickle sat quietly thinking nothing, but occasionally giggling.

At midnight The Cat said, "I'm tired. Roger, will you give Pickle a ride home?"

"Yeah," said Roger, "that'd be bedooplorp."

Roger and Pickle left in Putnam and The Cat went to bed.

So went the first meeting of Pickle and Roger. That was four months ago and now the three pals enjoyed a friendship (er, palship), as much as was possible for three slightly bizarre, socially inept, dim-witted misfits. Little did they know what unlikely events were in store for them. Little did they know...

It all began when Jenny, The Cat's little sister, told the three pals about the Internet. Well, not the Internet per se, the three pals were not that dim-witted, but about the fact that anyone can have a website on the Internet.

"Just anyone?" asked The Cat.

"That's ridimulope," scoffed Roger.

"What?" queried Pickle.

"Yeah," assured Jenny. "Just ask Jake if you don't believe me."

So they did. They asked Jake. Jake, who was older and wiser. Jake, who had graduated from high school. Jake, who had a job at a computer parts company. Jake, who knew how to act normal.

"Yeah, I guess anyone can, if they know how to do it," explained Jake.

"How do you do it?" asked The Cat.

"Yeah, how?" echoed Roger.

"What?" said Pickle.

"Well, I don't know how to do it, but there's a guy at work named Gary who can do it."

Jake said he'd get Gary's phone number for The Cat. And he did. The very next day. The Cat then called Gary and arranged to meet with him the next Saturday.

When The Cat told Roger and Pickle about it, Roger was practically stunned since he couldn't imagine The Cat taking such initiative. He could only say, "Plarniffle!" Pickle immediately accepted the idea, he giggled, leaned back in his chair, put his arms on top of his head, and mumbled, "What's it like to be on the Internet? Does it hurt?"

On Saturday the three pals drove in Putnam to Gary's. Roger let Pickle drive, even though Pickle didn't have a driver's license and wasn't taking any of his medication. Pickle did remarkably well behind the wheel, although it turned out that when it came to using his feet on the pedals he was completely and inexplicably uncoordinated to the point of hopelessness. So The Cat sat next to Pickle and controlled the foot pedals himself while he counted the white lines on the highway. Eventually they got to Gary's, having caused only a slight dent on the single car they had sideswiped along the way. "Mastarplick," said Roger.

Gary told the three pals about creating a website and even showed them a computer. Of course, they had seen a computer before, but now that they knew that anyone, even they, could have a website, they looked at it as if it were a three-headed dog.

The Cat counted all the words on the screen, lickety-split; Roger daydreamed about what kind of website they might create (something about plastics, he imagined); and Pickle giggled at the idea of squeezing his large frame into such a small monitor.

On the way home The Cat said, "We should do it."

"But I'm kinda large. And it costs a lot," said Pickle, who giggled and stuck out his tongue.

Roger was firmly committed and said, "Pitanwick! I have my money from work. We could use that."

That was how it began. The game was afoot for the three pals.

The Cat met with Gary a number of times, gave him some money that he got from Roger, and told Gary to create a website called SpaceWizards.com.

The three pals now spent most of their time planning their website. They decided it had to be about science fiction. The Cat would be the manager, the boss of things, Roger would make up words and stories, and Pickle would add humor. They made up a story about outer space, a battle between good and evil, and a secret society of interplanetary explorers who had special powers. Their main character, Hunk Man, had super strength and could transport himself through space and time at the speed of light. The three pals made crude little drawings and sketches of their superheroes, rocket ships, laser guns, space creatures, explosions, and exotic planets. Pickle's drawings were especially, err… ingenious. They gave all of these to Gary, who was the Web master for SpaceWizards.com.

But Gary said that The Cat should have a computer too, with Internet hookup, so he could make changes to their website. Gary could get him all set up for about five hundred dollars. But The Cat didn't have five hundred dollars. The Cat didn't know how to get five hundred dollars. The Cat started counting, counting to five hundred.

The next day, The Cat, Roger, and Pickle rode in Putnam to a warehouse-style sporting goods store. Jenny's birthday was soon and The Cat wanted to buy her a gift, maybe a tennis racket or a volleyball, although she didn't play either sport.

It was there, at the sporting goods store, where The Cat discovered his talent.

"Lookee there, that's some blarkum," said Roger, pointing at a promotional display – a large, clear plastic sphere full of golf tees. A sign read, "GUESS THE NUMBER OF GOLF TEES AND WIN $500."

The three pals looked. Pickle asked if the display was meant for him or for his brother. Roger repeated, "That's some blackum." And then added, "We should try to guess."

The Cat's eyes widened and his mouth gaped. He looked at Roger intently and gasped, "Guess? Shoot, I can tell you exactly how many tees are in there!"

"What?" said Pickle.

"Outmodiferonset!" said Roger.

The Cat filled out the little white slip of paper. In the space that read YOUR GUESS _____, The Cat carefully wrote 2,919. He placed the folded slip into a slot in the top of a box. The Cat then bought some pink sport socks for Jenny and the three pals rode home in Putnam.

Three weeks later The Cat got a phone call informing him that he had won the contest. The three pals went to the store and saw a sign proudly proclaiming the correct number of golf tees: 2,919. The Cat's name was displayed as the grand prize winner.

The Cat had his five hundred dollars and he promptly gave it to Gary. Soon The Cat had a computer sitting atop his dresser. Every day he checked the SpaceWizards,com website, often adding things or changing the stories and pictures that were there. The site was not very popular, but it did get a few hits from transient Web surfers, sci-fi aficionados (nerdy teenaged boys), and a few of the Internet-obsessed.

"Cool," said The Cat. "We have our own website. Let's put our pictures on it."

"Yeah," said Roger. "That would be way starleckickity."

Pickle giggled and wondered, "Would people think the picture was of me or my brother?"

The three pals dreamed that some big corporation would buy their website for millions of dollars and they would have it made in the shade. They mused for hours on what they would do with the money. Pickle wanted to buy lots of popsicles. Roger said he'd quit his job, buy a big old RV, and travel out West. He particularly wanted to go to Montana. The Cat was happy the way things were and thought the money would be great only to make life a bit easier, to help his family, and stuff.

Each day The Cat updated the SpaceWizards.com website and each day he ventured more and more into cyberspace. It was difficult for The Cat to pay attention to all the information on the Internet since he spent most of his online time counting this and that on the screen.

One Saturday The Cat was showing his pals some other websites that he had discovered during his limited cyber surfing.

"Hey," interrupted Roger, "what's that weird word?" Roger pointed to an ad in the upper right corner of the monitor, an ad for eBay. "That's a coolisimo word – eeeebaaayyy!"

"Plant it now and see it grow," offered Pickle. "My brother would do it too."

The Cat for once in his life, perhaps the only time, acted spontaneously and impulsively. He clicked his mouse on the eBay icon.

"Auction? You mean buy things?" queried Roger.

"And sell, too," replied The Cat. "Hey, we could sell some of our junk and maybe get some more cash to keep up SpaceWizards.com"

It took a few months for the idea to sink in, but eventually The Cat asked Gary to help him list some of his bottle caps and other collectibles on eBay. Most of them didn't get any bids at all. But the bottle cap that said "Blue Egyptian Soda Water" turned out to be a very rare antique and was coveted by a small, very wealthy group of collectors. The Cat found it all inexplicable, but he watched in earnest and with overwhelming fascination as the bidding increased day by day. When the time limit was nearly up, The Cat was astonished to watch the bidding go through the roof! The final bid shocked The Cat into near silence.

When The Cat had recovered a bit, he told his pals. Roger was stunned and could utter only, "eeeebaaaayyy!" Pickle didn't completely understand what was going on. He stood giggling with his arms draped loosely over the top of his head. He was wearing a white

T-shirt that read SPACEWIZARDS.COM, which he had lettered himself using red crayon. The letter R was printed backwards. Pickle said, "I bet you thought my brother won the money."

"Yeah, I did," said The Cat.

The Cat accepted the highest bid for the Blue Egyptian Soda Water bottle cap and Gary made the arrangements to send it to the buyer in Germany. He also arranged for a bank account for The Cat in order to handle the transfer of funds. It took about two weeks. Naturally eBay and the government got their shares of the purchase price, but the remaining amount was more than the three pals had ever dreamed. The Cat generously gave a share of the money to Roger and Pickle, and a smaller share to Gary. The Cat saved a big, round number for himself.

Later the three pals sat in their plastic lawn chairs, like bowling pins four through six, in the front of The Jaybirds' garage, staring out onto the afternoon happenings. Pickle was sucking on a popsicle, Roger had quit his job making plastic boxes and was leaving for Montana in a few days in his new Winnebago, and The Cat was smiling a contented smile.

As the afternoon sun crept slowly across a clear blue sky, the three pals sat in their lawn chairs, sipped Rolling Rock, and each in his own way contemplated the recent events that had changed their lives. Pickle was thinking about using his share of the money to build a grand amusement park. Roger was creating a new story for the SpaceWizards.com website, which, now that the word had been spread about The Cat's eBay success, was exceedingly popular, a cult hit. The new sci-fi story Roger was creating was inspired by *The Planet of the Apes*, except in Roger's version instead of apes it was dimwit humans that control the Earth.

And The Cat? Well, The Cat sat quietly counting to himself, as always. The Cat wasn't counting anything in the suburban neighborhood, he wasn't counting objects, he wasn't counting anything at all. He was simply counting. Totally preoccupied and smiling a contented smile, The Cat was slowly and meticulously counting to two million.

Top Ten List

"Every revolutionary idea seems to evoke three stages of reaction. They may be summed up by the phrases:
(1) It's completely impossible.
(2) It's possible, but it's not worth doing.
(3) I said it was a good idea all along."
— Arthur C. Clarke

"The only reason people get lost in thought is because it's unfamiliar territory."
— Paul Fix

"The great pleasure in life is doing what people say you cannot do."
— Walter Bagehot

"Never miss a good chance to shut up."
— Will Rogers

"Granted, most writers I know are a bit strange. Some, downright weird."
— Christopher Hopper

Top Ten List of the Most Common Moods or Temperaments Possessed by Fictional Characters (Read: Men) Who Appear in Short Stories or Creative Fiction or Short-Short Literary Works that Have Been Accepted For Publication in Today's Ultra-Hip, Postmodern, Contemporary-Styled, Non-Genre, Literary Journals

10. Petulance
9. Bewilderment
8. Ennui
7. Angst
6. Ironic Detachment
5. Sullenness
4. Piquancy
3. Sardonicism
2. Knowing Bemusement

And the number one most common mood seen in creative fiction today is.....

1. Anhedonia

Longest on the charts:

18. Apathetic Nihilism

Rising fastest on the charts:

12. Sarcastic Disdain

The Invisible Man

"The public have an insatiable curiosity to know everything, except what is worth knowing."
— Oscar Wilde

"We live in a strange world where people don't try to know who we are, rather they go by what they think we are!"
— Ramana Pemmaraju

"Anyone who says he can see through women is missing a lot."
— Groucho Marx

"We are an impossibility in an impossible universe."
— Ray Bradbury

"I have an existential map; it has 'you are here' written all over it."
— Steven Wright

The Invisible Man

Spencer was invisible. As far back as he could remember, he had always been invisible, at least part of the time. He first became aware of it in childhood, but he noticed it had gotten worse as he got older. Now Spencer found that he was invisible nearly all the time.

Spencer lived in a big city. When he walked down the street, although there were dozens of people nearby, not one of them could see him. No one looked at him at all! Spencer found it quite amazing. No one ever greeted him, though hundreds of people passed by him daily. They all stared into space or right through him. Also, when Spencer entered an elevator, no matter how many others were there, they all stared persistently at the numbers above the door. No one saw Spencer. No one spoke to him or reacted to him. When inside a building, the same was true. He was invisible. He could walk the halls amongst other people and not one person would look at him or acknowledge his presence. If Spencer attempted to enter a room, quite often there would be people standing and chatting in his way, congregating right in the doorway. When Spencer arrived, they did not move, they did not look at him, they did not acknowledge his presence; they simply stood unmoving and continued chatting without a glance at him. Spencer was invisible.

Spencer also noticed that when he was talking to others they usually could not hear him. When he spoke, others looked away, fiddled with their clothes or fingers, or started conversations with others; they did not respond whatsoever to what Spencer said. Apparently Spencer was not only invisible, Spencer was also inaudible. Spencer talked, but no one seemed to hear him. He could ask questions, tell jokes, or relate funny events, but nearly every time, the people around him did not respond, did not make eye contact, did not see or hear him. In fact, they often began talking to others while Spencer had not yet finished a comment. Spencer was invisible and inaudible.

One day Spencer stopped using deodorant. Since he was invisible and inaudible, he reasoned that perhaps he also was inolfactible. And, yes, it was true, no one seemed to notice. No one told Spencer that he smelled bad. No one at all. Spencer moved invisibly, inaudibly, and inolfactibly amongst others. No one noticed him. The Invisible Man.

Spencer was aware that, just like Claude Rains who pl yed the Invisible Man ch racter in the movies, he did in fact leave footprints. When walking in the snow or on the beach, for exa ple, Spencer looked behind and s w his prints. Unli e the case with Claude Rains, however, no one else seemed to notice Spencer's fo tprints. To other people, Spencer s emed not to exist. Spencer mov d in his milieu without being ackn wledged, recogn zed, approached, or ad ressed by anyone. It was as if he didn't exist. Well, exc pt for the footp ints. Oh, and a mir or reflection that S encer could see. Others did n t seem to be aw re of t e reflec ion, h w ver.

Sp ncer oft n wond red w at was hap eni g to him. W s he like the Inc edible Shri king M n from the movies who had encounte ed a str nge mist at sea that ca sed h m to gra ual y vanish? Had Spen er be n engulfed by some stra ge m st, too? He c ul n't r me ber it. Alt ough, there was ne tim as a ch ld when he w s cau ht in th rain a d got very wet. Co d it hav be n acid r in hat caus d hi to g adu- al y beco e inv sib e? Sp cer o ten mull d o er h s fa e, but h dn't the fai test id a wh t ca se hi to be i vi ible or w t he cou d do abo t it.

S e c r som g e, i u ion nt.
ion d; he ey. T on
fr goi en. W th , rt
h un t n. S , t r y wa g i s e i
ve o o li e i nny. as
o rs ch m. St , a s t y o
S lly h
e d id
e. He

altho . Rig th und
er t
visi b e at
ally bu her ost,
getti inst
, nce
on plea th ion.
, ty inv t. m,
me or ; fortu

ne ace. ed. Ju
r tt

ee s.
nei

Sp

e

y.

Another Scotch

"Hell is other people."
— Jean-Paul Sartre

"All my life I've wanted to be somebody; I realize now that I should have been more specific."
— Lily Tomlin

"I don't know why we are here, but I'm pretty sure that it is not in order to enjoy ourselves."
— Ludwig Wittgenstein

"The secret to happiness is to face the fact that the world is horrible."
— Bertrand Russell

"He who laughs last has not heard the bad news."
— Bertolt Brecht

Another Scotch

He made a clever, insightful quip. She looked down at her cheese.

He quoted a philosopher. She stared blank-faced at him, then quickly looked away.

He tried to catch her gaze, but she demurred.

Then she asked him what TV shows he liked. He said he liked old classic movies. She was adjusting a button on her sweater while he answered. She offered no response.

She asked how long he had been on computer dating. He said not very long, that he didn't like it and wanted to quit. Then she made fun of a man whom she had met online who believed that a nice date might be going to a Red Lobster restaurant. She made a disgusted face. She wanted a professional man, she insisted. Her eyes widened a bit. He then suggested that maybe they should go to Red Lobster on their next date. She was cleaning a spot off her wine glass with her napkin and did not hear his ironic suggestion, didn't get the sardonic humor, didn't understand his point. Snobbery is a hierarchy. Everyone is a snob, it seems, from the top on down, each in turn disdaining those considered beneath. He decided not to bring up this boring point of view.

She asked why he didn't like computer dating. He said it didn't seem like dating at all, rather it seemed to him like shopping. Computer shopping. Shopping for people. When he wrote to women, if they responded at all, it was with what seemed a command, Where's your photo? They demanded to know what he looked like before they would communicate with him. That seemed shallow and superficial, he said. They weren't even polite about it, he added. She replied that she wouldn't write to someone who didn't have a photo. Okay, he said, I guess that makes sense. He took a sip of wine.

She told him of a male friend who went through 165 women on computer dating before finding one he liked. Her male friend had counseled her that finding a companion was like work. You had to do the work, to put in the hours and the proper analytical search, in order to find a desirable mate. She smiled and looked at him.

He replied that this was exactly his complaint. People are not products. Relating to other people should not be a work project. Dating should not be like choosing a refrigerator or a pair of pajamas. There is no romance, poetry, or humanity in such a cold system, he said.

He then smiled and suggested that in a few years when computers are conscious, when machines are sentient… (slight pause while looking at her with expectation in his eyes…. but, she was studying her nails, she didn't respond, there was no reaction on her face; curious, he thought)… then computer dating will be perfect for machines, for computers, he continued. The computers can shop for one another on their own online dating site. Then he kidded in a mock computer tone of voice: "Where is your photo? Show me your photo!"

She apparently did not hear his little amusement, his bon mot. Rather, while he was joking she was intently studying an attractive woman who was walking past their table. She slowly looked the passing woman up and down, assessing her clothes, her weight, her shoes and hair. When done, she recounted the tale of a female friend who met a nice French man during a trip to Spain. Yes, he said, that seems a bit more like what I would prefer, a bit more human, more romantic. As usual, he felt old-fashioned, out of date.

The bill for the cheese and wine came. She stared at him, smiling a tiny smile, saying nothing, sitting quite still, not reaching for the tab or for her purse. He handed the waiter a credit card. He added a tip and signed.

Now for the denouement, he thought. He walked her to her car. They stood awkwardly near her car door. There was an ungainly hug during which she twisted her body and head away from him in a manner that felt coarse and discomfiting. They said goodbye.

He walked to his car and watched as she drove away. He sat in the driver's seat and stared at his face in the rear view mirror; he pondered: person or product?

Finally, after a minute's reflection, he drove home. There he poured himself a glass of scotch, put on his reading glasses, and grabbed a book.

It was a mystery.

The Strange Disappearance of Mr. Bonkers

"You're entirely bonkers. But I'll tell you a secret. All the best people are."
— Lewis Carroll

"The world is full of magic things, patiently waiting for our senses to grow sharper."
— W.B. Yeats

"Nonsense is good only because common sense is so limited"
— George Santayana

"I plan on living forever. So far, so good."
— Anonymous

"You're not going to get weird on me, are you?"
"How exactly would I get weird on you?"
"I don't know, but the way you just said weird felt a little weird to me."
— Thomas Pierce, Hall of Small Mammals: Stories

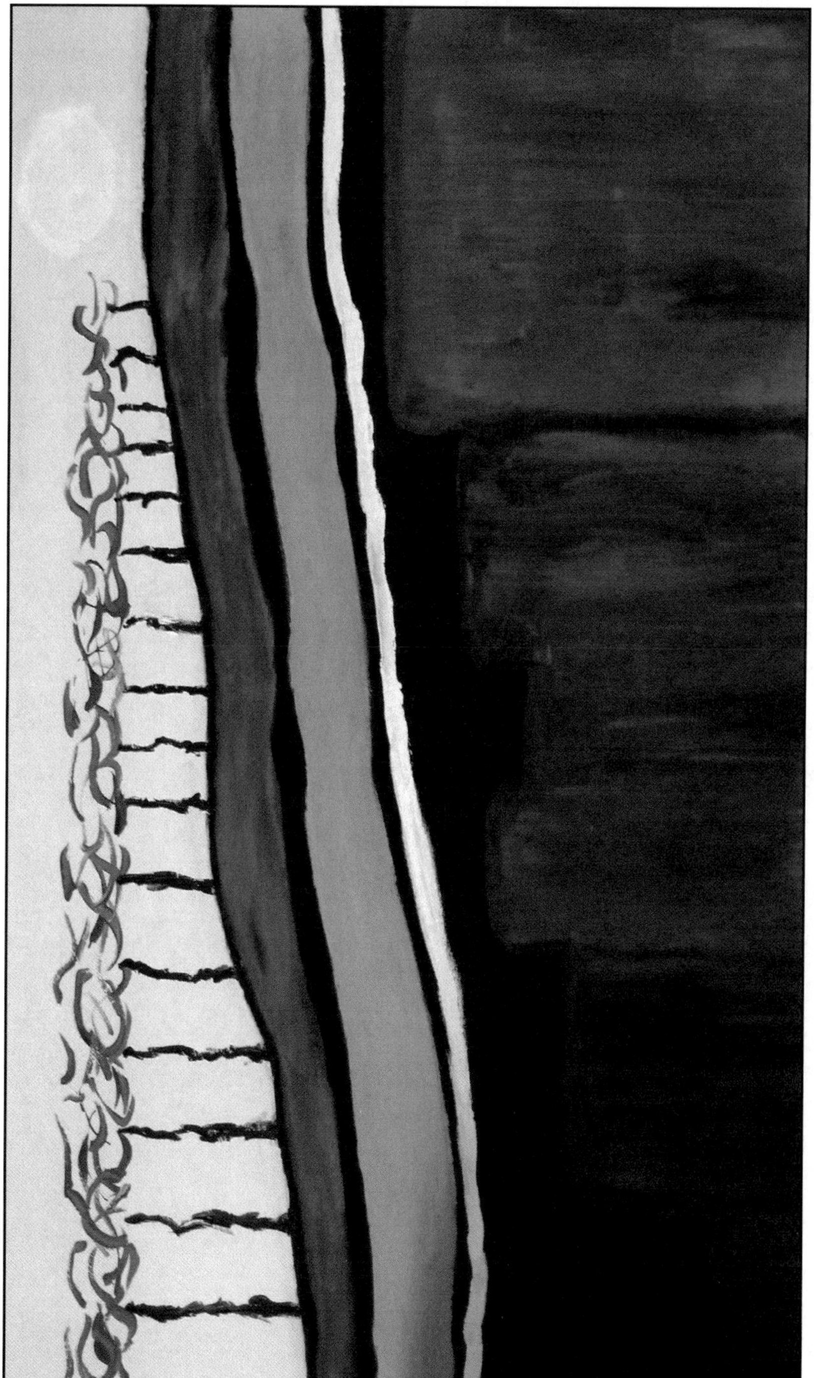

The Strange Disappearance of Mr. Bonkers

It had been quite a while, Mrs. Bonkers mused, since she last saw her husband, Mr. Bonkers. People say that things happen suddenly, like "suddenly one day he was gone," but the disappearance of Mr. Bonkers didn't seem sudden at all to Mrs. Bonkers. It definitely seemed gradual. Although, to be fair, her memory really was quite confused on the matter. Mr. Bonkers clearly wasn't around now, but Mrs. Bonkers could not recall how long it had been since she had last seen him. How long had it been? Mrs. Bonkers vaguely remembered seeing Mr. Bonkers around the house about a year ago. Or, so she thought. He's certainly not here now, so far as Mrs. Bonkers can tell. She just doesn't remember seeing him around for quite some time.

Mrs. Bonkers came from a small family and never had many friends. She does have one sibling, however, a sister, a Siamese twin named Katinka. Mrs. Bonkers is named Irinka. The sisters are very close. In fact, Mrs. Bonkers met her husband, Mr. Bonkers, through her sister Katinka. You see, they had previously been married to each other, Katinka and Mr. Bonkers. They had been married for about three months. The marriage did not work out because Mr. Bonkers claimed that Katinka was not his type. He didn't go for conjoined twins, he had explained. Still, ironically, shortly after their divorce Mr. Bonkers started dating Irinka. People are funny like that.

Mr. Bonkers and Irinka got married shortly after they started dating. Katinka was the maid of honor at their wedding, which was convenient. Fortunately, Katinka did not seem to hold a grudge about her conjoined sister marrying her ex-husband, Mr. Bonkers. However, during the wedding ceremony a strange, perhaps revealing, event happened. When it came time for Irinka to say "I do," her left arm (well, her only arm) inexplicably jerked forward and Irinka punched Mr. Bonkers hard in the stomach. Mr. Bonkers bent over, gave a cough, and his face turned bright red. Katinka turned her head to the side and smiled, maybe even giggled a silent giggle. Then the wedding ceremony continued.

Now it had been quite a while since Mrs. Bonkers recalled seeing her husband, Mr. Bonkers, around the house. She just hadn't noticed him missing for who knows how long? It's funny how that goes. It was odd, she accepted, but she had been busy with other matters and just didn't notice that he wasn't around, she rationalized. "Where could Mr. Bonkers have gone off to?" she sometimes wondered. But most of the time Mrs. Bonkers simply didn't think about the missing Mr. Bonkers.

One morning Mrs. Bonkers asked her conjoined sister if she had seen Mr. Bonkers lately. "No," Katinka replied. "Well, that's very odd," responded Mrs. Bonkers to the former Mrs. Bonkers, "it seems he was here a little bit ago, but now I seem to have misplaced him. I wonder where he could be?"

Katinka said nothing.

A few days later Mrs. Bonkers had a funny feeling about the disappearance of Mr. Bonkers and Katinka's reaction to it. Something nagged at Irinka. There were indications that something was off. For instance, when she had asked her conjoined twin sister if she had seen Mr. Bonkers lately, Katinka had merely said, "No," yet Mrs. Bonkers detected a slight tingling sensation in her spleen at that very moment, noticed that Katinka's face evidenced the glimmer of a tic – a slight spasm of the cheek muscle – and also noted that Katinka had turned to look away from Irinka's face, perhaps in an attempt to conceal the facial twitch. That seemingly minor, perhaps trivial, incident gave Mrs. Bonkers an eerie notion. She had the heebie jeebies. She felt that something surely was up. So, after a few days Irinka broached the subject again with her Siamese twin sister.

"Katinka, are you sure you have not seen Mr. Bonkers lately?"

"Yes, I am sure. I have not seen him around."

Katinka's eyes darted sideways and Irinka noticed the facial tic was there again. And, so too, was the tingling in the spleen of Mrs. Bonkers.

"Katinka, is there something you want to tell me?"

"No."

Well, that was that. No sense beating a dead horse. Katinka was not talking.

However, there was another unusual incident that bothered Mrs. Bonkers. Katinka was having some very frightening dreams as of late. You see, during sleep sometimes a dream or a fragment of a dream could seep from one conjoined twin to the other. The phenomenon is called 'dream seeping' and it is one of those idiosyncratic experiences known only to Siamese twins. Through this strange mechanism Mrs. Bonkers had observed that Katinka was having some unsettling, even downright scary, dreams lately. This matter was duly noted and filed in the subconscious mind of Mrs. Bonkers.

Some time passed and Mrs. Bonkers had mostly forgotten about the disappearance of Mr. Bonkers and the somewhat puzzling and disturbing reaction of her sister Katinka. Now it was spring and time to do some spring cleaning. This entailed a trip to the attic – an annual occurrence. The conjoined twins went together to the musty upstairs storage area to clean, arrange memorabilia stored there, and to throw out what they could stand to see gone – though, truth be told, each year more objects were placed in the attic than were removed. It was on this particular trip to the attic that Mrs. Bonkers discovered the reason for the disappearance of Mr. Bonkers.

While scavenging through the clutter that was scattered and piled in the dusty space, Mrs. Bonkers bumped into an assortment of old rugs. The pile of rugs moved in an odd way, as if something soft and squishy was beneath it. While Irinka was contemplating the odd lumpiness of the rugs, at that very moment Katinka pulled in the opposite direction and inquired, "Irinka, where is that old gray sweater we wore in high school?" Mrs. Bonkers did not answer her sister. Mrs. Bonkers was suspicious that Katinka was trying to distract her from the large mushy bump on the floor. Hence, Mrs. Bonkers continued staring down at the pile of rugs, although she was being aggressively pulled sideways by her sister. As a consequence, Mrs. Bonkers had to twist and stretch her neck awkwardly. That is the very moment when the dreams came flooding back to her, flowed into her consciousness – the dreams that had seeped through from Katinka, the scary, alarming dreams. Apparently the cockeyed wrenching of Irinka's neck had loosened the dreams from her subconscious mind and they now came tumbling into her awareness like lava erupting from a hot volcano and flowing down a mountain side. The memory of Katinka's dreams flowed from her subconscious mind directly into the conscious awareness of Irinka Bonkers.

The dreams were surreal. They involved strong emotions, sexual tension, and a vivid ambience of terror. One dream had lots of blood, another chaotic screaming, and still another powerful jealousy. This is what had seeped through from the brain of Katinka to the now conscious mind of Irinka. Well, you can imagine, the effect of the dreams bursting into her awareness while she was simultaneously staring at the curious bulge beneath the pile of rugs made Mrs. Bonkers feel a deep, all-consuming sense of anxiety. What could it all mean? At that very moment Mrs. Bonkers experienced an overwhelming, irresistible impulse to look under the uneven, lumpy stack, even while Katinka continued to pull at her in an attempt to distract her. Mrs. Bonkers became uncomfortably aware of her own fears of what might be creating the irregular bump beneath the rugs on the attic floor, and hence experienced not only a penetrating urge to look under the rugs, but, too, a deep dread of what she would find there.

And, that is when it happened. The flood gates burst open. It was the moment of truth, the kairos, the revealing crunch, the climactic instant, the big enchilada, the definitive answer to the strange disappearance of Mr. Bonkers. Irinka reached down toward the mysterious protuberance, struggling with difficulty against the reverse pull of Katinka, stretching her arm and half-body, pulling Katinka sideways with her, and then abruptly, unexpectedly, their feet gave loose and the two conjoined sisters lost their balance and fell, kerplunk, directly atop the irregular protrusion on the attic floor. Katinka screamed and appeared to suffer a minor seizure. Her eyes rolled back in her head, her mouth gaped open, and her half-body shivered. Irinka stared at her sister, speechless and confused, her mind now a jumble of unsettling thoughts and fears. Below her she felt the mushy, uneven lump. But then, remarkably, Katinka spoke. The words tumbled out of her. She could hold it back no longer. Her overpowering guilt propelled her to confession. She was as if in a trance, a psychoanalytic dissociative state, that compelled her to speak.

Mrs. Bonkers sat wide-eyed and listened keenly as her conjoined sister confessed the unbelievable events of the past year. Katinka began by dropping a bombshell: Katinka and Mr. Bonkers were having an affair! They had been sneaking around behind Irinka's back. Well, not exactly behind her back, rather a bit to the side. "But how is that possible," Irinka asked, "without me knowing?" Katinka then dropped another bombshell: she had concealed the affair by hypnotizing her sister. Katinka explained that she had seen an advertisement in the newspaper and signed up for hypnosis training sessions. She later had hypnotized Irinka and gave her a post-hypnotic suggestion to forget the hypnosis training they had attended. Oh, and of course, also commanded Irinka to forget about Katinka's affair with Mr. Bonkers.

Katinka continued her story while Irinka sat astonished, hardly comprehending the incredible tale now spilling from her sister's mouth. The affair had gone on for several months, Katinka elucidated, but reached a nadir when Mr. Bonkers once again claimed that he was not into conjoined twins and wanted to break things off with her. Katinka was devastated and could not tolerate the idea of losing Mr. Bonkers once again. In a state of frenzy and near panic, Katinka had poisoned Mr. Bonkers and placed his body in the attic beneath the jumble of old rugs. And, Katinka explained, again she had hypnotized Irinka and ordered her to repress all memory of the gruesome incident. That's when her horrible dreams began. Dreams driven by her deep sense of guilt.

Irinka stared at her sister in utter disbelief. How could this be? I thought Mr. Bonkers was true to me, she told herself. My sister, too. And then yet another bombshell transpired: Irinka felt the lump beneath her move. She also heard a muffled, moaning-like sound resonating from the moving lump. The sisters awkwardly clambered to their feet and stood glaring at the mass of rugs and the moving lump, their mouths agape and their faces frozen in stunned expressions. From beneath the pile of rugs slowly arose the lump, which fantastically proved to be Mr. Bonkers. Yes, Mr. Bonkers, inconceivably still quite alive. Katinka stammered, "I, I, I…" Irinka exclaimed, "It's alive, it's alive, it's alive!"

Apparently, the dosage of poison that Katinka had used had not been entirely effective. Mr. Bonkers was not dead, but had simply been in a mild coma. He was now awake and aware, though a bit drowsy and befuddled. Mr. Bonkers sat on the attic floor, the old dusty rugs across his lap, and he gawked at the twins for quite some time, slowly looking back and forth from Irinka to Katinka. Likewise, the twins silently goggled back at Mr. Bonkers with looks full of bewilderment. For a long time all was quiet in the musty attic. Finally, Mr. Bonkers broke the silence. He leaned forward, glared intently at the faces of the sisters, and then ardently asserted to Irinka and Katinka, "I'm starving!" For a long while the twins continued to stare dumbfounded at Mr. Bonkers, and then at last Irinka said, "Well, of course you are, dear. Come to the kitchen and we will fix you a nice bite to eat."

Mr. Bonkers arose clumsily from his long-held spot on the dusty attic floor, brushed himself off, and then he and the twins wriggled down the attic steps to the hallway below. The twins shuffled into the kitchen and Mr. Bonkers sat at the dining room table awaiting a meal, his head still a bit cloudy after being comatose for so long, but the mental fog was eclipsed by his teeming hunger.

The conjoined twins stood before the kitchen cupboards, each in a similar mindset of deep thought and reflection mixed with disbelief and confusion. Mrs. Bonkers reached for the bread while

Katinka twisted her body enough to grasp the tea kettle. Katinka then placed a cup on the counter directly in front of the two conjoined sisters. Irinka was busy preparing a sandwich but felt the tug of Katinka bending down and reaching under the counter. When the former Mrs. Bonkers stood up she was holding what appeared to be a dark brown bottle marked with three large red Xs.

Irinka stared at her sister in astonishment and perplexity, and then meekly inquired, "Is that poison?"

"Why, yes, it is," responded Katinka.

"Well," replied Mrs. Bonkers, "be sure to use a double dose this time."

Simon Says

"This world is but a canvas to our imagination."
— Henry David Thoreau

"I have no fear of making changes, destroying the image, etc., because the painting has a life of its own."
— Jackson Pollock

"The true work of art is born from the 'artist': a mysterious, enigmatic, and mystical creation. It detaches itself from him, it acquires an autonomous life, becomes a personality, an independent subject, animated with a spiritual breath, the living subject of a real existence of being."
— Wassily Kandinsky

"The most interesting painting is one that expresses more of what one thinks than of what one sees."
— Mark Rothko

"Art finds her own perfection within, and not outside of, herself.
She is not to be judged by any external standard of resemblance."
— Oscar Wilde

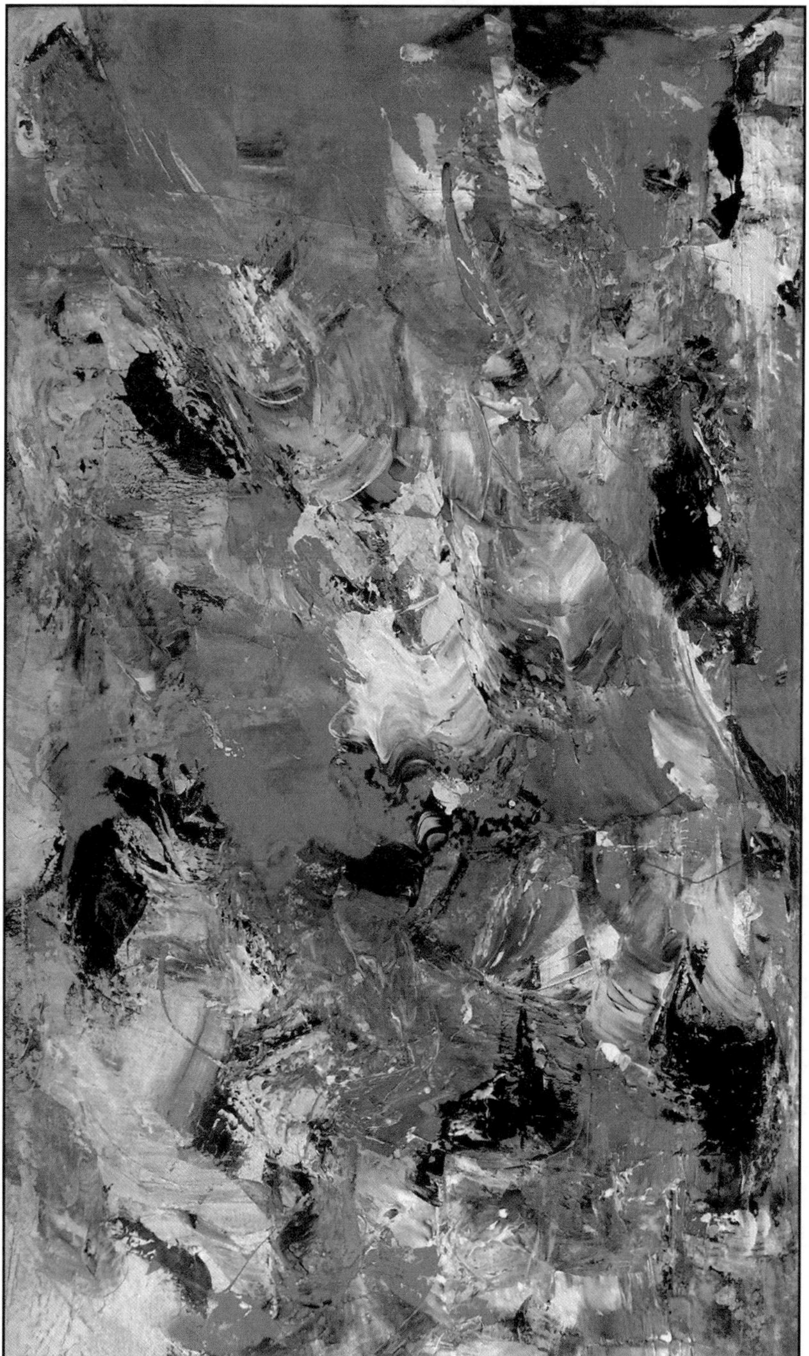

Simon Says

Let me begin by saying that everything in this story, all the places, settings, characters, events, and so on – everything – is completely, entirely true. Absolutely true.

Oh, wait, no, no, gosh, I'm so sorry, why did I say that? I mean everything is false! Not true. Made up. Everything in this story is false, absolutely, entirely false. Fictitious. Invented. Fake. As they say in the movies – the people and events in this story are not real nor are they intended to represent any real persons or any real events.

Yes, totally true. Oh, no, no, oh my gosh, I did it again, so sorry, really, really sorry, of course I mean totally false. Yes, everything is false. Absolutely false. Everything in this story is false.

Oh, no, but wait, wait just a minute, let me think about this… some of it must be true, I mean, of course the characters and events in this story represent reality in certain aspects, in certain, umm, details, of course. I mean, the people in the story will not be aliens, or furniture, or plastic yoyos, or whatever – they are people! People with the same physical features, mental and emotional states, hopes and desires, and other characteristics, just as you and me and everyone else. Yes, of course, some things in this story are true. The characters, they are people like you. Just like you. Yes, of course, just like you.

Well, wait, wait again, let me think this through, they, I mean the characters in this story, are not exactly like you, naturally. That would be weird. I mean, what if by pure coincidence one of the characters in this story was you, or, I mean, was exactly like you, or was a representation of you, I guess? I mean, in words, of course, not physically, not in body reality. But, I mean using words, the character described was you, or like you, just like you in description. Wouldn't that be weird? What is the probability of that happening, I mean that you would be reading about a character that is you? What are the chances of that? I don't know. I certainly don't know. But I know it would be weird. Well, at least I think it would be weird, wouldn't it? Isn't that right? Wait, was that the phone? Was that my phone ringing?

Can a piece of art be just what it is? I mean does art, a painting or a story, for example, have to represent something else, have to be interpreted by the mind, or can it have a reality of its own, live on its own terms? If you look at a painting, it is just colors on a flat surface, right? Does it have to be interpreted as a representation of a tree, a flower, a portrait, a figure, or anything from the real world, the world of our visual experience? Can't it just be paint on a flat surface? Does art have to represent? What about a story? Can it just be letters and words on paper, can it be itself, live on its own, or does it have to represent something real, something outside of the ink and paper?

No, I don't think that was my phone. Was it yours? Anyway, back to what I was trying to tell you: everything in this story is true. No, no, no, darn, I can't believe I did it again! Duh – why do I keep saying that? What is wrong with me? What I am trying to tell you, of course, is that everything in this story is false. Yes, false. Well, except that some parts are true, of course, as I was trying to explain, in the sense that these elements of the story represent reality sort of, that is, in a small way, a normal way. Okay? Is that right? I don't know, I'm just not sure how to say it, how to explain it, it's too confusing, I'm just lost, I don't know what I think, but, well, okay, let's just begin…

Simon sat at his desk preparing his lecture. He only had 20 minutes before class, but he had given this lecture so many times before that 20 minutes was plenty of time. He only had to remind himself of the sequence of ideas and the few revisions he had recently made to the PowerPoint slides. That wouldn't take long. Simon Pharaoh had taught microbiology for twenty-three years. Today's lecture on cell division was a snap for him. His department assistant, Marie Newman, walked past his office door and glanced at Simon. Their eyes met for just a split second. She then continued walking, entered her office, and sat at her desk. Marie's office was right next to Simon's.

Simon thought about Marie for a moment, and then swiveled his office chair and stared out his office window at the gloomy winter landscape, gray, mottled sky, and slick, frozen tundra, now empty, motionless, lonely. A forsaken land, he thought. There were no people, no animals, no movement, no sun, no clouds, only grayness, darkened, filthy snow, ice nearly everywhere, and black, leafless, life-less trees and bushes. A barren world, Simon mused.

Oh, but of course there was the vast parking lot full of dirty, icy cars wearing the salty white of winter and dangling chunks of frozen, unyielding, packed snow that hugged the cars' wheel wells and drooped like thick, crusty stalactites. It was no Norman Rockwell scene. No, certainly not Norman Rockwell. Seemed to Simon more like Edward Hopper. Or even Hieronymus Bosch right now. This is it, thought Simon, this is my life. What was the point of all that education, research, publishing, writing and so on? This was the result, the reality? This is what I get? And, what is there to do about it? What is there to do?

Simon looked back at his computer screen that displayed the PowerPoint slides. The images of cells he saw there in slide after slide suddenly looked to him like modern, abstract works of art, squirmy, amoebic, glistening, fundamental – like the early 20th century paintings of Kandinsky. Simon thought about Kandinsky's thesis that these non-representational, colorful, wiggly shapes could touch the viewer's spirit, could reach the inner self, could bring about an emotional, spiritual, maybe religious experience, could undeviatingly pierce the soul bypassing the realistic representations of nature and beam directly to the viewer's inner phenomenological essence. Beam me up, Wassily.

Right, thought Simon. Straight to my soul. He glanced through the sequence of slides hoping – trying – to achieve, to experience, to evoke an artistic/spiritual awakening, a moment of clarity, to arouse, to excite, to conjure a rapture of higher consciousness. But, no, nothing stirred in him, nothing spiritual, nothing reached his essence. Gradually the slides again appeared to Simon to be simple cellular structures.

Simon quickly checked the window again to see if there was any activity outside, any life, but no, it was the same, like looking at a photograph, he thought, rather than real life. Nothing had changed. Nothing moved. There was no vigor, no vitality, just deadness. Nothing changed, Simon thought. Nothing but time, time passing. Time passing at a rate of one hour per hour, apparently. How did anyone know? How could anyone know? Simon sighed and looked back at his monitor.

In a few minutes he was ready. He closed the PP program, rose from his chair, and retrieved his laser pointer and bottle of water. He locked his office door on the way out and briskly walked down the hallway nodding at Marie sitting at her desk as he passed by. Marie.

Simon Pharaoh walked at a quick pace, though age had slowed him in recent years. He greeted the people he encountered with a nod or brief "hi" or "hello," though no one greeted him in return, instead they walked like zombies from A to B, eyes glued to the floor, or more commonly to their cells, heads bowed as if in worship to their phone god.

To avoid going outside, Simon walked downstairs to the lower level in order to get to the next building – there was a tunnel connection to Twombly Hall – the subterranean passages protecting him from the barren winter ice-land outside. Then up the stairs to room 230. Simon entered the lecture room from the rear door and walked toward the front on the left-side aisle passing the many students crowded into the uncomfortable seats surrounded by cement walls and floors and expansive, plastic fluorescent lights. A prison, he mused to himself, as he did every time he walked this regular route and entered this room. Every time.

About half-way down the aisle Simon glanced at the podium in front of the classroom and then stopped abruptly in his tracks – he froze. What he saw was very unsettling, very disturbing and incongruous. What could explain it? What could it mean?

Simon stared in silence and without movement. What Simon saw was himself at the lectern presenting his lecture. At first he was unsure, wasn't clear about what was happening, but as he studied the scene he soon realized that, yes, it was him alright, it was Simon Pharaoh presenting his lecture on cell division. He stared in puzzlement for a moment and then looked up at the big screen on the wall behind the other Simon and, sure enough, there he saw one of the Kandinsky slides bigger than life on the big screen, colorful and plasmic, integral, like a real Kandinsky painting, but inexplicably still arousing no emotional or spiritual insight at all – to Simon it was just a simple body cell. No emotion. No religion. Simon looked again at the lectern and again saw and heard himself standing there explaining cell division to the microbiology students, who, by the way, were stoically, robotically writing notes in their laptops or notebooks.

Simon stared, not moving, mouth agape. He didn't have any idea why this odd experience reminded him of the desolate winter landscape outside his window, but it did. Then slowly Simon looked around the classroom where he saw the students diligently taking notes, apparently uninterested or unaware of his presence standing awkwardly in the left-side aisle.

And then, out of the blue, Simon was calm. For reasons that surely no one could fathom, not even Kandinsky, Simon became nonchalant, was not at all concerned, became fully accepting of what was happening, as if it were all entirely normal. Alright, thought Simon, I guess I am already giving the cell division lecture, so I guess I can go back to my office now. Which he did. Simon turned and walked up the left-side aisle, exited room 230, and re-traced his path back to his office, nodded at the department assistant, Marie, as he passed her office, entered his own office, and then sat down in front of his computer.

I'm sorry to interrupt the story, but I think I'd better remind you that everything in this story, I mean the characters, places, events – everything – is entirely, absolutely true. You've got to be kidding me! I actually did it again. Of course, I mean false. Absolutely false.

That's weird because, I mean, I was just thinking that I should break into the story and remind you and so on, and I told myself that I had better be careful, to be sure to get it right this time, that for sure I should not say that the story is true, not like I did before, you know, and I can't believe that even after reminding myself not to do it, I still did it! What in the world is causing me to do that? That is just so strange!

Okay, as you must know by now what I am trying to tell you is that everything here is false. Yes, false. Well, not everything here, I shouldn't have said that; for example, not what I'm saying to you right now – that isn't false; no, that is true. Well, I guess, so is this story, that is, in some respects, some details, as I told you before, the story is, in a sense, true. But, wait, I just had a weird thought: by any chance you aren't Simon or Marie or a microbiology student, are you? If you are, then, well, you know, that is truly a nutty coincidence, and it means that a lot of this story really is true, is certainly true. Absolutely true. But, if you are not, you know, then, well you know… so, okay, back to the story…

Simon was calm. He wondered why what had just happened didn't bother him very much. Shouldn't he be perturbed, or at least concerned? He looked out the window – it was the same. Dead. Static. Simon got up, left his office, walked past Marie, nodded, and continued down the hall, down the stairs, through the subterranean labyrinth and this time entered the Miro building. Simon walked up the stairs to the offices of the language department, past the office of the department secretary, Joan Pollock, nodded at Joan, mouthed a simple "hi" to go with the nod, and continued into the office of Scandinavian language professor Hans Krasner. Simon flopped down into the dark maroon-colored, comfy chair (why do language teachers get soft, cushy chairs?) across from and facing his colleague Hans.

"Hi," Simon said in a low, unassured voice.

"Hi," said Hans. "What's up?"

"Well," Simon began to explain, still in a low, unassured voice, "a weird thing happened, and I think might still be happening."

"What's weird is that you are here and not giving a lecture," replied Hans. "When I first started teaching, not here, but at another University, I knew this guy, Walter, a physics professor, who quite often forgot to go to his classes. No one really noticed. None of the students complained. I'm not sure Walter even noticed. It's like when I was working for the railroad during college, the bosses were so bureaucratic that they didn't even know what they were doing, they were like cyborgs, oblivious to what everyone else was doing except for some bureaucratic details, minute, unimportant details, well, important to them I suppose, they talked and acted and made decisions as if people weren't really people at all, like people were objects, just commodities that needed to be counted, tallied, accounted for, objects that could be fired or promoted, given raises, or be arranged, talked about, planned about, as if they weren't people at all..."

Hans was droning on, as he often did. That was one of the things Simon liked about Hans. Simon now was staring right at Hans, but his mind, of course, was elsewhere. He was thinking about Marie, and about what had happened with the other Simon, and about the cold, dearth landscape which now coincidentally became inescapably manifest through Hans's office window, directly behind Hans, who continued droning on. Simon slowly turned his gaze from Hans and peered at the sterile world outside, focusing on the grim panorama. Nothing had changed, he noticed. Nothing had changed. Simon looked back at Hans who was now remarking about the disturbing and unrelenting lack of humanity among humanity.

"I went to my lecture," Simon interrupted, "but when I got there I discovered that I was already there, giving a nice presentation with lots of beautiful slides, and so on, so I left, and I came here."

"That's good, that's how it should be," remarked Hans. "The bean counters will note that you, an object, a commodity, did something within the broad context of what it is that beans do, and everything will be in its right place, no one will..."

Simon was half listening and half wondering about Marie. What did the glance mean? Was there something there?

Hans continued, "... beans will be arranged, classified, filed, then forgotten, later when the beans are out of sight the bureaucrats will plan and scheme about the beans, thinking of them and treating them merely as pawns, things, items, gadgets, nothing else, never people, always intending…"

Simon again was half listening and half absorbed in numb preoccupation when out of the corner of his eye he saw someone approaching Hans's office door. Simon turned his head and saw himself entering Hans's office. This new Simon then saw Simon sitting on the comfy maroon-colored chair looking up at him, stopped, stared – a confused, mask-like look on his face – then straightaway turned and left the office doorway and disappeared down the hall.

Simon looked back at Hans who apparently had not noticed the other Simon and was still orating his philosophical conceptions concerning human vicissitudes.

Oh, sorry to interrupt again, it's just me, sorry to bother you, but I was just thinking, you're not Hans are you? That would be a good one! Did you recognize yourself? No? But surely you noticed that you have some qualities of one or more of the characters, right? I mean, the story is partly, in some details, true, after all, isn't it? Well, maybe, I guess. Okay, sorry, so sorry to interrupt, just a thought, you know, okay, back to the story…

"Did you see that? Did you see who was at your office door?"

"No," said Hans, "was there someone there?"

Simon said nothing for a moment, his eyes were glazed over in a mesmerized stare, his mind stuck in deep, mystified thought. Then finally he stood up and said, "I guess I'd better get back to my office. I think the weird thing is still happening. Don't worry, I'll be okay. I need to look up something. See you later."

Simon nodded bye to Hans, waved a small wave, and walked out of Hans's office door and back through the tunnel pathways toward his own office, walked by Marie's office, nodded to her, and then sat in front of his computer. He had not seen himself along the route, not even once, but was bafflingly indifferent to the whole thing by now. He just didn't seem to care, one way or the other. In one way he was glad that his lecture was being given. Or, was it? The confusion was a bit vexing.

Simon reached for his keyboard, clicked some keys, and watched as the google machine displayed many links to a condition called autoscopy in which people saw themselves outside their own bodies, saw doppelgangers, doubles, often doing the exact same movements, but in mirror image, as the people themselves, a sort of disembodied hallucination. Autoscopy was common in folklore and mythology, and not rare in modern psychiatric practice. Although scientists did not have a clear understanding of its causes, stress seemed to be a common trigger.

Simon minimized the browser on his computer screen and sat staring at his screensaver image of a mountain, sky, trees, and a serene lake. That looks nice, he thought. For comparison, Simon turned and looked out his office window. Still the same. No change. Solid gray sky, dirty cars, cold, austere wasteland. Simon looked back at the screensaver.

Then Marie walked into his office.

"Got a minute?" she asked in her cute voice.

Listen, it's me again, sorry to interrupt again, but I was just thinking of something that I wanted to mention. You don't mind, do you? You know, these characters are not real, you know that, right? I mean this is just a story, right? You get that, don't you. Wait, was that my phone again?

Anyway, as I already told you, these people, places, and events are real. Oh my gosh, no, no, not again, sorry, I mean not real, not real, not real! Don't get mixed up! I don't want you seeing yourself reading this story – that might be upsetting to you, I don't know, maybe, probably, I think, I mean, I guess. Don't go seeing yourself in the story or seeing your doppelganger reading the story, okay?

Also, I just want to warn you that this is not a normal short story. I mean, don't get up your hopes about some poignant, meaningful message or moral or nice, endearing ending. That just isn't in the cards, you know? I mean, what could happen? Really, what could happen? Okay, sorry to bother you again, but just saying…

"Yes, come in, sit down."

"Thanks."

"Hey, how was the art fair last weekend?" "You went, didn't you? Did you buy anything?"

"Yes, I mean, no," answered Marie. "Yes, I was there, but no, I didn't buy anything. The weather was nice and the art was okay, but nothing struck me. I just stopped to ask about your budget. Anna K. says she hasn't received a budget request from you. It was due last week."

"Oh," Simon uttered slowly, thinking. "Oh, I see. I think I handed it in. Let me think. I will check. I'm sorry, I've been a bit absent-minded lately. I will get it to her. I will take care of it."

"Okay, thanks," said Marie. "Umm, there is another thing, umm, I wanted to mention," she continued. Marie shifted in her chair.

"Yes," queried Simon a bit nervously, "what is it?"

"Umm, yes, well, umm, it's about Joan. Joan Pollock. Hans's assistant."

"Yeeesss?" Simon had no idea what this was about.

"Umm, well Joan has sorta got this weird idea that you are flirting with her. That you visit Hans as a diversion to flirt with her. She doesn't really mind – I mean, you are both single. But, she has mentioned it to me and kinda asked me to find out. Unfortunately, I just couldn't think of any subtle, sneaky way to find out if you were interested in Joan, so I thought I would just come out and ask." Marie looked away from Simon, as she felt a bit embarrassed by the situation. She had a squishy look on her face.

"Well," Simon stumbled for words, "I think Joan is great, but, no, no, I am not conscious, umm, not aware that I have been flirting with her. But, does she want me to?"

Look, I'm really sorry to bug you again, but what in the world is going on? Who is it that keeps interrupting this story? I am the author and I don't understand who it is who is pretending to narrate this story. It is very odd since I did not intend there to be a narrator for this story. That is not supposed to be part of this story! Who is doing that? Who is it? It seems this interrupting person is pretending to be me! Is that what is going on? Who is it, do you know? It is surely a very strange, very unsettling thing. Who would butt into a short story? People should mind their own business! What could it mean? I'll tell you right now, I intend to get to the bottom of this!

Marie left Hans's office and returned to her office. Nothing had been decided about what to tell Joan. Marie agreed to let Simon think about it for a while and they would talk again. Marie would have to think of some way to put off Joan's queries for a little while.

Simon watched Marie leave his office and then sat quietly at his desk pondering this new event. It had been quite a day. Simon once again swiveled in his chair and faced his office window. But this time, instead of looking out the window, through the glass, Simon found himself involuntarily perceiving the window and the outdoor scene as one large flat surface. For some reason, his eyes and mind were not seeing a normal three-dimensional view of the window and the outer vista; the depth had dissolved and Simon now perceived a collapsed singular surface.

The 2-D scene that now penetrated his mind, engaging, even hijacking, his conscious perception, seemed to Simon to be very much like a Mark Rothko painting – large rectangles of solid colors. The window frame and transom were a sleek, glossy black, the upper portion of the glass was an uninterrupted, smooth, light gray, the lower window was a plane of lustrous, silky white with hints of yellow and orange, and, here and there Simon glimpsed a strip or splotch of azure blue or cerulean green. Simon sat and gazed in awe at the Rothko painting that hung before his eyes and permeated his mind.

The artist Mark Rothko himself had declared that he was, in fact, not an abstract painter. He claimed to paint emotions, to express affective experiences, much as Edvard Munch had done, but using large planes of color in lieu of people. Rothko also claimed that many viewers cried when they saw his paintings, which proved to him that they were experiencing the same emotional stirrings that he had experienced while he was creating the vast fields of color.

Simon sat still and quiet, absorbing and enjoying the spectacle before his eyes. He wondered, can we make sense of the odd experiences of life, the enigmatic, quirky, fragmented events that we encounter, or should we just accept them with a sense of resignation, of apathy, maybe even enjoy them? Can there be order in disorder, purpose in randomness, hope in disillusionment, can there be energy, life, in a thing itself, or must it represent something else?

Suddenly a large black bird flew past Simon's office window, and the spell was broken. Again, Simon stared at the bleak winter landscape.

Quirks of Nature

"Learn the rules like a pro, so you can break them like an artist."
— Pablo Picasso

"Every portrait that is painted with feeling is a portrait of the artist, not of the sitter."
— Oscar Wilde, The Picture of Dorian Gray

"Surrealism, then, neither aims to subvert realism, as does the fantastic, nor does it try to transcend it. It looks for different means by which to explore reality itself."
— Michael Richardson

"Realism falls short of reality. It shrinks it, attenuates it, falsifies it; it does not take into account our basic truths and our fundamental obsessions: love, death, astonishment. It presents man in a reduced and estranged perspective. Truth is in our dreams, in the imagination."
— Eugène Ionesco

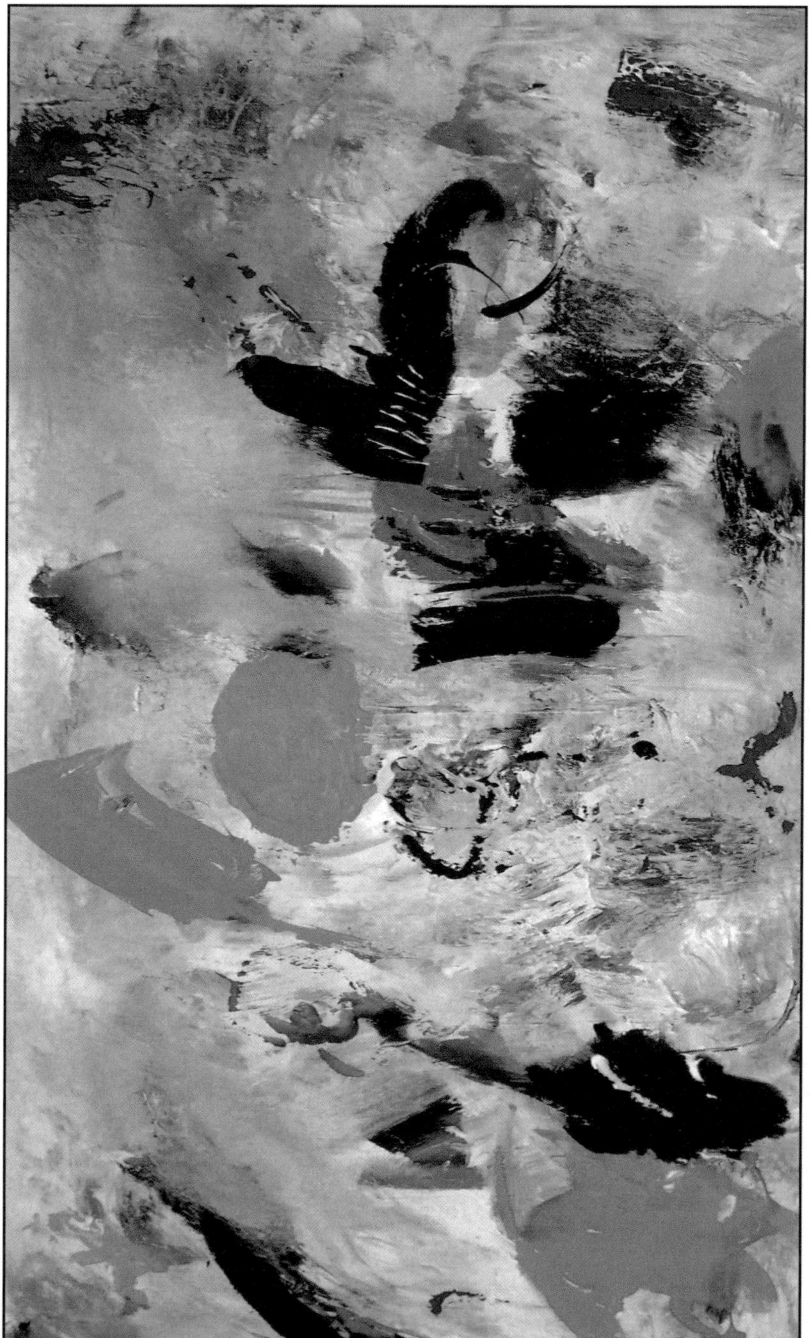